He looked u ... he ballistic windows on

He didn't think. He just reacted. The only reason for one of those windows to open would be that they'd been spotted, and were about to take fire.

Snapping his rifle to his shoulder, he leaned around Bianco's shoulder, put the faint, red chevron in the ACOG, still illuminated despite the fact that the optic was so old that the tritium had to be half depleted already, on that dark rectangle in the top of the tower, flipping the weapon to "semi" and squeezing the trigger as soon as the chevron settled.

The M4 thundered in the otherwise quiet night, spitting flame in the dark as Bianco flinched away from the muzzle blast. Wade leaned into the rifle, dumping four more rounds into the opening even as Kirk opened fire on the other tower, if only to cover Wade's back.

They were committed, now.

BRANNIGAN'S BLACKHEARTS

BLOOD DEBT

PETER NEALEN

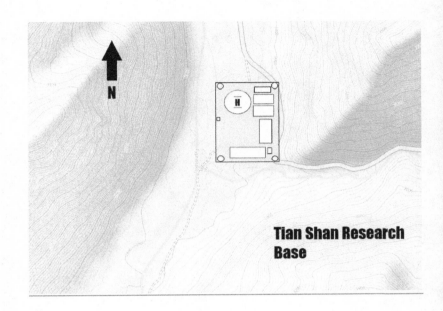

Tian Shan Research Base

CHAPTER 1

Vernon White was just glad that they were finally in the truck and heading up into the mountains. It promised to be a rough ride, as the old Soviet Ural truck had clearly seen better days, but at least he and the rest of the team were in the covered bed and out of sight. Max, Travis, and especially Sam, lean and crooked as he looked, could blend in with the Russians in Kyrgyzstan far better than a tall, muscled, bald-headed black man. Bishkek had been bad enough. Kochkor had been far worse. Even the rest of the team had caught stares there. The Kyrgyz themselves were a Turkic people, not Russian, and all the MMPR Special Projects team were either too pale or too dark.

He looked around the inside of the truck bed. Max hadn't changed much since their first mission together, on that ill-advised trip into the Anambas in the South China Sea. He never tanned, instead turning bright red for a few days before returning to a "lighter shade of pale." He'd always been hefty, and that hadn't changed, no matter some of the austere environments that Mitchell Price's special tasks had taken them to.

Sam hadn't changed much, either, except to get skinnier and more sullen. He'd never been a particularly personable individual, and if he hadn't been as good on the ground as he was,

1

the rest of the team might have kicked him to the curb a long time ago.

That, and the fact that he knew things that Mitchell Price didn't necessarily want getting out into the public sphere. Better to keep him close and well paid.

Travis, the new guy, wasn't one that Vernon had quite figured out. He was quiet, almost as pale as Max, with a reddish-blond beard that almost covered the mag pouches on his plate carrier. He stuck out like a sore thumb, and Vernon still didn't know exactly what had qualified him for the Special Projects team.

It was a continuing sore spot with Price. While the man had come in at the eleventh hour and pulled the survivors out of the Anambas, calling in all sorts of favors and spending a shitload of money in the process, they'd had a problem with how little information he pushed down to his contractors back then, too. He always had a *master plan*, but they were always left trying to guess what it was while they carried it out.

One of these days, the debt we owe him isn't going to be enough.

Sure, they'd done some good work with Price, following up on the *highly* sensitive information they'd retrieved from Yuan's body on the island. The former PLAN frigate captain turned pirate had been using that information to blackmail Beijing to keep the PLA off his back. From some of what they'd found in that blackmail file, there was good reason that the CCP didn't want it getting out. It hadn't worked out for Yuan, but they'd sure made good use of it.

Vernon didn't know if more of that information had led them to Kyrgyzstan or not. He suspected so, since what little intel Price had handed down had echoed what had led them to Chad and the Humanity Front's biological weapons experiments there, a couple years before. The team didn't know for sure if it was the Humanity Front up in these mountains, but some of the limited brief fit the profile.

His eyes strayed toward the front of the truck, where Price was in the passenger seat next to their guide, a local named Boren. Boren bothered him. He had ever since he'd joined them planeside in Bishkek before heading down to Kochkor, where they'd linked up with the rest of their support element—all local, of course. The man seemed a little too sly, a little too eager to please, while being unable to disguise the fact that he knew something his clients didn't. Vernon didn't trust him.

"I know." Max had followed his gaze. The big man wasn't just cursed with pasty pale skin and a spare tire that never seemed to go away, no matter his diet or exercise, but he had a surprisingly high-pitched voice for his size. "I don't like it either."

"Like what?" Travis looked over at them, his eyes a little wide. Sam just looked disgusted and turned his eyes out the back of the truck as they trundled up into the hills. There wasn't much to look at. Just the rolling hills already starting to show a dusting of snow as they climbed higher, out of the valley dominated by the massive lake of Issyk Kul. The landscape was open and desolate as the truck rocked and creaked its way higher into the Tian Shan mountains. But Sam apparently thought it was more interesting than trying to explain things to the FNG.

Max leaned back against the sidewalls. "We're *way* out in the cold here. We're way too close to Russia *and* China to get the whole MMPR—and affiliate—operation out here." He jerked a thumb toward the cab. "That means we've got to rely on local contractors, just to keep our footprint small. But local contractors aren't always all that reliable, and if you can pay them, somebody else can, too."

"Who'd be paying them out here?" Travis's words were a little disturbed as they went over a bump or a rock, and everyone in the back was bounced painfully off the slat seats.

"Russians. Chinese." Vernon ticked his fingers off. "Whoever's got the resources to reopen an old Soviet base that nobody seems to have much data on, without the Kyrgyz government looking too deeply into it." He shrugged. "Take your pick."

"You think it's a trap?" Travis's eyes seemed to get even wider, if that was possible.

Max shrugged. "It's certainly possible. We've seen it before." He grinned and patted the Gilboa M43 hanging between his knees. "Welcome to Special Projects, kid."

Sam muttered something and spat over the tailgate, just in time to almost take the steel lip in the chin as they hit another bump in the poorly-paved road.

***

They didn't make it much farther than that.

Vernon recognized the growling roar as it passed overhead and shook the truck, even as they lurched to a stop. He'd been around or aboard too many helicopters not to recognize it.

He could also tell that it wasn't a Kyrgyz Mi-8 or Mi-24. It was too quiet. And when he ducked his head to look under the canopy, he saw a lean, sleek shape, sporting not only a fast-moving main rotor but also a pair of pusher propellers on the ends of double wings. He'd never seen a bird like that before.

That kind of narrowed down who was up there. There weren't too many organizations that would have that kind of next-gen tech in the Tian Shan Mountains.

He and Sam were already lifting their rifles as the shooters, dressed in unfamiliar green, gray, and brown camouflage and carrying squared off, blocky rifles, started to pile out of the helo. He opened fire, dumping 7.62x39 rounds toward the bird, as Max went between him and Sam, diving over the tailgate without bothering to try to drop it.

Vernon heard Max hit the ground, even as the strange shooters scattered and returned fire, bullets zipping through the canvas near his head, one of them hitting the hoop overhead with a loud *bang*, scattering splinters over him. Sam followed Max out as the big man scrambled off to one side and opened fire from the prone near the two rear wheels. The truck wasn't going to provide any cover whatsoever, and if the door gunner behind the minigun just ahead of those twin wings opened up, they were going to be mincemeat.

4

Fortunately, the shooters appeared to have been caught by surprise when the Special Projects contractors had started shooting at them. They returned fire wildly as they dashed for the brush on the sides of the road, giving Vernon the chance to get out while Sam and Max maintained covering fire.

So far, this fight had rapidly degenerated into a wild spray-and-pray, but as long as that minigun stayed silent, Vernon was going to count his blessings.

He hit the ground hard but maintained his balance, then threw himself off to the left and flat on the ground as more bullets smacked into the truck where he'd just been. He could hear more fire from the front of the truck, but he didn't dare look behind him as he sighted in on a man in full cammies, plate carrier, high-cut helmet, and balaclava, all in that matching, green, gray, and brown pattern, sprinting toward a rock just uphill. Vernon's shot caught him mid-stride, and he stumbled, the follow up taking him through the throat. The man tumbled onto his face, both gloved hands going to his neck.

The roar of a second bird intensified behind him as Price bellowed, "Peel left!" Despite all the time the PMC magnate had spent in offices and meeting halls over the years, the man had proved to be surprisingly skilled in the field, but right then, Vernon had to take his eyes off the enemy for a second to figure out which way *left* was supposed to be.

He couldn't see Price, which meant he had to be on the other side of the truck. But he *could* see the second helicopter, or hybrid, or whatever it was, as matte black as the first, circling overhead. It looked like the bad guys had tried to block both sides of the road before their target had turned out to be a little pricklier than they'd expected.

Sam was moving already, and Vernon was quickly glad that he'd pushed up just slightly, because it meant Sam could get between him and the truck without moving in front of his barrel. He took another shot at a running camouflaged shooter, missing by a hair as the man dove onto his face behind a fold in the ground.

There wasn't much cover in that valley aside from microterrain, but the sheer volume of fire flying in both directions was brutal, and both sides' accuracy was suffering from it. Sam sprinted a few yards and threw himself flat, as Travis started to try to make his own dash. He didn't get far. He'd just passed Vernon when a bullet took him in the side with a *thwack* that Vernon could hear even over the gunfire. His choking scream died quickly as he dropped.

Max sprinted past then, followed quickly by Price. At almost the same time, as the second helo growled overhead, the door gunner opened fire on the truck, a stream of tracers tearing through the vehicle lengthwise with an angry, buzzing roar, sparks and pulverized metal flying as the old Ural was practically cut in half.

At least we've only got shooters on one side, now. Vernon gasped in the thin air as he ran for the creek bed off the side of the road, where Sam and Max were already set up, blazing away at their attackers. Another round *snap*ped past his head, alarmingly close, just before he dove through the low bushes along the bank and into the shrubs along the bank of the streambed. A faint trickle of water gurgled through the lower part of the bed, but most of it was dry, aside from the dusting of snow.

They were now out of sight of the enemy, but all it would take would be one gun run from one of those helos, and they were dead.

The gunfire had momentarily died down, as neither the Special Projects contractors nor the enemy shooters had targets. Right at the moment, Vernon couldn't see either helo, but he could hear them clearly enough.

"Where's Boren?" Max didn't look over his shoulder as he asked the question, having positioned himself where he had a narrow window through the brush where he could see the road just behind the smoking ruin of the smashed Ural.

"He tried to grab my weapon as soon as the birds showed up." Price's voice was bland and slightly wry, despite how hard he was breathing. "He didn't survive the attempt." He was digging

6

in the go bag at his side, finally coming up with the satellite phone they'd brought, hitting the speed dial for their QRF. Vernon didn't think that there was a hope in hell that the Quick Reaction Force was going to get there in time, but what else were they going to do?

Sam took a shot at a moving figure trying to run up to the high ground above them, and the shooter disappeared. "They're trying to flank us."

"They won't need to with those birds in the air." Vernon had eyes on one, watching as it banked around to the south, turning back toward them. It was surprisingly quiet, and with those pusher props, it was *fast*. He watched it, wondering if he could get a round through that windshield. He wasn't nearly as confident in the 7.62x39 to get a kill shot on a moving helo's pilot as he might have been with a heavier round.

He also wondered just why the bad guys hadn't simply burned them down with those miniguns as soon as the fight had started. He had his suspicions, and he didn't like them much.

Price threw the phone in the dirt with a curse. "Those sons of bitches. The signal's getting through, but they're not picking up. Must have been bought off."

Before anyone could make the observation that naturally followed, that weird, fast-moving helo roared by, the gunner tearing through the brush with a long burst of minigun fire, just off the creek bed. All four men ducked as they were showered with debris.

"*Mitchell Price!*" The voice on the loudspeaker had a faint French accent. "*You are cut off and alone! Surrender, and you will not be harmed!*"

"Fuck off." Sam, true to form, wasn't inclined to go quietly into that good night.

Price wasn't going to react that quickly, though. Vernon glanced at him, and saw that their boss was frowning, looking down at the dirt in front of him as he thought it over.

Looking up at the helo as it circled back around—or maybe that was the second bird—he couldn't help but think that

7

surrender was not their best option. He didn't believe that they "wouldn't be harmed." Not with this bunch, if they were who he suspected.

"I'm sorry, gents." Price looked up and around at them. "I might have gotten us in deeper than we were ready for, this time. It was just supposed to be recon."

Sam's look of disgust was eloquent enough.

"I'm who they want. I'll do what I can to protect you." He started to stand up.

Vernon's mind was racing. They'd been sold out—he was pretty sure of that. And the timeframe meant that he couldn't be sure it was just Boren who'd been behind it.

It had become obvious over the last few years that while Price might hold onto as much control of his PMC empire as possible, there were elements within it that were less than trustworthy. It was *possible* that Boren and his little company had been paid off in advance just to call ahead and warn about anyone showing too much interest in the abandoned Soviet base. But the fact that they knew it was Price…

He grabbed the phone as Price put his rifle down and stood up. Fortunately, he had the number memorized. There was one man Vernon would really, truly trust with all their lives, even though he'd sworn he'd never go back to the private military contracting world again, not after the Anambas.

Sam was spitting curses as he flipped his sling over his head and put his rifle down. The bird was circling around again, descending toward the road, and more of the shooters in their unfamiliar camouflage were starting to move up. The phone rang in Vernon's ear, every passing second feeling like an eternity. *Come on, come on.*

It went to voicemail. "Dan, it's Vernon. Look, we're in deep shit. I need you to get in contact with a retired Marine Colonel named John Brannigan. Tell him that we've been taken hostage, and that the target is in an abandoned Soviet base in Kyrgyzstan." He rattled off the coordinates quickly, as the helo landed on the road and the shooters closed in. "I'm about to get rolled up, so I can't tell you any more, but tell him that it's our old friends from Chad. Hector Chavez, with John Paul Jones Consulting, will know how to contact him."

Then they were too close, and he had to drop the phone. It was over.

For now.

CHAPTER 2

Dan Tackett heard the phone vibrating on the workbench, even over the faint strains of Charley Crockett coming from the small speaker on the shelf above, but he ignored it. *One thing at a time.* He wasn't going to leave the job half-finished just to answer the phone.

He finished tightening down the housing and stepped back from the bike appreciatively. Hondas weren't his favorite to work on, but he was good at it, and he had to admit that this Shadow Phantom was a nice-looking bike.

Looking around the shop, he nodded. It never quite ceased to amaze him, even after five years, how much he'd managed to build. He knew he couldn't have done it without Mitchell Price's payoff after the Anambas mission had gone horribly awry, but all the same, there'd been a time when he'd wondered if he'd ever be good for anything but packing a gun in dangerous and far distant places.

It had been that wonder, as he'd been working a dead-end job and trying to maintain the lifestyle he'd had before his first wife had died, that had led him to that ill-fated contract. After the hell he'd gone through on those islands, cut off, hunted, sure they'd been left out to dry, he'd promised that he'd find another way.

11

And he had. This shop was all his, and he was doing a hell of a booming business. He glanced at the three other bikes lined up against the far wall for repair, knowing that there were about twelve more after that on the waiting list. He was *good* at this, and while it meant long hours, he returned the repairs fast, and he was rapidly building a name for himself in the local community and beyond.

He heard the car in the driveway outside. Cassie was back with the kids. He swiped a rag off the bench and started getting the oil and grime off his hands as he looked down at the phone, activating the lock screen with a knuckle.

He frowned. He didn't recognize the number. It didn't look like a US number at all. But whoever was calling, they'd left a voicemail.

Probably another scammer. But he was curious. Satisfied that he had most of the grease off his hands, he lifted the phone, unlocked it, and listened to the message.

He felt himself go very still, as a voice out of the past, scratchy and distorted but unmistakable, nevertheless, begged him for help. Cassie, with Tom in tow, eager to see what his dad had been working on, found him like that, the phone in his hand, his eyes far away.

"Dan?" Cassie Tackett knew that look. She'd worn it herself, more than once. She and Dan had gotten together about a year after the mission to the Anambas, a mission where they'd both nearly been killed. They'd been married less than six months after they'd started dating, and Tom, at least, had taken to his stepmother eagerly. Amy had been a bit of a harder sell, but Dan and Cassie had developed a bond that was a rarity, and Amy was a good kid. She'd come around. "What's wrong?"

Dan forced his eyes over to her, then just wordlessly handed her the phone. She looked down at the number next to the voicemail, frowning. "Who is it?"

"It's Vernon." Dan was frankly surprised at how even and steady his voice was, after what he'd just heard.

Cassie looked up and searched her husband's face. "He's not coming over to visit, is he?" Vernon and Max had both been by a few times over the years, though they had rarely talked about what they were doing for work. They both knew that both men had agreed to keep working for Price after the PMC magnate had pulled them off the island just ahead of the PLAN's commandos. Neither had asked, and neither man had volunteered. But they knew that it wasn't tame, whatever they were doing. It couldn't be.

"He needs help." Dan met his wife's eyes, almost afraid of what he'd see there, but he saw only Cassie. Only the compassion and the certainty that had been the only thing to get her through that nightmare on the Anambas, when most of the other female "operators" had folded, panicked, or been killed out of hand.

Cassie nodded and listened to the message. "Do you know anything about this Brannigan guy? Or Chavez?"

Dan shook his head. "Never heard of either of 'em. But I've been out of the game for a while, and if Vernon says to get in touch with them…"

Cassie nodded. "Tom, go inside with your sister for a minute. I need to talk to your father."

As soon as Tom had shut the door behind him, though the eight-year-old boy had been watching his dad with some amount of trepidation on his face, she took both of Dan's hands in hers. "I know that look. I know what you're worried about. I know we both promised that we were done with all that. But it's *Vernon*. For all we know, it's Max, too. We both owe them our lives. As much as all of us owe *you* our lives." She squeezed his hands. "This is different."

Dan nodded. It was going to suck, leaving the kids behind, after promising he'd never leave again, but his wife was right. There was an obligation there.

He couldn't help but wonder if Vernon had known that he'd place that on his shoulders when he'd called him. But he knew the big man too well, after those days and nights in the jungle. That wasn't Vernon's way. He wasn't manipulative that way. If it had been Jenny, now…

It had been a long time since he'd thought of that cold-hearted, vicious woman. She'd disappeared into the jungle, never to be seen again, all her Machiavellian schemes and tough chick attitude swallowed up by the harsh realities of combat.

He squeezed Cassie's hands in return. "I'll go look up this Chavez guy, see what I can find. We might be on a short timeline."

He looked down at her. "You're not going this time. I've got to, but I need you to stay here with Amy and Tom. They *could* stay with Roger and Darlene, but…"

She nodded, though she started to tear up a little. "That might be a little too much like last time. I understand." She dashed a tear away from her eye. "I'm not up to another tramp through the jungle, anyway." She hugged him suddenly, squeezing tightly. "Just be careful, okay?"

***

It was a good thing, John Brannigan reflected, that he was a regular at the Rocking K Diner as it was, and had met numerous old buddies, Marines and otherwise, there over the last few years since he'd built the cabin up the mountain. Otherwise, people might start to ask questions about his regular meetings there, usually followed by his absence for several weeks.

Hector Chavez was sitting at the usual back table, which Ginger and Mama Taft had practically made his private reserve. Hector was looking a little healthier than the first time he'd come out here. He'd lost weight, and he was dressing more like a local these days, as opposed to an outsider in a suit. Hector had been a hell of a Marine Officer, and would have made a decent general, if his heart hadn't prompted an early retirement.

Just as well for everyone involved that he hadn't pinned on that star. His own maritime security concern was relatively lucrative, but more importantly, he'd turned into one hell of a facilitator for the much more covert mercenary band who called themselves Brannigan's Blackhearts.

The man sitting next to him was younger than either of them, probably in his late thirties, early forties. Brown haired, clean shaven, he was fit, without a paunch under his t-shirt. His hands, folded on the tabletop, were a working man's hands, scarred and calloused.

But his eyes were different. He was watching everything in the room, checking movement, and the visible assessment he made as Brannigan approached betrayed an alertness that Brannigan had usually only seen in seasoned gunfighters. This guy was a meat-eater.

He shook Hector's hand as he slid into the seat, Ginger already right behind him with his usual cup of coffee. "How's the family, Hector? This one of your new proteges?"

"Family's fine." Chavez waited until Ginger had left with a smile, after patting him on the shoulder. "And Mr. Tackett here isn't one of mine. He's the client."

Brannigan just looked over at the younger man, his eyebrow raised. "Really."

Tackett was studying him, too. Brannigan knew what he saw. An older man but still hard-muscled, six foot four with broad shoulders that strained the shoulders of any shirt that fit him otherwise. He'd gotten a haircut recently, so his gray hair was cropped neatly short, his thick handlebar mustache a matching silver.

Tackett leaned forward, clasping his hands in front of him. "A friend of mine is in trouble. He gave me your name, said that you could help me go get him out. His name is Vernon White."

Brannigan's eyes narrowed. Something about that name rang a bell.

"He's been working for Mitchell Price for the last several years." Tackett chuckled wryly and ran a hand over his face, so he didn't notice the recognition in Brannigan's eyes. "Hell, *I* worked for Price for a while, too, before we knew that he was actually running that show." He took a deep breath. "I don't know a lot of details. He was clearly under fire when he called me on a sat phone and left a voicemail message. He said they were in trouble, they

15

were in Kyrgyzstan, and to get in touch with you." He looked up at Brannigan, a pensive look in his eyes. "He said to tell you that it was 'our old friends from Chad.'"

Brannigan felt a shock go through him at that. He glanced at Chavez, who just nodded. Tackett had already told him, but from the look on Tackett's face, he hadn't told him exactly what that meant.

If the Humanity Front had come out of whatever hole they'd crawled into after Argentina, then it was damned near a certainty that the Blackhearts would take this job. Especially if it meant helping the guys who'd helped them take down the Front's biological weapons experiments in Chad.

"Do you know where in Kyrgyzstan?"

Tackett nodded. "He sent me a grid. It's supposed to be an old, abandoned Soviet base."

"Sounds like someplace those assholes would set up," Chavez noted as he took a sip of his own coffee.

"What assholes?" Tackett looked from man to man, frowning. He took a deep breath. "Look, it's obvious that you guys know more about what's going on than I do. I've been out of the game for a while. I swore I'd stay home after we got back from... well, from the last job I did. We went through hell out there, and I was going to stay home with my kids. But Vernon and I... Like I said. We went through hell. I owe him my life."

Brannigan leaned back in his seat, cradling his coffee cup in his hands. "What do you know about the Humanity Front?"

Tackett's eyes narrowed. "They're a big shot NGO, I know that much. Everybody wants to cozy up to them, establish their philanthropist cred." His eyes widened slightly. "Wait. You mean..."

"Yeah, their philanthropy's a front. We met up with your boy Vernon, along with Mitchell Price and a few others, in Chad a while back, looking into the disappearance of some doctors from the WHO. Turned out they'd gotten in the way of a Humanity Front biological weapons test." He sipped the coffee. "That was

16

when we found out that they were also the ones behind the attacks in the Southwest a few years back."

Tackett's eyebrows climbed toward his hairline. "Holy shit. Never heard about any of that."

"That tends to happen when the terrorist group has bottomless pockets and most of the elites of the world are eating out of its hand," Chavez observed dryly.

"So, I've got a question." Brannigan pinned Tackett with a stare. "If this Vernon White is working for Mitchell Price—which he was the last time we saw him—why call you? I would imagine that Price has some pretty considerable resources of his own. Why would he call you and ask you to find us?"

Tackett spread his hands. "Hell if I know. And believe me, I've been trying to figure it out, myself. Sure, Vernon and I trust each other. Hard not to, after what we went through. The only *possible* explanation I can think of is that Vernon thinks that Price's organization is compromised. Hell, I don't even know what kind of resources *you*'ve got."

"More than you'd think, but fewer than you're probably expecting or hoping for." Brannigan ran a hand over his mustache, thinking. This was a thorny problem. If the Humanity Front really *was* stirring again, he wanted a piece. But he seriously doubted that Tackett had the resources to even begin to pay for this kind of op. "We tend to operate on the down-low, doing deniable jobs in shadowy, unpleasant places."

"Sounds about right." Tackett winced a little. "I can't pay you. I'm sure Price can, but I'm hardly in a position to access any of his accounts."

"Don't worry." Chavez grinned. "We've had some dealings with Price before. And I've got some really good lawyers. We'll take it out of his hide."

"So, you'll do it?" Tackett still looked tense, even though Brannigan had already essentially said yes.

Brannigan nodded. "Provided enough of the team are on board. We'll need you to provide whatever intel he gave you. The message itself would be good. We might be able to figure some

17

things out from it. I've got a couple nerds on the team who can tease all sorts of things out from recordings, and even the sat phone number."

Tackett nodded, though now he was looking at the table. When he looked up, his jaw was set and his eyes were hard. "You've got it. There's just one condition. I'm coming with you."

Brannigan didn't react, except to raise an eyebrow. It wasn't exactly in their SOP to bring a client along, but Tackett wasn't their usual client. He also remembered Vernon talking about someone named Dan, whom he'd credited with saving his life. He suspected this was the very man. He clearly wasn't soft, clearly had a history as a gunfighter, and they'd taken new Blackhearts on based on almost as slim a recommendation. Hell, he'd hired Herc Javakhishvili purely on Ben Drake's say-so.

"Fair enough." He waved Ginger over to take his order. He was hungry. "It's going to take a couple days to get the team together. Keep in touch, and I'll give you the time and place where we'll do our planning and knock the rust off with some drills."

Tackett looked relieved as he nodded. Brannigan glanced at Chavez, who nodded slightly as Ginger came up, smiling, her pad already in her hand. He'd get started on the logistics as soon as possible.

So, the utopian psychopaths are at it again, huh?

I wonder what nightmares they're cooking up this time.

exterior—but the Blackhearts were still vastly more important to him. As was the work.

"See you tomorrow, then." Brannigan hung up first, and Bianco turned back to the convention hall, pocketing his phone and pondering how he was going to tell Tom that he was about to leave the entire game launch in his hands.

***

Ignatius Kirk leaned back in his easy chair, blowing a cloud of cigar smoke toward the ceiling. His thick, red beard, shot through with gray, cascaded down his chest. "Whatever happened to Armando?"

Tom Burgess, one of Kirk's oldest friends, his long, dark hair pulled back in a ponytail, his own beard currently trimmed short, took another sip of Kirk's whiskey. While he wouldn't have put it past the old, cantankerous, solitary SF NCO to distill his own, this was Pendleton, and smooth as glass. "He bought it about three years back." He grimaced slightly. "Shot himself."

"Dammit." Kirk leaned forward, the cigar still clamped in two beefy fingers, and poured himself another finger of the bourbon. "I never heard." He swirled the amber liquor in the glass then took a deep gulp. "Too damn many of us checking ourselves out."

"He had some serious money troubles." Burgess had had much the same reaction when he'd found out. Armando Real hadn't been the first vet that either of them had known who'd committed suicide, and probably wouldn't be the last, but it wasn't something they ever got used to. It was always a shock. And a disappointment. "His wife left him and took just about everything. He'd just gotten fired from his last gig—alcohol, I think—and so he had nothing. Nothing except that old Browning Hi Power he was always wishing he could take on contract with him."

"I guess it's kinda fitting, him going out that way." Kirk took another swig. The barrel-chested man could put some booze away without showing any effect. Burgess had been astounded at how much Kirk could drink, the first contract they'd done together. "He sure loved that gun. More than anything else in the world, I thought, sometimes."

"Maybe." Burgess's phone buzzed. He glanced down in some surprise. "Your cell disruptor on the fritz?" Kirk lived in a camouflaged cargo container house, deep in the woods, and was notorious for being more than a little paranoid. He wasn't unstable about it, but he didn't like company—with few and rare exceptions—and generally didn't like electronic noise around his place, either.

"I turned it off while you're here." At Burgess's raised eyebrow, he shrugged. "Thought maybe you might be getting a call. It's been a while."

Burgess looked down at the phone, then up at Kirk. "Well, your crystal ball's sure on point." He answered the phone. "We got a job, Colonel?"

"We do indeed. Usual place for briefing, tomorrow. Can you make it? Or are you in Africa again?"

"No, I'm CONUS at the moment." He looked up as Kirk got his attention, jerked a thumb at his own chest, and nodded. When Burgess tilted his head questioningly, Kirk nodded even more firmly. "I'm at Kirk's place. He says he's in, too."

"Is he sure?" Brannigan didn't sound like he'd object, but Kirk had gone down with a sucking chest wound in Argentina, and the recovery had been long and hard.

"He's giving me that look that says if I want to leave here in one piece, I should say yes, Colonel." Burgess grinned as Kirk rolled his eyes, already heaving himself out of his chair and heading toward the back of the house, presumably to pack. "We'll be there."

***

Erekle Javakhishvili dropped his duffel on the floor and shut the door behind him, looking around at his little apartment. He sighed.

He was tired. It had been a long flight—or flights—back to the US from Georgia, and while it had been good to see his cousins again, he was glad to be home.

34

The target was a slightly lighter silhouette in the shades of green that filled his scope. The PVS-14 mounted just ahead of his LPVO worked a lot better than he'd expected, but it was still slightly dim.

That much more of a challenge.

The target paused, just under the rocks and standing in the gap between two patches of sagebrush. He wasn't going to get a better shot. Letting his breath out, he squeezed the trigger smoothly, straight back.

The shot broke cleanly, the crosshairs right on the coyote's heart and lungs. The suppressor coughed loudly in the quiet desert night, and the scavenger gave a yip as the 5.56 round tore through it, flipping over before tumbling to the dirt.

A chorus of yipping howls rose above the desert floor as the rest of the pack sounded the alarm and scattered. Gomez stood up and started toward his kill.

It was a big coyote, easily four and a half feet from nose to tail. Gomez looked down at it through the second set of PVS-14s that he'd dropped in front of his eye after he'd gotten up, then scanned the desert around him with what might have been a faint sigh.

Truth be told, he was getting bored. He wouldn't have necessarily expected it, after all that the family had been through. The Gomez Ranch had been a battleground for years, ever since the Espino-Gallo cartel had decided to take it over as a staging point for their drug traffic to the north. The Blackhearts had buried the Espino-Gallos, but other cartels that had tried to fill the vacuum they'd left behind had been a problem.

But that was increasingly in the past. Word had gotten around that to try to cross the Gomez Ranch was a short trip to a shallow grave in the desert. The drug traffickers and their various scum hangers on had decided discretion was the better part of valor and found other routes.

There is no hunting like the hunting of man, and those who have hunted armed men long enough and liked it, never care for anything else thereafter. Gomez had been familiar with the

Hemingway quote for a long time, but it seemed that only recently had it really begun to apply to him. It had been a while since Colombia, and he needed some action. Shooting coyotes in the desert wasn't quite good enough anymore.

He started back toward the house. He hadn't brought a phone out to go coyote hunting, and he had a sudden thought that maybe there might be a message from Joe, or the Colonel. He didn't have far to go, and the house was dark except for a single lamp lit in the living room. It was getting late, and most of the cousins who were running the ranch these days called it a night shortly after sundown. Only Gomez's restlessness had taken him out into the dark to shoot coyotes that night.

Checking the phone sitting on the table, he saw that there was a message. It was short and to the point. *Got a job. Our old friends might be involved. Usual place, tomorrow.*

He didn't hesitate, but quickly texted back, *I'll be there.*

CHAPTER 5

"*I'm about to get rolled up, so I can't tell you more, but tell him that it's our old friends from Chad. Hector Chavez, with John Paul Jones Consulting, will know how to contact him.*" The recording ended with a *click*.

"So, that's all the information I've got." Tackett spread his hands, almost apologetically. "I know it's not much. All I've got to go on is that phone call from Vernon. I haven't been a part of Price's operations in years, so I don't know exactly what they were doing up there."

"We've got some idea." Flanagan looked around at the rest. They were gathered in Brannigan's cabin, rather than their usual campsite. It was still pretty cold at altitude, and there was a storm moving in, lashing the trees overhead with wind and spattering mixed snow and rain against the cabin's windows.

"That's what Colonel Brannigan said." Tackett knew that Brannigan was retired, but he'd noticed that most of the Blackhearts still referred to him as "Colonel" or "the Colonel," so he'd go along with it. "But I still don't know exactly what their mission was, or what kind of setup they did beforehand. Again, all I've got is a phone call and a set of coordinates."

"We've done work on less." Santelli had kept to the back, leaning against the wall with his beefy arms crossed over his chest. "The brief for the Tourmaline Delta wasn't much more detailed."

"At least then we knew that we were going after terrorists in a possible hostage situation." Wade was a bit less sanguine about it. "I mean, sure, this Vernon dude seemed like he was okay when we worked with these guys in Chad, but it's been a while, and Price isn't exactly pure as the driven snow."

Burgess snorted. "Neither are we."

"Maybe not, but we haven't taken some of the contracts he has." Brannigan was grim. "Yes, we've worked together. Worked against the Front together, for that matter. And at least he hasn't taken contracts with the Chinese."

"He'd end up in a Chinese work camp the moment he did." Tackett was sure of that, and his words were firm. "After what we pulled in the Anambas, if they have any idea that he got that blackmail file, he's got to be Public Enemy Number One."

"That's the general impression we got, working with him in Chad," Brannigan agreed. "There were Chinese operatives there after him, too. But he's taken jobs training Gulf dictatorships, as well. Which tells me we can't entirely trust him."

"I don't trust *him*." Tackett leaned on the table. "Never have. That's why I declined his offer when he pulled us off the island. I trust Vernon, though. We've been through shit together that most people never even imagine."

"You're sure he wasn't in any way under duress?" Flanagan was leaning against Brannigan's counter, in a similar stance to Santelli. "I have to ask, since the Front knows about us, enough that they sent attack dogs after us a few years ago. They're why a friend of ours is currently under permanent twenty-four-seven care." Expressions around the table got hard and angry at that. There wasn't a single Blackheart who didn't hold a grudge for what had been done to Sam Childress.

"If he was, he was doing a damned good job of hiding it." Tackett shook his head. "Again, I trust Vernon. If he'd been feeding me a prepared story at gunpoint, he'd have found a way to let me know. I could hear helicopters in the background, and I might have heard Max's voice, though I couldn't make out what he said. It really didn't sound like they'd been rolled up yet."

Brannigan looked up at Santelli and Bianco. "Either of you managed to get us some imagery yet?"

Bianco shook his head, his expression sour. "It's pixelated to all hell. There *might* be something up there, but it's far enough into the mountains that nobody at Google wants up-to-the-minute imagery, or gives much of a damn for clarity. That whole area is low-res to the point of being useless below about twenty thousand feet of eye height."

Brannigan's eyes narrowed. Tackett watched him carefully. The Colonel was clearly thinking through the implications. "Either it's not considered of interest, or somebody doesn't want anyone looking at it too closely." His mouth tightened behind his handlebar, then he looked at his watch. "Carlo, start getting some flights set up. For all of us, including Dan here. If you can reach out to anyone in the area to arrange for weapons, comms, that sort of thing, do it."

"That's going to be difficult." Bianco looked a little pained. "I can Tor up and see if there's anyone in the region on the Dark Web who might be in the business, but Kyrgyzstan isn't known for its enlightened gun laws."

"Just do what you can." Brannigan laughed shortly and humorlessly. "There's got to be one hell of a black market coming out of Afghanistan these days. See what you can find. I might have some back channels to work, too." He looked at his watch. "As for the rest of us, we'll run drills in the morning." He looked up at Santelli. "Can we have flights going wheels up in two days, no later?"

"It'll be expensive, especially with no retainer up front, but it's doable."

Brannigan might have smiled slightly. "We've got an ops budget already."

Santelli frowned, then his expression cleared and his eyebrows climbed. "You called Abernathy and told him who's involved."

Brannigan nodded. "Needless to say, he was *very* interested. We might even have some overwatch, if he can get

43

assets in position soon enough." His expression turned grim. "With the Front involved, we are definitely not going to be alone.

"Because if they're sticking their heads out of their hole again, at least their terrorist division, then it means they've got some kind of nasty surprise in store, and Abernathy agrees with me that we want to get in front of it as fast as possible.

"Now, get some rest and be ready to knock some rust off in the morning."

**

Snores echoed from the guest room, where most of the Blackhearts were bedded down, either on the bed, the couch, or just the floor. Curtis and Jenkins had grumbled a little, but Santelli had snapped at both of them before Wade had been able to get his mad on.

Now Brannigan, Santelli, and Flanagan were gathered around the table, lit only by a single lantern. Each man had a glass of good whiskey in front of him. Not enough to get drunk, but enough to help the conversation along.

"What do you gents think?" Brannigan looked around at the three men he probably trusted the most in the world.

"About the mission?" Flanagan took a sip. "Or about Tackett?"

"Both. Either." Brannigan leaned on his elbows on the table.

"I think he's sincere." Santelli leaned back in his chair, swirling his drink in his glass. "I did some digging before coming out here, and I know Vinnie did, too. Price's staff are in a quiet panic right now. They don't know where he is, but they're trying really hard not to let anyone know. I even used the special line he gave us after Chad. Nothing. He's straight-up disappeared."

"That does tend to make me think that this is all on the up-and-up." Flanagan took another sip. "And if it really *is* the Front, then I don't think we can afford *not* to go take a look."

"I'd agree," Santelli said. "Whatever they're doing, if they're hiding in an old, supposedly abandoned Soviet military base in Kyrgyzstan of all places, then it can't be good."

44

"Nothing they do is good. Not even the stuff they get applauded for." Brannigan felt like spitting. He'd had plenty of experience with "humanitarian" NGOs in Africa during his lengthy Marine Corps career, and he had seen them do a lot to make themselves feel good, but little to actually help the people who were suffering. There were exceptions, of course, but he'd seen far more damage done via second and third order effects— quite often simply empowering the thugs and raiders far more than the people who really needed help—than he'd ever seen benefit. And the Humanity Front was no exception. They were less concerned with helping people and more concerned with propagandizing their version of the "brave new world" they were trying to build.

Once one looked under the hood, the means of building that "brave new world" were uglier than most.

"What about Tackett himself?" He wanted both men's opinions.

"We're pretty sure he's the 'Dan' that that Vernon guy told us about in Chad, right?" Santelli looked from Brannigan to Flanagan.

Flanagan nodded. "He fits the bill."

"Well, if he's half the warrior that he got made out to be, he might well be an asset." Santelli drained the last of his glass and set it on the table. "Seems a little weird taking the client along as a strap-hanger, though."

"It is," Brannigan agreed. "And I'm not entirely sold, either." He finished his own drink, got up, and stretched. "Run him through his paces tomorrow. Let's see what he's made of. If he can't keep up, then he gets to stay back, client or not. I don't give a damn about his conditions if he's going to be a liability."

Flanagan nodded as he stood up. "We'll put him to the test, Colonel. Don't worry about that."

***

"I love you, too, Amy. Have a good night. And try to be good for your stepmother."

45

The sigh on the other end of the phone was probably about the closest Tackett was going to get to assent from his daughter. It wasn't that she didn't *like* Cassie. She just didn't like to consider Cassie her mom. It had resulted in some friction over the last couple of years. Amy wasn't going out of her way to antagonize her stepmother, but she wasn't eager to please her, either.

Cassie took the phone back. "Thanks, Dan. I don't know how far it'll go, but thanks."

"She needs to be reminded sometimes." Tackett sighed for his own part. "It's been five years. She wasn't all that old when Julie died. She shouldn't be acting this way."

"Five years isn't all that long, and a mother can't ever really be replaced." Cassie's voice was understanding. "She doesn't really understand why we ended up together, either."

In some ways I hope she never does, because that wasn't an experience I'd ever wish on my kids. Cut off, far from support, being hunted by Chinese commandos and pirates both, those days in the jungle had been a nightmare. He and Cassie had bonded through the shared danger and suffering, but that didn't make it any easier.

"How are you doing?" Cassie sounded worried.

"I don't know. We've got some training to do tomorrow. It sounds like these guys do some drills before every job." He glanced up at the cabin. He was sitting in his truck, mainly for some privacy while he called home. He could appreciate Brannigan's hospitality, but he hadn't wanted to try to talk to his wife and kids with the others listening in, even if they were being polite about it. He was very much an outsider, and he was well aware of it.

These guys also appeared to be much more of a trusted, coherent team than the last set of contractors he'd worked with. There had been divisions and suspicions among the MMPR contractors that had ultimately turned deadly. He had seen nothing like that from this group. "They all *seem* pretty dialed in. I just hope that I am, too. It's been a while, and from some of what I've heard, these guys have been out in some hairy stuff a lot more

46

recently than I have." He didn't want to talk about what he'd heard from them about the Humanity Front. He hadn't told Cassie that part. She'd only worry, especially if she knew the kind of resources the opposition could bring to bear.

Presuming that it really was the biggest NGO in the world they were up against. He still hadn't quite wrapped his brain around that.

Cassie chuckled a little, though. "Dan, you might not have been out in combat since we got back from the Western Pacific, but remember, I know how much you spend on ammo and training. You still haven't been able to quite turn it off, and I haven't worried about it because we're both carrying the same scars."

Tackett had to quietly chuckle in agreement. The truth was, they almost always went to the range together. A certain degree of paranoia had come back with them from the Anambas, and neither one had been entirely comfortable without weapons close at hand. Even after five years, they carried the mental scars from the islands, along with the handful of physical ones they'd brought back.

"You'll be fine, babe." She got serious, which was about the only time she used names like "babe." "I know you will. You can't let Sam, Vernon, and Max down. And you won't." She took a deep breath. "Bring them home."

"I will."

CHAPTER 6

"Contact!"

Flanagan flung the makeshift artillery simulator, essentially the biggest firecracker they could have found, and it detonated just up the hill from the small hide site with a deafening *boom*. In seconds, the Blackhearts were moving.

Gomez was first, bursting out of the small circle of trees, one of Brannigan's ARs in his shoulder. He dashed about ten yards before turning and throwing himself flat, sighting in on one of the steel targets that Brannigan had set up in somewhat more difficult to spot points along the hillside that they'd been using as a training ground for the last several years. True to Gomez's reputation, he rang the steel with the first shot, as Jenkins, Burgess, and Bianco ran past him.

Flanagan watched from the hill just above the trees. It was his turn to be an observer, while Brannigan took his turn in with the team. They'd thought about just going ahead and running the whole team at once, every time, just to get the training value in for everybody, but Santelli—who Flanagan couldn't help but notice was in with the rest of the team, despite his recent turn toward logistics and information support—had insisted that with a new guy, they needed to have *somebody* standing off where he could devote his full attention to evaluation. So, Flanagan and the Colonel were trading off as observer/evaluator.

He watched Tackett especially closely as the team peeled out of the hide site, alternating taking the steel targets under fire as they covered their bounding retreat across the scrub-strewn slope toward the trees on the far side of the meadow. The rest were falling into the rhythm quickly enough, as they should. This wasn't a first-time thing for any of them. While they'd needed some time working together to make sure everyone was on the same page at first, this was just blowing some of the dust off their skillsets, and reminding everyone what they were doing. The Blackhearts hadn't brought in a new guy since Hank, and the younger Brannigan was doing fine.

Flanagan smiled faintly behind his thick, black beard as he watched. Hank Brannigan was keeping close to Tackett, almost shepherding him. Nobody had told the former infantry officer to do that, but he was simultaneously trying to be like the mostly NCO Blackhearts and trying desperately not to be the FNG anymore.

Still, Tackett was holding his own. He had Brannigan's SIG550—which he'd seemed to appreciate the most, picking it up with a distant, almost wistful look in his eye—and so far, he'd dinged every steel target he'd shot at. His movement was good, his situational awareness was on point. Even as Flanagan watched him, he came off sights, looked over his shoulder to check fields of fire and make sure he wasn't about to run into another Blackheart's muzzle, then got to his feet and dashed a short way toward the next bit of microterrain cover.

The man knows what he's about. Of course, if this was the guy that Vernon White had talked about, that stood to reason. It was gratifying to see it, though, rather than just hear about it.

The Blackhearts continued their Australian Peel back toward the trees, and Flanagan paced them, walking upright and making sure he was well away from their line of fire. He trusted all of them—even Jenkins—to watch their shots, but it paid to play it safe.

"Consolidate!" Brannigan's bellow echoed across the meadow, and they started to fall in toward his position under a massive, lightning-blasted fir that stood out among the rest of the trees. He looked out and up the hill then, met Flanagan's gaze, and nodded.

Flanagan nodded back. The drill wasn't over. He reached into his pocket, pulling out another firecracker and a small remote.

He and Hank had helped Brannigan set these targets up the year before. They hadn't used them in training yet, so they would be a surprise to the rest. It annoyed him a little that Hank knew what was coming, but here was no getting around that. Besides, the kid wasn't *that* much of a kid anymore.

Lighting the firecracker, he tossed it off to the side, downhill from the just-formed perimeter. It blew with a deafening *boom*, and he pushed the button on the remote.

Six pop-up steel targets flipped upright in the trees just downhill from where the Blackhearts had consolidated. "*Contact!*"

Tackett actually spotted the targets first. He dropped three with as many shots, the reports almost blending together into a single roll of thunder. Flanagan felt his eyebrows climb toward his hairline. That was some good shooting.

Tackett held his position, dropping two more targets, as the rest of the team rolled out, bounding through the trees and up the hill, paralleling the edge of the meadow. They didn't go as far this time, and by the time Tackett was up and moving, Brannigan was already calling for consolidation.

Flanagan nodded appreciatively. Tackett might not be a Blackheart, but if they were going to have a strap-hanger, it was looking a lot like he'd be an asset, rather than a liability.

***

Midday wasn't the ideal time for this kind of thing, but there was a limited time window they had to work with. So, as the Blackhearts moved carefully through the trees toward the trailer set up at the top of the meadow, they had to be extra careful to avoid being spotted.

They didn't have a lot of camouflage. They'd mostly showed up in civilian clothes. Tackett had brought some, but he didn't have their experience with this sort of thing. Unless Van Zandt's quiet intel agency or some other shadowy ally—such as Erika Dalca's underworld operation—was getting them in, they usually had to source their gear and equipment on the ground, and that meant avoiding packing anything that might draw attention to themselves when they got through Customs.

They hadn't even taken camouflage fatigues on the Azerbaijan job, even with the Russians facilitating their entry.

Of course, that had been a double-cross, anyway, so it probably hadn't made that much difference.

Gomez padded from tree to tree, using the faint breeze to mask what little noise he was making as much as he was using the shadows and the concealment offered by the woods to shield himself from the trailer. He paused under a surprisingly thick spruce with branches most of the way down to the forest floor, taking a knee and glancing around him.

Jenkins stood out the most, and even he was bounding carefully from concealed position to concealed position. Curtis hustled past, bounding forward, making too much noise, but still probably not enough to get them compromised.

Tackett, though, was a ghost.

Gomez was looking right at where the man should be, judging by his awareness of the rest of the team as they'd made their approach from the last covered and concealed position. There was no sign of him. Gomez's black eyes narrowed as he scanned the undergrowth. There he was. Crouched in the shadows beneath another spruce, he was almost perfectly concealed, camouflage or no camouflage.

The man knew his stuff in the bush. Gomez had to give him that. He was almost as good as Gomez himself, who had been in a constant, low-level competition with Flanagan and Childress from almost the beginning to be the foremost sneaky woodsman in Brannigan's Blackhearts. If Tackett hadn't been an outsider, he might be in the running, himself.

Gomez turned his attention back forward. He wasn't there to evaluate Tackett. That was for Flanagan, Santelli, and

Brannigan. He was there to do his part of the training, show the Colonel that he hadn't gotten slack during their down time, and get ready for the mission.

Easing around the tree, he picked his next piece of cover and figured out the route that would keep him concealed on the way there. The shadows in that part of the woods were deepening, now that it was getting into late afternoon. The chill hadn't lifted enough for his Southwestern blood, but Gomez had been a Recon Marine, in addition to being half Mescalero Apache, so he wasn't going to complain. Or even shiver.

A few paces got him to the fallen tree, and he only caught glimpses of the trailer through the foliage as he moved. His concealment had held.

In ones and twos, the Blackhearts were spreading out in a rough crescent around the trailer. Those higher up, including Curtis and Bianco—their two team machinegunners, though they didn't exactly have belt feds at the moment—would hold in place and form the base of fire.

A moment later, Flanagan was on his feet and moving toward the door, his FAL up and pointed at the door. Wade, Gomez, and Tackett fell in behind him, covering each corner and window, as they moved quickly—but not quite at a run—to the trailer.

The trailer itself had seen better days. It wasn't going anywhere anytime soon. The tires were all flat, and the fiberglass walls had been bullet-riddled several times over.

This wasn't the first time the Blackhearts had used it as a target site.

Flanagan stopped just short of the door, keeping his rifle trained on it. Wade and Gomez had fallen back just a little, putting Tackett in the Number Two spot. That was deliberate. Brannigan had told them to before they'd started this little iteration.

Tackett didn't even hesitate, but stepped out, keeping his own weapon tucked under his arm and trained on the door, without flagging Flanagan in the process. He reached up, tested the handle, then yanked the door open.

Flanagan went in fast, and Tackett was right on his heels. The FAL barked deafeningly in the small space, and Flanagan yelled over his shoulder, "Small room!" Neither Wade nor Gomez needed the call, but it was a procedure they'd all carried over from the mil. The two of them pushed to cover the corners, anyway.

"Clear!" Flanagan called out, and Tackett echoed the announcement. "Coming out!"

"End-ex!" Brannigan's roar echoed across the clearing. "Bring it in on the trailer!"

The Blackhearts didn't take their time. It was getting late in the day, and the first flights were heading out early the next morning. Brannigan still beat most of them to the trailer, standing there with his arms folded.

"Fair enough performance, gents. Unfortunately, without more intel—not to mention time—we couldn't build anything like a mockup of where we're going, but we just needed to make sure we're all still on the same page, tactics-wise." He looked over at Tackett. "We also needed to make sure that you could hang with us, Dan. So far, it looks like you won't be a liability."

Tackett looked like he might be a bit uncertain as to whether that was a compliment or not. Gomez wasn't given to smiling much, but the corner of his mouth twitched upward just a little.

Brannigan and Flanagan then took the opportunity to go over just a few things that needed to be improved. The whole point was to knock the rust off skills that weren't always used, after all. It would have been surprising if there *hadn't* been any after action points.

Finally, Brannigan looked around and checked his watch. "That's going to have to be enough. Let's clean up and get ready to move. Morning comes early."

CHAPTER 7

Pain.

For an eternity, that was all that Vernon knew. Electric shocks coursed through his body, and he was pretty sure he'd just about bitten through his tongue. It was hard to tell, with all the other agony pulsating through his very bones. The heat skyrocketed, until he could barely breathe, only to plummet until he was shivering uncontrollably, at which point he'd get another shock.

He had no idea how long this had been going on. He couldn't see anything, and he wasn't sure if he had been blindfolded, or if the room was just that dark. Or if he was even in a room, or…somewhere else. Even when he roared and bellowed his defiance—almost always answered with another shock that locked up every muscle—he could barely hear his own voice. It was as if his surroundings drank every syllable, every noise.

Was he sitting? Or was he standing? Or lying down? He couldn't tell anymore. He tried to curl up into the fetal position, but he couldn't. He couldn't touch his own legs or arms. It didn't make any sense. It was almost like he was floating in space, without any control over his body.

A flicker, then, appeared out of the corner of his eye. *Oh, no. Not again.* Whenever the darkness had been somewhat relieved, whenever he'd been able to see or hear anything, it had been bad. And getting worse.

Shapes and colors started to come out of the dark, though he couldn't focus on any of them, as they sort of slid away as soon as he turned his eyes toward them. Strange sounds began to echo through the blackness. Howls, screams, disturbing drones and beats that clawed at his mind. Were there eyes out there, staring at him? Again, when he tried to focus on them, they disappeared.

He yelled and screamed, trying to drown out the horror show noises, but once again, he couldn't hear himself, but only the muffled interior sounds vibrating through his chest and head. His voice was lost in the vacuum around him, while the demonic sounds pressed in on him.

Leering faces that flowed and melted into ever more nightmarish shapes came out of the dark to laugh at him, as another round of shocks locked his body into a quivering spasm. They faded as quickly as they came, but they kept coming. He could have sworn he'd seen the Devil, along with people that looked like lizards, and others sprouting masses of tentacles from their mouths while third eyes appeared in their foreheads.

"What do you want from me?!" He still couldn't hear the scream, but only the faint echo of his voice inside his head. His throat felt dry as the Sahara, even as his head swam, and the heat started to climb again. Or was it getting colder? He couldn't tell anymore.

Then a new figure came walking on the void, clearer than the rest of the phantasms that tormented him. The screaming and crying got louder, and he suddenly wondered if the sound was outside of himself, or if he was making it, and if that was why he couldn't hear himself talk.

As the figure got closer, it bent over him, as if he was lying down, though he had been pretty sure he was standing up. Or sitting in a chair. What was happening?

It all got worse when he looked up into his own face.

It was and it wasn't his own face. He recognized his features, but the look in the eyes and the cast of the expression was so full of contempt, loathing, and hatred that it was as if he was looking at an entirely different person. Someone he'd never been, even through all the years of...

Of what? Panic started to well up in his chest as he realized he couldn't remember much of anything beyond this awful, dark void swimming with horrors. Was he himself? Or was he really this cold-eyed, evil-looking sonofabitch staring down at him?

The doppelganger spoke, then, but the words were as muffled as his own had been. He couldn't make out what he was saying. Was that the truth? Was that other him really him, and that was why he hadn't been able to hear himself? So, then, who was he?

Despite himself, he started to scream, and scream, and scream.

He still couldn't really hear it.

***

Boyd wasn't the man's real name. At this point, he would have had to think a little to remember what his real name was, he'd spent so much of his adult life using one alias or another. Ordinarily, he didn't really care.

But watching the man twisting in the sensory deprivation tank, hooked up to electrodes and a steady drip of psychotropic drugs, while the soft-looking techs and researchers in their white lab coats carefully monitored his brain waves and vital signs, adjusting the sounds being pumped into the earphones affixed to his head and messing with the temperature, he couldn't help but feel some unease at that lack of identity. He knew all too well what was being done to the captured contractor, and it made him wonder a bit about his own sanity, when he had to dig around in his memory to dredge up who *he* really was.

He looked down at Doctor Karesinda, the pretty blonde who was heading the experiments up. He was pretty sure that wasn't her real name, either. Physically, she was one of the most stunningly attractive women he'd ever met. But there was something about her, something that went beyond the gleam in her

57

eye as she tormented their prisoners and test subjects, that was decidedly repellant. As dead as he knew his own soul was—or would be, if he believed he had any such thing—she really wasn't human anymore.

He'd still take his turn whenever she inevitably knocked on his door and invited herself in. She'd been using his security team room as her own stable of gigolos since they'd gotten there, and he wasn't opposed to it. Again, physically, she was a stunner. But he wouldn't be able to avoid wondering if he was just another test subject.

He'd certainly be careful about his drinks and his food for the foreseeable future. Who knew what she might try to slip one of them before an evening's recreation, just to see what would happen?

Karesinda touched another button on the touchscreen in front of her. "He's reacting, but not quite the way we want. He's still holding on to some thread of his primary personality." She bit her lip. Under any other circumstances, the gesture might have been sexy as hell. Given what he was looking at, Boyd found it vaguely irritating. "We need him to dissociate, or this will have been a waste of time."

"It might be a waste of time, anyway." Boyd crossed his arms over his chest. "Somebody like that, a trained warfighter, isn't going to crack easily. He's used to pain and discomfort. You need someone a bit more…pliable."

The look Karesinda turned on him was at once contemptuous and apparently dumbfounded that the hired monkey had dared to venture an opinion on things beyond his purview, such as researching how to break a man's mind with drugs, torture, and sensory deprivation, to turn him into a pliable tool.

"That, in fact, makes him the ideal subject for this experiment, Mr. Brody." He was sure she had called him by the wrong alias on purpose. Doctor Karesinda didn't make mistakes. She was telling him exactly how important he was. "Adjusting a weaker individual's personality is easy. We've been doing it for years. To create a truly dangerous operative, one who can be trusted with higher-level tasks, we need to learn how to manipulate this kind of personality. Which is why we are here." For a moment, she put on her pretty girl mask, and patted him on the arm. "You and your team *are* to be commended for taking these alive. It has sped the process up *considerably*. We would have needed to go much farther afield to capture subjects like this if these contractors hadn't come looking for us. Even the local Kyrgyz soldiers haven't been *quite* sufficient for our needs."

Boyd wasn't sure he liked the sounds of that. How long before the "researchers" decided that they had enough security contractors that they could start pulling from his team for more test subjects?

Once again, he resolved to check his food and drink *very* carefully for the duration of this assignment.

"Let us worry about the research, Mr. Brody." She patted him on the arm again, condescendingly. "That's what we get paid for, while you get paid to keep the reactionaries away from this facility. You do your job, and we will do ours."

Boyd kept his expression carefully controlled as he turned toward the door. Karesinda was already ignoring him, his irrelevant intrusion into her twisted work dismissed, turning back to adjusting the drug levels and the timing of the electroshocks as the captured contractor writhed in the tank, his limbs restrained in such a way that he shouldn't feel the restraints, his mind going somewhere dark and nightmarish as the drugs teamed up with the most unpleasant stimuli that Karesinda and her coven of weirdos could dream up.

The expression on her face was downright aroused, which Boyd found the most disturbing part of the entire interaction.

***

The team room was almost a refuge, though it wasn't as much of one as it might have been. The client had forbidden their security contractors to lock any interior doors, which meant they had constant access to any space the contractors might have called "private." So far, the only intrusions had been the female researchers coming into contractors' bedrooms when they felt like it, but while that had been a source of some leering fun, Boyd couldn't help but think that they were just being fattened up for something else.

After all, these Humanity Front types almost all thought of the gunslingers as little more than occasionally useful knuckle-draggers, who were there to be used and otherwise contemptuously disregarded as relics of the past. He found that a little amusing, given how much of the Front's work had been done in the last few years by Flint's Special Purpose Teams, but he'd been in the contracting world for long enough—even before hiring on with the Front—to be somewhat resigned to the attitude. It was everywhere.

It was getting late. The rest of the team was either out on patrol or bedded down for the night, so the team room was empty. Boyd didn't feel like going to sleep, not after what he'd just watched, so he slumped down on the couch and turned on the TV.

He almost immediately regretted it, since the movie that was still in the Blu-ray player was *The Cell*. He turned it off after a couple of minutes and plugged in the PS5.

But even ripping and tearing through demons for the next half hour didn't settle his mind.

What the hell are you doing here? You're not Flint. You're not even that freakish German, Winter. He wasn't a true believer. Oh, sure, he was pretty sure that the Front was going to get their way, eventually. He'd seen enough, working for them over the last few years. They had people everywhere, in every governmental, financial, and entertainment entity that mattered a damn. They were slowly, steadily, pulling the world the way they wanted, and he'd become convinced that it was better to take their money than possibly get in their way.

Or become their guinea pig.

Might be a little late for that.

Of course, he knew why he was there. It was just hard to face, sometimes.

Gabby's a greedy, extravagant bitch, and you still don't want to break up with her, even if you have laid three of the "researchers" here over the last few weeks. And you know damned good and well that if you try to cut away at this point, they'll burn you down. You've done things that would get you The Chair if anyone found out. And they will *make sure someone finds out.*

Or would they? He thought about it as he ran down another passage, pausing just long enough to rip an imp in half. No, they probably wouldn't. At the very least, he'd probably meet with a terrible car accident, or "commit suicide," presuming he didn't get rolled up by a black bag squad in the middle of the night and find himself in that poor bastard's place in the isolation tank.

He shuddered for a moment, just long enough for the hell knight to crush him and the menu screen to come up again. With a grunt of disgust, he tossed the controller aside, grabbed a nearly-full bottle of vodka off the little bar they kept in the team room, and headed for his room.

At least Karesinda would probably be occupied for a while, so he wouldn't have to hide his disgust while he banged her.

CHAPTER 8

Brannigan did his best to look bored, if slightly impatient, while the shrimp of a Kyrgyz Border Guard, dressed in snappy, pressed camouflage utilities and a flat-topped field cap, examined their passports. He glanced over at Wade, who was actually doing a pretty good job of not staring murder at the Kyrgyz security, which was surprisingly light. Wade's ice blue eyes and generally aggressive stance tended to make him intimidating even when he wasn't trying to be, and right then wasn't the best time to rub one of their "hosts" the wrong way.

"Purpose of your visit?" The little man actually spoke English, though not well. Given the fact that Manas had been the primary staging point for Coalition forces going into Afghanistan for years, it probably shouldn't have been much of a surprise.

"Hiking in the Tian Shan mountains." That elicited a narrow glance, as the little man looked him over, then Wade, then Tackett. Brannigan had told Santelli to make sure that their client and strap-hanger was on the same flight with him. It looked like Tackett was going to be an asset, but best to keep an eye on him, nevertheless.

He knew why the border guard was giving him the side eye. Usually, hikers in Central Asia were professorial types or hippie college kids who were convinced that the world was their oyster and nothing bad could happen to them. This guy had to have seen enough meat eaters go through Manas over the years that he had to be a *little* suspicious. Wade was a walking billboard for "cold-eyed killer," Brannigan himself was big and mean-looking, clearly fit for his age, and had been through plenty of combat himself. Even Tackett, as average-looking as he appeared at first glance—five foot eleven, lean without being overly muscular, brown haired and clean shaven—carried himself with the unavoidable readiness that combat soldiers always did. Nobody was going to mistake the three of them—or any of the rest as they filtered in—for the usual clueless tourists who wanted to see the mountains and thought that all the talk about jihadi threats was just scaremongering.

The border guard didn't comment on their unusual appearance, though. He handed their passports back. "The Tian Shan mountains are dangerous during this time of year. If you get hurt up there, it can take a very long time to reach you. You should be careful."

Brannigan nodded as he took the passports and handed them off to Wade and Tackett. "We will. We've had some experience with these sorts of trips."

Boy, is that an understatement.

He'd wondered if Customs was going to inspect their luggage, but the border guard had simply asked if they had any prohibited items or anything to declare. They didn't, and they'd said so. For a moment, Brannigan wondered if Jenkins or Curtis had brought something they shouldn't have. Neither man was known for his better judgement. But despite the occasional issues—and in Curtis's case, they all seemed to be off the job—both men were professional enough they wouldn't have tried to smuggle something into the country that could compromise the mission.

Glancing over his shoulder, Brannigan saw Kirk and Bianco gathering their bags from the single luggage carousel in the terminal. They paid each other no mind. It might already be suspicious enough to see several groups of men in their thirties to fifties, clearly in good shape and alert, all showing up to go hiking.

Any more association with each other while in Bishkek might work against them.

It wasn't just the Kyrgyz government he was worried about, though Brannigan was keeping an eye on the airport security as they walked out of the terminal and into the cold, gray spring day outside. If the Humanity Front was involved, he suspected that they had eyes and ears everywhere, most especially at the airport.

He hadn't seen anyone who pinged his radar yet, but knowing the Front's technical resources, it was entirely possible that their surveillance was entirely electronic.

He wondered how often the power went out in Bishkek, and how that would affect technical surveillance.

There were a handful of taxis in the parking lot outside the airport terminal. The trees that lined the road, those that weren't pines, still didn't have their leaves yet, and the Tian Shan mountains loomed in the distance, white where they didn't disappear into the clouds. Through the trees, Brannigan could just see the old USAF transit facility, where thousands of US troops had stayed while waiting for military flights into Afghanistan. It looked quiet and dead now, nothing and no one moving through the paved lanes between the semi-permanent structures.

"Taxi or bus?" Wade shifted the weight of his pack on his shoulder. Since they were supposed to be hikers, they'd all brought commercial backpacks rather than suitcases or duffels.

"I read that it's harder to get ripped off if we take the bus." Brannigan was already heading toward the Marshrutka 380, a white minibus with "Manas 380" in Cyrillic letters on a sign propped up in the window.

The bus was empty except for the driver, a wizened little man with a white mustache, wearing a heavy, dark blue jacket and a fur hat. He glanced at them when they got in, especially as Brannigan's and Wade's size set the vehicle to rocking on its shocks, but otherwise paid them little mind, especially as Brannigan handed over thirty som for the ride.

65

They waited a little longer. They weren't the first ones on the ground, and Brannigan had to assume that most of the others who'd already arrived had moved out into town. Behind them, Kirk and Bianco were getting into an ancient-looking yellow Lada with a "Taxi" sign on the roof. He was pretty confident that Kirk wouldn't get ripped off. The man knew the ways of scams and baksheesh well. He'd been around.

Finally, the driver put the minibus into gear without a word and lurched into motion.

The ride was an interesting one, that was for certain. The old man behind the wheel seemed to have an utter disdain for the laws of physics, and they probably came within inches of crashing into another vehicle many times. The road wasn't exactly smooth, either, and the bus's shocks had clearly seen better days.

Both Brannigan and Wade just rode out the bumps, the sudden accelerations, the abrupt swerves, and the equally sudden and hard braking. They'd both spent plenty of time in the Third World of late, and they were about as used to this kind of driving as any Westerner could get.

Brannigan watched Tackett, though. From what he'd said, he'd been out of the game for a while, and if Price's operation in Southeast Asia had been as fancy as it had sounded, he probably hadn't been on this side of the tracks in even longer. But if the man was disturbed by the Kyrgyz bus driver's recklessness, he didn't show it. He leaned back in his seat and closed his eyes.

Brannigan and Wade shared a look, and Wade shrugged. It was a good sign, really. Given what they'd seen of Tackett's performance on training day, this just reinforced the impression that the man was a seasoned operator. Southeast Asia clearly hadn't been his first go-round.

Brannigan was tempted to do the same. Jet lag was a bitch, and while he'd slept on most of the flights over the Atlantic and Europe, that didn't change the fact that they were a good thirteen hours off from home. The next few days were going to be rough.

But a time sensitive mission was a time sensitive mission. Tackett's friends probably didn't have a lot of time, if they were still alive. And if the Front was involved...

Truth be told, that was what had Brannigan more focused. He'd come to respect Vernon and Max during the Chad mission, but he considered shutting down whatever the Front had going up in those mountains more important.

He caught glimpses of the snow-laden Tian Shan mountains through the windshield as they plummeted down the highway toward the Bishkek skyline, wreathed in smog. Somewhere up there, some of the nastiest enemies he'd ever faced were hatching some new nightmare.

I'm coming for you, you bastards.

***

It took several more buses to get to the Hotel Futuro. The place looked weird as hell from the outside, with the entire second story forming a sort of sectioned billboard overhanging the sunken first story, with a whole bunch of wooden poles appearing to hold up the front, though none of them were exactly straight. The place looked solid enough, so Brannigan suspected the poles were there for some aesthetic reason that only the architect could really fathom.

Check in went quickly enough, even though the clerk didn't speak much of any English. He and Wade had enough Russian to make the transaction work, and then the three of them were heading upstairs to their suite.

The suite was compact, but clean and modern. The interior walls were a dark gray, but there were lights inside the fake wood wainscoting, and the window let in plenty of light, though it was the gray of the overcast, early spring day. There wasn't much room around the king size bed, though when Tackett went exploring, he found that the love seat by the window folded out into a twin bed with a very thin mattress. There was no space between its side and the foot of the main bed, but none of them would have to sleep on the floor.

At least, not for the one night they expected to stay there.

Brannigan dropped his pack on the bed and opened it, fishing out the radio and switching it on. It was a commercially available job, though one that ordinarily required a ham radio license in the States. It probably did in Kyrgyzstan, too, but they didn't intend to spend so much time on the radio that they attracted government attention.

He powered it up and checked the battery. Plenty of juice. They'd brought these in part so that they wouldn't have to source radios locally—the weapons and gear were going to be bad enough—but also so they could communicate without having to go through the rigamarole of buying cell phones in Bishkek. In most countries, especially in a post-Soviet republic, a passport was necessary to buy a SIM card, which would have put a record on their traffic. None of the Blackhearts wanted that to happen, so they'd stick with the radios.

Maybe someday they'd have to get some convincing fake passports for missions like this one.

The hiking cover would have been their explanation if the border guards at Customs had searched their luggage. Cell phones wouldn't have been that useful up in the mountains, anyway.

Checking his watch, he decided to risk it. "Woodsrunner, Kodiak." It was possible that Flanagan, Curtis, and Burgess hadn't gotten to their hotel yet, or were otherwise in a public place where they couldn't have the radio on, but he thought they'd probably had enough time.

"Send it." Flanagan's voice was scratchy but legible.

"We're checked in. Just getting a head count."

"We're up." Flanagan broke squelch once. "We got eyes on Pancho Villa, Guido, and Noob on the way here."

"Roger." Brannigan broke again. "Shady Slav, Kodiak."

"This is Shady Slav." If anything, Javakhishvili's accent had gotten thicker. "I have Ventura with me. We're in our hostel. It's actually nice, for a post-Soviet hellhole."

"Good copy." Brannigan checked over the roster in his head. "Gamer, Kodiak."

"This is Lumberjack." Kirk's callsign had become obvious as soon as Curtis had seen his beard. "We just got into our room. Gamer's getting set up to make contact with our boy."

"Roger. Pass the word when you get it."

***

To Bianco's surprise, the hotel had internet, and from what he could see, it was pretty fast. Fast enough that even when he activated the VPN then started his Tor browser and headed into the .onion site where he'd made contact with their guide and facilitator, it didn't even really slow down much.

Fortunately, he hadn't had to do a lot of digging. While Abernathy's unit—whoever they were; Bianco still wasn't sure— had been too tasked out to do much out in Kyrgyzstan, at least not for a few days, they'd provided the Blackhearts with a contact, and the information to get in touch with him securely. The dark web was the most secure place, given what they were looking for.

Bianco had poked around in the dark and scary parts of the internet a little bit in the past. He was always leery. There were some very, very bad people who used the dark web. But in a potentially hostile country, with the Humanity Front involved, he couldn't think of a more secure way to contact this guy.

We are on the ground. Time and place?

He waited. There was no telling when their contact would check the site. They might not get an answer until morning.

But just before he backed out, the return message came through. *0815 tomorrow, Kara-Jygach Park. Have a newspaper in your left hand. I will be in a leather jacket with a fur cap on, at the north end of Lake Pionerskoye. When you shift the newspaper to your right hand, I will take my cap off.*

Bianco decided that was probably enough. While the VPN/Tor combination was extremely secure, with the Humanity Front involved, he couldn't be sure that someone *wasn't* trying to listen in. He backed out, shut the laptop, and looked up at Kirk.

"We've got our meeting."

"Good." Kirk hefted the carbon fiber stiletto he'd carried in his boot. Bianco currently had an identical weapon hidden behind his belt. They weren't really good for anything but stabbing, but they'd become the Blackhearts' go-to self defense weapons when they couldn't carry guns. "Let's hope that Hauser's trust isn't misplaced."

CHAPTER 9

Flanagan felt out of place. Not that the early morning bothered him. The cold didn't either; he was dressed for the weather and for their surroundings. But he was a six-foot-tall, broad-shouldered Westerner in a city without a lot of Westerners. Most of the people he'd seen were Kyrgyz, all decidedly Asiatic, Turkic people, smaller, browner, and with pronounced epicanthic folds around their eyes. A six-foot, green-eyed Irishman stood out. A lot.

He was keeping to the trees as much as he could, for just that reason, but he still had to avoid *looking* like he was sneaking and lurking.

Scanning the western bank of Lake Pionerskoye, which was currently little more than a pit with some large puddles of standing water, surrounded by a dirt walking path and some playground and exercise equipment, some of it falling down, all of it peeling paint and rusting, he took in all the people he could see out and about. A couple of younger men in tracksuits were going through a calisthenics warmup on the far side, and he noted them carefully. They were just about the right age to be security forces.

There weren't that many people out and about at this hour of the day. It was the middle of the week, even for the large population of Muslims in Kyrgyzstan, for whom Friday was Sunday. Most people were going to work.

He spotted Javakhishvili walking past the workout crew. Their Georgian medic slowed and stopped, watching, then approached them and started talking. Flanagan hid a faint grin as their self-proclaimed "Shady Slav"—even though Georgians weren't really Slavs, Javakhishvili could move seamlessly between most former Soviet populations—stripped off his jacket and joined the young men in their routine. He was well placed to keep watching the meeting site and the surrounding area, while simultaneously maintaining closer surveillance on their most likely competition.

Got to hand it to the man. He knows his shit, and he's a damn chameleon.

Bianco was walking up from the southern end of the "lake," bundled up against the morning chill and carrying the morning's *Vecherniy Bishkek* in his left hand. He was dressed largely like a local, though the young man's sheer size made him stand out a bit. There'd been some debate over the radio the night before about who should make contact, but Bianco had been the one in communication with their facilitator, so he was the man on the spot.

Flanagan had spotted Kirk, Burgess, Jenkins, and Brannigan by the time Bianco moved past him. Curtis was staying back in the hotel, along with Hank, keeping an eye on local police frequencies, for what it was worth with the language barrier. If the rest of the Blackhearts—except for maybe Javakhishvili—might stand out a little, Curtis would have been a little too glaringly obvious. They hadn't seen a single other black man since getting on the ground.

Wade and Gomez were nowhere to be seen, but Flanagan knew they were there, stationed off to the north to keep an eye on the other approaches through the park.

If the Front, or the local security forces, decided to crash the party, there was a limited amount they could do, aside from call a warning and bombshell away. They all had their various

72

covert and improvised weapons. Flanagan himself was carrying one of the carbon fiber stilettos as well as a roll of quarters that made for a good load for a fist. But if it came to it, better to scatter and break contact than get in a fight.

He checked his watch as Bianco continued toward the meeting site. Two more minutes.

**

Bianco had been in combat in all kinds of places, usually with minimal support. He'd been scared every time, but he had always managed to push that to the back of his mind. Almost always, anyway. There'd been that one time in Chad, but he'd gotten over it, and had even survived getting cut off, alone and unafraid, in the jungle in Colombia. He'd been in far worse scrapes than walking through a park in a place that wasn't an active warzone, despite some recent terror attacks aimed at embassies in Bishkek.

So why am I so damned nervous?

He thought he'd caught glimpses of the other Blackhearts, but he was so focused on trying to spot their contact that he couldn't be sure. He knew they were there, but right then that was small comfort. He was as exposed as he ever had been, out in the open, barely speaking any of the local language—and even then, that was Russian he'd picked up from Herc, not Kyrgyz—and about to try to conduct a covert action in broad daylight.

Movement in the trees ahead caught his eye, and then a deeply-tanned man in jeans, black and white shoes, a black leather jacket, and a black Russian fur hat walked out of the lane to the north, turning down the path that encircled the dried-up lake, pausing next to one of the fallen concrete platforms just a few yards away from the walled compound at the tip of the lake.

Forcing himself not to gulp or otherwise appear nervous, Bianco shifted the newspaper to his right hand.

As he did so, he realized that the man wasn't looking at him, and he wondered if he'd just blown it. A moment later, though, the man reached up and took his hat off, scratching his short black hair before turning and walking casually down into the trees. Without any other course of action being obvious, Bianco followed him, noticing Flanagan only a couple yards away, doing the Slav squat while he looked out at the lake and smoked a cigarette. Bianco hadn't even known Flanagan smoked, but he realized after a moment that he didn't, that he was putting on a show for anyone watching.

Once he got deeper into the trees, even though they were hardly completely concealed from any observers, the man in the leather jacket stopped, lighting up a cigarette of his own. "So, you're the one looking for some special guide services in Kyrgyzstan?" He had a decided Australian accent, though he was fairly brown, with black hair and brown eyes. He wouldn't pass for a Kyrgyz, but he didn't stand out that much, either.

"Vinnie." Bianco stuck his hand out, and the man shook it, studying him closely.

"Carter." He took a deep drag on the cigarette, watching Bianco expectantly.

"We've got some hiking in mind." Bianco wanted to look around, make sure they weren't being watched or followed, but he knew that would only give the game away. He had to play this cool. Counter-surveillance was all on the other Blackhearts now. "Pretty far off the beaten path."

Carter was watching him, his eyes cool and appraising. "Well, I know most of the paths in this part of the world, beaten or otherwise."

"You've been in Kyrgyzstan a long time?" Bianco knew he had to feel this guy out, despite Hauser's recommendation. Abernathy's operator hadn't given a lot of details, and Brannigan had made it clear that they needed a bit more information.

The Australian expat chuckled. "You could say that."

"Australian Commandos?" It was a guess, but it seemed like a safe one.

Carter's face went still for just a moment. "Once upon a time. I've been private sector for a lot longer."

"You came highly recommended." Bianco decided to probe a little more. "We're not just concerned with finding our

74

way in the mountains. There's been some instability that we're a little concerned about, and our mutual friend said that you've got your finger on the pulse around here."

"Well, that depends on a few things." Carter started walking and Bianco had to accompany him, though he thought he saw Wade up ahead, leaning against the little building that formed a gateway to another trail moving back into the woods. "What kind of information are you looking for?"

Bianco suppressed the urge to gulp. This could all go bad in the next few moments. If Carter thought he was about to get burned…

"Anything that you wouldn't find in the local newspaper." He hefted the day's edition of *Vecherniy Bishkek*.

Carter laughed, a short, sharp bark. "That would fill libraries, my friend. You're going to have to narrow things down a bit."

He's not going to make this easy, is he? Bianco kept his expression and his mannerisms as calm, collected, and casual as he could. "Outsiders with lots of resources coming and going." He reached into his pocket, slowly and carefully, and pulled out a photo, holding his other hand—the one with the newspaper—up placatingly when Carter tensed. "Possibly any sign of this man?"

Carter was a pro. He didn't react visibly as he looked down at the printout of one of Mitchell Price's publicity shots from the website one of at least three PMCs the man had headed up—Bianco had lost track of which one was the most current, and he didn't think that this picture was from that website, anyway—but only studied it for a moment before looking up and studying Bianco carefully.

"You know who that is?" Carter asked.

"Very well. What do you know about him? Specifically, what he might be doing around here?"

"You're on very dangerous ground, my friend." Carter scanned their surroundings quickly and surreptitiously, almost imperceptibly. Bianco was momentarily proud of himself that he'd spotted it.

75

"So, you do know something about him." Bianco pocketed the picture.

"I know a lot. None of that information is free, though." Carter seemed to be reconsidering the wisdom of this meet. "And it bloody well isn't a subject for conversation in public, even out here."

Bianco spared a glance around, himself. He hadn't heard any alerts that they were being watched or otherwise monitored, and he hadn't seen any cameras. That didn't mean they weren't there—there was a reason it was often referred to as *Universal* Technical Surveillance—but he'd been looking on the way up the path. "Is there somewhere secure where we can talk? About information and... *other* logistical requirements?"

Carter paused a moment. "What *other* logistical requirements do you have in mind?"

"We plan on going hiking in the Tian Shan mountains south and east of Karakol." Bianco saw the flicker in Carter's eyes at that. "We packed light, so we're going to need *all* the equipment we'd need up there. For any contingencies that we might run into up in the mountains."

Carter clearly got it, then. He scanned their surroundings once more, though he was trying to be subtle about it. Maybe he spotted one or two of the other Blackhearts, maybe not. He dropped his voice. "Do you have any idea what you're talking about getting into?"

"More than you can imagine." Bianco was generally a big, genial, slightly boyish sort, but he was still a combat vet, a trained soldier, and a hardened killer. He wouldn't be a Blackheart otherwise. "It's not our first go-around."

Carter seemed to take that in for a moment. "If it weren't for our mutual friend, I'd probably tell you to get lost and never try to contact me again. This is some heavy shit you're getting into. But I trust him, despite some of our differences in the past." He sighed for a moment. "Meet me again in five hours at the end of Ulitsa Tursun Byara. The south end. I'll walk you in to my safehouse from there." He rubbed his chin. "How many?"

"About a squad in total." Bianco didn't need either Flanagan, Santelli, or Brannigan to tell him that giving concrete numbers at this point was a bad idea.

Carter visibly suppressed a grimace. "Tell them to come in ones and twos, and spread it out. Over an hour, at least."

"We'll be careful. Like I said, it's not our first rodeo."

If that was any consolation to Carter, he didn't show it. "Five hours." He turned and walked away into the trees.

Bianco stood there for a moment, then remembered that he needed to make himself scarce, now that the meet was over. Glancing around, he headed north and east, toward the edge of the park and away from either Flanagan or Wade. He needed to catch a taxi or a marshrutka.

When he glanced over his shoulder, Wade had already disappeared.

CHAPTER 10

With the entirety of the Blackhearts finally assembled in Carter's safehouse, an old, two-story plastered house with a steeply peaked, green tile roof, Carter retreated into a back room. Having taken his jacket off as they entered the warmth of the house—though it was heated by electric mini-splits rather than a regular furnace—they'd all seen the grip and low-slung slide of an Arsenal Strike One 9mm jutting from an appendix carry holster. That currently made him the most heavily armed man in the safehouse.

Tackett caught a glimpse of several computer monitors showing camera feeds from all the way around the house and the attached barn, just before Carter closed the door behind him. "He's checking that we weren't followed."

"Solid security practice." Brannigan didn't seem bothered by it. None of them did. Tackett reflected that while he had plenty of experience, he'd always been part of a larger crew, and didn't have the Blackhearts' track record in this kind of covert, underground operation with only a handful of bodies to rely on. While those days in the jungle in the Anambas had been hairy as hell, and with a limited number of teammates to rely on, it hadn't been quite the same as sticking one's head into the lion's den and relying on potentially treacherous local contacts.

Though this Aussie wasn't all that "local." He might have gone native, but he'd clearly been making his living facilitating things for Westerners, on several levels. That surveillance room was state of the art. Tackett might have been out of the business for a few years, but he could still recognize that much.

He looked around the room. The Blackhearts all seemed relaxed, though after a moment he saw that looks were deceiving. Wade, Gomez, Javakhishvili, and Burgess were posted up on the windows, none of them actually silhouetted in the openings, but watching every approach to the house. Carter might be checking his surveillance, but the Blackhearts were already on security with the tools at their disposal.

Brannigan, Santelli, Flanagan, and the others were positioned around the room where they could appear to be sitting and waiting, but where they all had eyes on the door Carter had disappeared into. Flanagan was actually positioned where he could come out of his chair and tackle Carter as soon as he came out of the door, just in case.

Finally, the door opened, and Carter came out with a folder in his hands. None of the Blackhearts moved, and Tackett could see that Carter noticed, too. A speedy glance across the room and he'd registered every man's position and attitude, as disguised by nonchalance as they were.

Carter understood the sort of men he was dealing with. The fact that he appeared more nervous about what or who was outside than these hired killers in his safehouse spoke volumes to Tackett.

The Aussie sat down on his threadbare couch against the whitewashed, plastered wall. "Okay. It looks like we got here clean, though with the CCTV cameras all over this bloody city, it's still kind of a tossup. The Chinese have been cozying up to install camera systems here, just like almost every other damned city from here to Suez. *And* they've got facial recognition software along with it. I don't know how much you've been read in, but I wouldn't trust the Kyrgyz police as far as I could throw my mum, and she weighed three hundred pounds."

"So, what can you tell us?" Brannigan watched the man like a hawk as he leaned back in his chair and watched their contact.

"The same thing I told your mate Vinnie, here." He waved at Bianco. "You gents are in way over your heads, if this is all you brought. What gave you the idea to come here in the first place?"

Several eyes turned toward Tackett. He leaned forward where he was sitting on a stool in the corner. "Several of my friends were working with Price. One of them called me just before they got rolled up in the mountains. We've come to get them out."

"And throw a monkey wrench into whatever their captors have going up there." Brannigan apparently figured that was a safe bit of information. Maybe that was rapport building.

"I'd ask when this was, but it's irrelevant." Carter tossed the folder on the kitchen table. "You should get on the first thing smoking and head home." He held up his hands. "Look, I can tell you're pros, but this is beyond you. Trust me." He looked at Tackett. "Your friends are gone. I'm sorry. That's just the way it is. Nobody who's disappeared in those mountains in the last few months has been seen again."

Brannigan shook his head. "Not good enough. I could care less about Price, but Dan's friends are also friends of ours." He leaned forward, his elbows on his knees. "But all of that is window dressing. We've got a pretty good idea who's up there, and we've got a score to settle with them."

He fixed Carter with an icy stare for a moment, then leaned back and folded his arms. "So, why don't you give us the rundown of these last few months, and what you know about what's going on up in the mountains above Karakol."

"Like I told your mate, that kind of information isn't free, and it isn't cheap." Carter pulled out a chair at the kitchen table and sat down.

"You've been paid, if you check your accounts." Brannigan's voice was cold.

Carter blinked, then got up without another word and retreated into the back room. Flanagan shifted his weight, ready to move, but Brannigan shot him a warning glance.

Tackett was impressed with how much these men communicated without saying a word. He would have killed to have a team like this during the Anambas job.

Carter came back out a moment later. "Well, I'll be damned. You've got some resources." He sat back down at the table. "Nothing like the people you're up against, though."

"We know. We've crossed paths with them before. So, what do you know about their operations here?" Brannigan wasn't giving out anything more than he already had. Carter might maintain that information cost, but that went both ways.

Carter looked around the room, his eyes settling on each man in turn. Finally, with a deep breath, he tapped the folder. "I've been trying to find out who they are since they first showed up. So were the local authorities, for about a week. Then they suddenly seemed to lose interest."

"Bribes big enough to buy an entire city will tend to do that." Flanagan had leaned back in his chair, his ankles crossed in front of him, yet he still seemed to be ready to come out of his seat in a moment.

Carter could only nod. "That was the only explanation I could come up with, too. The handful of contacts I've got around here who tried probing either disappeared or were picked up by the police and told in no uncertain terms that they needed to mind their own business.

"I do have a local source in the police who told me that they've got someone high up reporting to them, and that they possibly have extra technical surveillance around the city." He looked around at them all again. "I guarantee they're watching the airport. They have a few people quietly set up in the old Manas transit area."

Tackett frowned. He hadn't seen anyone there, but if they were using remote sensors and drones, then they wouldn't have needed to expose themselves to watch the airport.

"So, they probably already know you're here. Whoever they are." When he didn't get much of a reaction, Carter shrugged and kept going. "That's just their stay-behind, too. Most of them went up into the mountains." He opened the folder and pulled out several printed, black-and-white overhead photos. "As a further example of just how much money these people have to throw around, you can't get *any* recent imagery of that area of the mountains. There's an old, abandoned Soviet military base up there. I think it was used for some weird experiments by either the KGB or the GRU back in the day. Six months ago, you could find overhead imagery of it. There were always weirdo explorer tourists who wanted to go up and look at it. I've even been up there a couple of times. It wasn't much. A helipad, four Quonset-style hangars or warehouses, two concrete permanent buildings. The guard towers were rotting away, and if there was more foliage that high in the Tian Shan, the whole place would have been overgrown years ago.

"Now, though?" He tapped the stack of photos at his side. "Good luck finding anything newer than old U-2 overflight photos, or KH-11 shots from the Cold War. *Everything*'s been scrubbed. I can't find any newer imagery, and believe me, I've tried."

"That sounds about right." Santelli was nodding.

Carter started to look a little frustrated at the blasé reactions he was getting from the Blackhearts. "Look, mates, do you realize what I'm saying?"

Brannigan raised a hand before he could get going. "Yes, Mr. Carter, we do. We know exactly what we're up against. If our information is correct, then the mysterious new tenants on that base are working for the Humanity Front."

Carter blinked even harder at that. He frowned. "Wait. You meant the insufferable hipster cunts raking in billions of dollars every year and getting fawned over by every celebrity and politician on the bloody planet?"

Brannigan nodded grimly. "The same. That's just the shiny, happy face they put on for the glitterati and the press.

They've got big plans. We've only scratched the surface so far, but we've managed to put a dent in those plans, largely by staying small, stealthy, and hitting them where they don't think they can be hit. They were behind the terrorist attacks in the Southwest a few years ago, and when the Tourmaline Delta platform blew up? That was them. We *almost* managed to stop it.

"Since then, we've crossed paths with them a couple of times. They were experimenting with biological weapons under the guise of a humanitarian medical mission in Chad. And we chased one of their benefactors to an underground base in the Altiplano, where they were doing some weird stuff with human enhancement."

"They kind of went quiet after that," Flanagan put in, while Carter frowned down at the photos on the table, taking it all in. "Until now, if our intel's right." He looked over at Tackett. "From what his friend told him, they're up to something up here, and even if we can't get those guys out, we're here to shut down whatever new hell they're cooking up." He shook his head. "In a Soviet research base, of all places."

Tackett understood. There weren't many things the Soviets might have been doing in the mountains of Kyrgyzstan, far from Russia itself. None of them were likely to be particularly savory.

Carter was still frowning down at the floor, calculating. Finally, he looked up and nodded. "Well, I still think you're crazy. And coming from me, that's saying something. I've been in Central Asia off and on since 2005. Your mate Vinnie guessed it. Came here with the 4th Battalion, Royal Australian Regiment, then went private sector in 2007. I've been here ever since, though Kyrgyzstan had to become something of a fallback after that cock-up in Afghanistan."

He chuckled almost silently. "I'd guess that's how I got mixed up with you lot. I might have done some scouting and facilitating for various special operations units in the region over the years. Including working with a lad named Hauser."

The chuckle died, and he sighed. "If I can't talk you out of it, I guess I'd better earn my pay. What all do you need?"

"Weapons, ammunition, demo, optics, night vision, load bearing gear, the works." Santelli was taking over as the retired sergeant major. "Also transport, chow, extra batteries, and a couple radio repeaters if you can get them."

Carter shook his head. "Repeaters I can't do. Sorry. Pretty sure I can float the rest, especially for what you paid. It won't be fancy. Mostly castoffs from the Afghan National Army that some friends managed to get out of the country via the black market. The smuggling industry in this part of the world is *wild*." He stood up. "Come with me. I think we had ought to move quickly, in case you were spotted and identified. After all, if you've crossed swords with these people before…"

"No objections here." Brannigan stood up, and the rest followed suit as Carter led the way down the back hallway toward the attached barn.

*****

It took some doing to get the crates out. Carter had them buried in the dirt floor, underneath a couple of ancient tractors that looked like they shouldn't have even started, let alone moved. But they did, allowing access to the corrugated steel sheeting covered in dirt that concealed the hole.

There were a lot of crates down there. When Brannigan considered the fact that this was a safehouse, and not Carter's primary bed-down site—if even had one—then the extent of the man's operation became even more impressive.

Hauling the crates up, Carter cracked one of them open. Neatly secured in racks inside were twelve M4s, each with an ancient, chipped and worn ACOG on the top rail. Carter unfastened one of the securing rails and pulled a rifle out.

"They're Afghan Commando castoffs, so they're not in the *best* shape, but they're in better shape than the M16A2s or AK-47s that we could get from the regular ANA. No 203s, but I couldn't get any grenades for them, either, so that's a small loss." He started hauling what appeared to be a much heavier crate out of the hole. That one was stacked with loaded STANAG magazines.

"Any belt feds?" Curtis was peering down into the hole.

"I've got a couple of RPKs." Carter shrugged. "Couldn't get any SAWs. I think the Taliban and a few of the warlords managed to snap most of those up."

Curtis grimaced. "So Joe gets a proper American weapon, and I get stuck with ancient Russian castoffs that have been in Afghan hands for forever."

"You *could* take a rifle." Flanagan was watching him with a raised eyebrow.

"That would be settling, Joseph, and Mama Curtis's baby boy does not *settle*." With a grimace, Curtis held out a hand. "Give me the Russian relic."

"Seems to me that *settling* for an RPK just because it's a machinegun is still *settling*. Don't you agree, Hank?" Flanagan was barely hiding a grin.

"Don't you start!" Curtis stabbed a finger at Flanagan, then stabbed it at the younger Brannigan a moment later. "You keep out of this, Junior!"

Hank raised both hands. "I don't want any part of this particular lover's quarrel."

"*You take that back!*" Curtis advanced menacingly on Hank, who was desperately trying to stifle a grin of his own even as Flanagan laughed out loud. Carter was looking around at the lot of them like they were crazy.

Then Carter's alarm went off.

It wasn't much. Just a beep and a flashing red light on the wall, as one of his early warning systems got tripped. "Fuck!" He dashed toward the house, even as the Blackhearts hastily handed out the weapons and loaded them.

A moment later, Carter was back. "Kyrgyz police. Looks like a SWAT team.

"And they're definitely coming here."

CHAPTER 11

Boyd frowned as he watched the Kyrgyz police command center. His own Kyrgyz wasn't great. In fact, it was next to nonexistent. Which made his presence feel increasingly pointless, but the word had come down from the client that, since a Person of Interest had pinged on the Bishkek CCTV system's facial recognition system, he needed to supervise the takedown.

Under different circumstances, he might have been a little worried about the fact that the client was even plugged into this Third World shithole's surveillance system, but that was one more reason he was working for them. He'd seen this kind of reach demonstrated before, and it had convinced him that it would be a better idea to work *for* that kind of power and influence rather than get trampled by it.

Because the end result was inevitable, regardless of what he thought about it. The client had way too much money and too many connections. There was no way anyone was going to fight that. They'd already won.

His Kyrgyz handler, a stocky man named Nuraliev, spoke just enough English that they could sort of communicate. So, when the radio suddenly erupted with anxious traffic, Boyd turned to the shorter man with a frown.

Nuraliev, for his part, didn't seem all that happy to be playing babysitter to the taller Westerner in khakis and a dark blue collared shirt, openly carrying a Glock 17 on his hip, unlike just about anyone else in the country except for the police and the army. He ignored Boyd until the contractor asked, "What's going on?"

The dark, stocky policeman tilted his head and listened. "Sounds like target had tear gas grenades hooked to tripwire in door."

Boyd felt his stomach do a flip. This already wasn't good. This was supposed to be a sweep and clear, and he'd assured the researchers in charge of both projects back at the base that it was probably nothing.

Of course it isn't nothing. Not when Mitchell Price himself came out here. Dammit.

"We need to get reinforcements in there. Is the cordon in place?" He realized he was talking a little too fast, as Nuraliev frowned, trying to catch up with the English. Or maybe he wasn't frowning because he was trying to understand what Boyd was saying, but simply because the outsider was telling the Kyrgyz police what they were supposed to be doing.

When Nuraliev didn't bother to answer, Boyd pulled his phone out of his pocket. That got some evil looks, but the client had made it clear, via a *lot* of money in the right hands, that he was free to come and go and do as he pleased. The security violation of having a smartphone, even one as advanced and secure as his issued one, in a secure command center, went right along with letting a Western contractor carry a gun in the same command center.

"Get me a drone feed over the target." He wanted to cuss about the fact that they still didn't have an app that could automatically do that without having to call up to the base via the helicopter-dropped repeaters they'd sowed all over the mountains. Maybe eventually.

After all, what the security team wanted was less than important to the organization's researchers, and the researchers had the final say as to what happened with the organization's assets in Kyrgyzstan.

It took a few moments before the video window opened. The police radio was still making noise, though he couldn't catch more than a word or two. It sounded like they'd run into something else on the inside, once they'd donned gas masks and gotten past the CS in the entryway. They were definitely in the right place. They had to be. If the target wasn't there, why have defenses built in, especially defenses that even the local organized crime probably didn't have?

Unless we just stumbled on a different operation. He had a sudden cold feeling of dread that maybe they'd stumbled on a different client operation. It was possible. He couldn't say what all they were interested in in Kyrgyzstan, but he doubted it was just the operations on the base. They'd poured far too much money into this place to only worry about one installation.

What if I just sent the Kyrgyz police after one of the Special Purpose teams? That would be bad. Granted, he'd had no way of knowing. The Special Purpose teams never talked to anyone except the Board. That wouldn't save him, though.

Trying to beat back the images of himself being put in a shallow grave, Boyd peered at the live video on the small screen in his hands. The Kyrgyz SWAT vehicle was in front of the gate leading into the house, the gate itself wide open. The house's front door wasn't visible, being sheltered by the overhang over the porch, but as the drone moved to adjust its angle, he saw a flash through the windows, and a moment later, the radio erupted with still more frantic calls.

"What just happened? Was it an IED?" He looked up at Nuraliev, who had stepped toward the bank of radios, listening carefully.

The Kyrgyz cop didn't answer immediately. The yelling on the radio was nothing more than noise to Boyd. After a moment, though, he shook his head. "There was flashbang."

Boyd frowned down at the feed, then killed it and stuffed the phone back in his pocket. The drone was useless. "Where is the cordon set up? This is bad."

The police chief looked over and barked something in Kyrgyz. Nuraliev looked at Boyd levelly. "This is Kyrgyz police operation. Your advice is one thing. You cannot give Kyrgyz police orders."

Boyd looked around the room and knew that, no matter how much money the client had thrown at these people, he was not in a position of power here. He gritted his teeth and kept watching and listening.

I'm going to have to get the react team moving soon.

***

The shouts and yells echoed from the front of the safehouse and Brannigan looked over at Carter. "Had some nasty surprises set up out there, did you?"

The former Australian commando smiled wanly. "A few. There are a lot of threats here, not just the possibility that the government might get squirrelly. They're not exactly paragons of personal liberty and trust of outsiders, but there are organized crime orgs and jihadi networks all over here, too. Having a fallback plan was only prudent." He was already heading toward the back corner of the barn. As he started to move boxes and tarps aside, he nodded toward the rear door. "That's also why that door is welded shut."

"What kept us from setting that off?" Santelli had his M4 in his hands, watching the door leading toward the house.

Carter looked over his shoulder. "The entryway tripwire was an IR laser that I turned back on after everyone was inside."

He'd barely finished speaking when the whole structure shook with a loud *boom*. "And there goes the flashbang, so they've tried entering the hallway." He kept hauling stuff out of the corner. "Somebody give me a hand here. We don't have a lot of time."

Flanagan, Wade, and Gomez were posted up on the door leading from the house. The rest of the Blackhearts, except for Javakhishvili and Kirk, who covered the back door, just in case, moved to help Carter.

More muted bangs and thumps were coming from the main house, along with muffled shouts in what was probably

Kyrgyz. "There goes the next round of CS." Carter grunted as he heaved the last pile of corrugated aluminum away from the corner, revealing a trap door set in the dirt floor. "They'll be at the door in a few seconds, if they've got gas masks, which they will." He grabbed the handle and heaved the trap door open. The frame was set into a concrete box that disappeared into the dark below, ladder rungs set into the cement. "We need to move."

Wade had his eyes on the barred steel door, his weapon in his shoulder, already geared up and ready to fight. "What's going to keep them from following us?"

"Trust me, mate, I've got contingencies for this. Not that I'm happy about putting them into effect, but they won't follow us." Carter was already halfway down the ladder into the tunnel. "Let's *go*."

Brannigan looked around. They had all the entrances covered, but a last stand against the Kyrgyz security forces was not a viable alternative at the moment.

"Let's go. We can trust Carter or we can't, but I don't expect gentle treatment from the Kyrgyz cops."

"We could take 'em." Wade hadn't moved, his weapon and eyes still focused on the door. "They've only got one entry."

"Not the mission, Wade." Brannigan understood the sentiment. Wade was not a man generally inclined to leave live enemies at his back, if he could help it. But getting into a firefight with the Kyrgyz police would only be counterproductive at that point.

If the Front had bought them off, that was bad enough. Brannigan knew from long experience, however, that there was a world of difference between local security forces acting on bribes, and local security forces chasing down someone who'd shot one or more of their own. They had a chance to get away reasonably cleanly, but if they held their ground and fought, the hunt would get that much more intense.

Wade understood that. He wasn't dumb. Perhaps the most aggressive of the Blackhearts, but none of them was a blunt instrument. So, he fell back with Flanagan toward the trap door, even as the door began to shudder as the Kyrgyz police started to hammer at it.

"Come on!" Carter was starting to get agitated, sticking his head back into the opening from below. "I can cut them off, but we have to go *now*."

The Blackhearts were already flowing down the ladder into the hole. The tunnel was dark and cramped, and even Curtis had to duck his head to keep from scraping his scalp on the ceiling. Brannigan, the last one into the tunnel before Wade, had to bend almost double.

Wade scrambled down the ladder, not without one last turn to cover the door as it shuddered with another *bang*, but he had to duck as Carter pulled on a cable and brought the trap door back down with another *bang*.

Carter reached up beside him and pulled on another cable. A series of *pop*s sounded, louder in the enclosed space now that the noise of the assault on the barn door had been cut off by the trap door, and sparks flew as thermite ignited, welding the metal trap door to the frame. It was going to take a plasma cutter to get through that. "Come on." He turned back toward the front, but the tunnel was narrow enough that he couldn't move to the front. "Just push until you get to another ladder." He'd barely finished speaking when he reached over and pulled another switch set into the concrete wall. "We want to move fast, too. Those welds aren't airtight."

Brannigan wasn't entirely sure what that meant, but then he remembered the CS trap at the entryway.

The tunnel would have been pitch black if not for their weapon lights. Brannigan was a little surprised that the lights still worked, but Carter had clearly made sure that the weapons were in good shape before burying them.

Gomez was in the lead, he thought, and they moved fast. Brannigan wasn't entirely sure what direction they were moving, but Carter had put a lot of work into this escape route. Sure, by his own account he'd been in the region for a long time, but this was something else. The tunnel went on for a while.

As Gomez found an exit and started to climb out, Carter seemed to read his mind. "No, I didn't build this tunnel. I fixed up some of the other stuff, but the tunnel was thanks to the drug ring that the Kyrgyz police rolled up and shot dead at another safehouse on the other side of the city a few years ago."

When Brannigan glanced back at him with a raised eyebrow in the splash of illumination from weapon lights, the Australian shrugged. "Waste not, want not."

The exit ladder led up into a small room in the back of what appeared to be a tiny row apartment. The Blackhearts spread out through the apartment, guns up and searching for threats, clearing the structure before Brannigan, Carter, and Wade climbed out.

"Unless they've got drones covering everything, we should be good for a few minutes." Carter was already moving toward the front door. "I'd suggest making the weapons disappear for a bit."

The Blackhearts still kept eyes on the doors, the windows, and Carter himself as he cracked the door, peered out, then left the building and hurried to a windowless commercial van in the courtyard just outside. He hauled the side door open before climbing into the driver's seat. "Get in! Quick!"

Scanning the empty sky above for drones or helicopters, the Blackhearts flowed out and piled into the van, even as Carter ran to pull the steel gate open.

Wade hauled the side door shut as Carter swung the gate wide, and then their guide and facilitator ran back to the van, jumped in behind the wheel, and they were moving.

***

Boyd had pulled the phone out again. He couldn't make heads or tails of the Kyrgyz radio chatter, and Nuraliev wasn't being particularly forthcoming. The drone footage couldn't be much less informative.

Nevertheless, it told him about as much as it had before. At least, until what looked like white smoke billowed out of the windows of the barn attached to the target house.

93

"What just happened?" He looked up as the radio went nuts. Something in the video caught his eye, and he looked down in time to see flames starting to come out of the barn windows as the smoke turned darker, while the Kyrgyz SWAT team piled out of the main house.

"Fire in barn." Nuraliev sounded like he wasn't terribly surprised.

"Fuck." Boyd turned toward the door. This was bad. Whoever had been in there, they were either dead or gone. And without bodies, he knew his bosses weren't going to accept the verdict of *dead*.

He had more work to do.

CHAPTER 12

The back of the van was dark, the only view out being through a small window leading onto the front seats and the windshield. Carter was driving like a madman, and the Blackhearts were thrown to one side or another of the completely stripped van with each abrupt turn, but as Brannigan braced himself against the floor and ceiling, peering out that window, he saw that Carter wasn't driving in any way that would make him stand out from the normal Kyrgyz traffic. This place was every bit as bad as any Middle Eastern or African country he'd been in.

Carter was staying away from the main roads, but it was apparent from what Brannigan could see that he'd only be able to do that for so long, if they were looking to get out of the city. Kyrgyzstan didn't have an abundance of backroads once a driver got away from Bishkek. Brannigan knew that much from the map study he'd conducted before they'd even left the States.

That was going to create some problems. And a few minutes later, as the residential area they were driving through got narrower and they were getting closer to the point where they'd have to get back on the highway, the problems became nearly unavoidable.

Carter started to turn, then stopped partway out into the intersection, cursed fluently and viciously, then turned back the direction they'd been going and kept moving. "I hope like fuck they didn't see that."

"What?" The small window gave Brannigan some view, but he hadn't been able to see around the corner.

"Checkpoints." Carter was still cussing quietly as he kept them trundling along the dirt road along the north side of the dwindling city. "That was fast."

"We gassed a SWAT team and set fire to the target. They're going to be looking." It was better than if they'd gotten into a firefight, but not by much.

"I was still hoping that we could get out before they cordoned off the whole city. They're a former Soviet republic. They're not *that* efficient." Carter took another turn toward the north, skirting around a hill covered in trees, the branches still bare from the slowly dying winter.

Brannigan didn't comment. Carter was obviously agitated, and the longer they drove, the less he thought that their contact's cussing was just about how close they'd gotten to a Kyrgyz checkpoint. "How separated were you from that safehouse?"

"Separated enough, at least on paper. The lease is on a pseudo, and it gets paid in cash every month. There shouldn't be anything to connect me to it. Still, they had to have hit it for a reason." He glanced over his shoulder for a moment, though he didn't take his eyes off the road long enough to actually look through the window. "This bloody facial recognition tech is causing all sorts of headaches, though. I don't know what drew them in, but they either IDed you or they IDed me, and decided to move. Either way, we're both burned. You're targets if they were after me, and I'm a target if they were after you."

Carter didn't say it, but Brannigan could fill in the blanks easily enough. "More than likely it was us, unless you've had some conflict or failure in security that put you on the Kyrgyz government's shit list."

"Nothing I know of. Hell, I helped out as a subcontractor with some training for the border guards just three months ago."

He shrugged. "Always helps to keep them off my back if I do a few favors from time to time."

Brannigan nodded, even though Carter couldn't see the gesture. "We've had some run ins with the Front over the last few years. It's possible that one or more of us was identified." It was more than possible, truth be told. They'd known they'd been flagged as soon as the Front's hitters had gone after Sam Childress in the hospital.

"That's great." Carter's voice was vaguely bitter. "That means I'm now on their hit list too. Thanks a million for that."

"There's got to be a reason you've stayed in this part of the world for this long." Santelli had braced himself in the corner, and while he couldn't see through the window, he could hear.

"Yeah. There's a lot of bad people still out here, and there's good money to be made facilitating the death or rendition of those bad people." Carter almost sounded resigned, as if he knew what was coming next.

"These are the worst people you've ever gone up against." Brannigan knew Santelli was entirely sincere when he said that. He would never have come along otherwise. "Consider this a change of mission."

"Can you afford the kind of money I've been making out here?" Even as he said it, Carter sounded like he was only arguing because he thought he had to.

"Our supporters can." Brannigan was sure that if he explained things to Abernathy, he'd approve the additional funds to bring Carter on as another gun, even if Price's organization didn't cough up after all this. "We'll get you your money, and we'll do our damnedest to get you out of the country. Quietly." That was going to require some interesting logistics, and he saw Santelli wince a little as he thought of that at almost the same time.

Carter took another turn south, slowing as he surveyed their options. Brannigan couldn't see much, but it looked like they might have a route to the main road, on the other side of the checkpoint. That didn't mean there weren't more out there. He suspected that if the existing cordon came up empty, the Front would insist—probably with plenty of money to back it up—on expanding the search to the surrounding countryside.

"Fine. Never liked those Humanity Front cunts in the first place, even back in the old days. And if they're doing bioweapon shit up there, well. I guess I've got to look in the mirror in the morning, don't I?"

As he spoke, he took another turn, and then they were moving past several more dingy, run-down cinderblock houses with corrugated metal roofs, set within similarly rickety-looking compound walls, and out into the fallow fields to the northeast of Bishkek. The road wasn't getting any better, still nothing but bumpy dirt and gravel, but Carter had at least slowed down a little, no longer needing to fight the traffic even in the residential parts of the city.

Brannigan didn't say much of anything else, keeping his eyes on their route despite taking one glance back to assess the rest of the team. Everyone looked about as cool and collected as they could after the close call they'd just gone through. Even Tackett was composed, leaning back against the wall, his eyes open and alert, and he seemed to be taking in every turn and every change of terrain.

The route through the fields turned south again soon, and then they were approaching a village. There wasn't much to see, on account of the trees and bushes that grew thickly around all the houses and other village buildings, but it didn't look like the police had gotten there ahead of them. They rolled through the village without incident, though they got a few looks from the local populace. It didn't appear that a lot of unfamiliar traffic went down that road.

Then they were turning onto the highway and heading east.

***

It took almost three hours to get to Kichi-Kemin. It should have been faster, but Carter was being careful, especially by moving to backroads through the fields and villages whenever he thought he saw helicopters or possibly drones. He was being cautious, which Brannigan could appreciate, but three hours was also a long time to spend in the back of a stripped panel van.

Finally, he pulled in next to what looked like a farm in the foothills above the village. He stopped a few dozen yards away, pulled out a phone, powered it on, and waited a moment before sending a text message. From where he stood, Brannigan couldn't see which encrypted messaging app he was using, but he was obviously not sending in the clear. He was also texting in Russian.

A moment later, he got a reply and started rolling forward again, as the gate to one of the long outbuildings rolled open. A man with an AK-103 stood by the gate as they trundled inside, then shut it behind them.

Carter shut the van off and turned toward the little window where Brannigan was watching. "Yuri's a friend. I won't say he's entirely trustworthy, but he won't sell us out once an agreement's been made. He damned well won't play games with the local security forces."

"What's his deal? Smuggling?" Brannigan suspected, given the other vehicles and tarp-covered crates in the former farmyard.

"Exactly. Which is why he'll keep his mouth shut around the police. He's got too much to lose." Carter cracked the door. "Let me talk to him first." He nodded in their direction. "I'll stay out front where you can see, and you've got enough rifles to make this very unpleasant if either one of us sells you out."

He didn't wait for a response, but stepped out and walked toward the stocky, bald man with a thick mustache and pronounced epicanthic fold in his eyes, despite his pale skin. The two men embraced briefly, then spoke quietly, noticeably right out in front of the van, right where Brannigan could watch. Wade and Burgess had cracked the rear doors, and were watching that direction, each man on a knee, muzzles down but cross-covering through the narrow gap.

The two men talked for several minutes, Yuri turning grim quickly. Carter kept talking, though, pointing to at least one of the vehicles parked in the yard, then gesturing toward the sky.

Yuri—at least, Brannigan assumed that was Yuri—didn't look like he liked what he was hearing, and he was getting steadily grimmer as the conversation went on. Brannigan resisted the urge to step back and train his M4 on the Russian smuggler. That might not be necessary, it would cut off some of his view of the rest of the farmyard—where several more men had gathered to watch and listen, though none were carrying long guns—and if Yuri could see clearly enough through the filthy windshield, it might just torpedo the entire negotiation.

Finally, Yuri nodded and said something Brannigan couldn't make out, though Carter looked more than a little sour as he turned back toward the van.

He leaned in through the open door. "We've got new vehicles and some more gear. I hope like hell your backers come through, because otherwise this deal is going to ruin me."

***

It was getting dark when they finally rolled out. They'd traded the van for a UAZ Hunter and a UAZ 452 "Bread Loaf" 4x4 van. They even had some night vision now, mostly ancient, grainy, barely functional PVS-14s—one of which had a cracked casing—and every man had a boonie hat, balaclava, and sunglasses to defeat facial recognition software if the Front's drones had the capability.

Carter wasn't driving anymore. Brannigan had taken the Hunter, and Wade was driving the Bread Loaf. It had been a tight squeeze, getting everyone in with their weapons concealed, but they'd done it.

Now they just had to get around Issyk Kul and into the mountains without being intercepted. Brannigan was sure that the Front knew they were there, now, and they probably didn't have to guess why the Blackhearts had suddenly showed up in Kyrgyzstan.

They could only hope that they weren't too late for Price and his team.

Not to mention whatever the Front was up to in that old base in the mountains.

CHAPTER 13

Boyd stormed into the main building, thankful that he could avoid Dr. Karesinda's house of horrors for this. Price wasn't being kept with the others. They had other plans for the PMC magnate, now that they had him in hand.

He strode past the main floor security desk, where a couple of his guys were on static security duty. He'd been on contracts where the static and mobile security were separate teams, but there was no such luck to be had here. Everybody did shifts at both. Except for Boyd, because he had to be at the "researchers'" beck and call at all hours. *The extra pay really ain't worth it.*

He skirted the offices and storage rooms that took up the bulk of the main building, one floor down from the barracks that housed the researchers and the security contractors. All separately, of course, until the female researchers wanted some recreation. The holding cells were at the far end, on the first floor.

Holding Cells. Officially, they were "Secure Guest Quarters." They were certainly a lot more comfortable than the concrete holes that the test subjects in the next building over were living in. But they were cells, nevertheless.

Only one was currently occupied, and Boyd checked that his pistol was secure before he punched in the access code. The

101

electronic lock clicked, the light turned green, and he pulled the door open.

Mitchell Price didn't look much like the impeccably groomed, smiling, clean-shaven man in an expensive suit on the cover photos for his various Private Military/Security Companies. Not anymore. His hair was clean but hardly combed, he'd grown a short, graying beard since he and the rest had been captured, and he was still dressed in the same camouflage utilities he'd been wearing upon capture, just without a belt or boots. Everything that had been in his pockets had been taken, as well.

Boyd shut the door behind him and stood at the entrance, watching Price as the older man studied him impassively. The PMC magnate was sitting on the bed, the TV they'd provided turned off, most of the luxuries untouched.

"Who was your backup in Bishkek?" Boyd knew he wasn't a trained interrogator. They had interrogators on the base, but they all worked for Dr. Karesinda, and there was no way in hell he was going to try to get them involved. There were two reasons for that. One was simply that if they *did* get involved, things would get ugly and weird quickly. Of course, they *wouldn't* get involved, because Price was a different prize, and the client wanted him in one piece and at least mostly sane. Which formed Reason Two.

"What the hell are you talking about?" Price hadn't moved. He leaned on his knees with his elbows, watching Boyd, unblinking.

Boyd didn't move either, though he mentally kicked himself for starting off that way. Price wasn't like the soft-clothed psychopaths he worked for. He didn't *want* this to become a hostile interrogation. They were more alike than it would have first appeared. They were both warriors. If he were being honest with himself, he respected Price a lot more than anyone else on the base.

"We know you got a message out. We know you have another react force. Who was it, and how much do they know?"

Boyd already knew this was getting out of his control. He could see it in Price's eyes.

The tycoon chuckled. "So." He leaned back a little, folding his arms, what might have been a faint smirk on his face. "You did have my local support staff infiltrated. Probably even before we touched down. What? Were they just on the lookout for someone who might be sniffing around, or were they watching for us, specifically?" When Boyd stayed silent, stony faced, he continued. "The only reason you'd wonder about a backup is if Boren and his PMC were already in your pocket. Probably somebody in my own organization, too. Which means that somebody *else* just pulled your briefs up over your head and you don't know who." He chuckled humorlessly. "Now, that's very interesting."

Boyd bit back the angry retort that came immediately to mind. He needed to reach this man, needed to persuade him to cooperate. Just beating him senseless wouldn't work, and it would only get him in trouble with his bosses.

What might happen to him then didn't bear thinking about. Karesinda would find a new use for him besides an occasional booty call.

Price leaned forward, studying him. "Tell you what. I'll make you a deal. Let me see my team. Let me see that my guys are all right, and I'll tell you what I know."

Boyd froze at that. He knew that was never going to happen. Even if they drugged the prisoners up enough that they could be puppeteered as vaguely normal, Price was likely to see through it. He might even ask them questions that the researchers couldn't prompt them to answer accurately. And if Price saw even a fraction of what those men were being subjected to…

Well, there'd be no cooperation after that.

"I can't do that." Boyd almost cursed as he saw the flicker in Price's eyes as the PMC tycoon's expression went cold and hard. He'd just given the game away, and Price was probably already calculating what exactly he'd do to all of them when he got loose.

103

Well, calculate away, old man. You're not getting loose. There's no way the organization is going to let you out on your own again. Like it or not, your fate is as sealed as it is for those poor bastards in Karesinda's testing rooms.

He abruptly turned and knocked on the door. The lock released with a *click* as the operator in the command post opened the door, and he stepped outside, resisting the urge to slam the door behind him.

That did not go according to plan.

Turning on his heel, he stalked upstairs, turned toward the command post, and let himself in. Cooker looked up from the movie he was watching on a tablet where he sat in front of the wall full of screens displaying not only the CCTV feeds from around the base but also the drone feeds from the regular patrols orbiting a few miles out. "What's up, boss?"

Boyd didn't answer right away, but stood over the watch officer, scanning each feed carefully. Nothing looked out of place. No infiltrators that he could see, either in visual or thermal. Of course, the dustup in Bishkek had only happened a few hours before. It was possible that the opposition hadn't gotten that far yet.

"I want security beefed up. Fifty percent on the perimeter, and tell the QRF to get ready to start patrolling." He could almost hear the groans and curses already, but if this installation got penetrated, it was going to be all of them in that tank instead of the captured contractors. "And double the drone patrols, too."

"That's going to put some strain on the charging apparatus." Cooker was already reaching for the radio, though. "The drones are already almost at half up, half charging. They haven't liked the altitude or the cold."

"I know. But we might have company coming, and I'd rather not get caught with my ass in the breeze when it shows up." Boyd didn't wait for a response, but turned and headed for the door.

He intended to take the first patrol out himself, and there was some prep to do first.

At least I won't have to answer the client's questions while we're out tramping around the rocks and the bushes, in the snow.

***

"Looks like we got off the road just in time."

The UAZs were parked on the side of the dirt road leading up into the Tian Shan mountains, about three hundred yards behind. They'd deliberately gotten off the highway and gone around the southern edge of the village of Novovoznesenovka, but spotting a weird, unfamiliar helicopter passing to the north, with two pusher propellers in addition to the main rotor, they'd decided to stop and push an OP up to the top of the nearby hill. That kind of tech was definitely out of the norm for Kyrgyzstan.

Flanagan and Gomez had been the natural picks, though Tackett had asked to come along. Flanagan had considered it for a moment, studying the man—who had been geared up and armed, still watching his sector even while he waited for an answer—then had glanced at Gomez. The quiet man had shrugged, and Flanagan had made the call to bring their client/strap hanger along.

He'd been further impressed on the climb up the hillside. Tackett had shown every bit as much awareness of the terrain and angles of visibility as the more seasoned Blackhearts, and he'd moved almost as quietly. He'd kept up without issue, too.

It was pretty clear that the man hadn't let his skillset slack since the Anambas mission he'd talked about. And if he'd successfully fought and evaded pirates and Chinese commandos through the jungle for days, he had to be pretty good in the bush.

There wasn't a lot of cover on top of that ridge. The foothills of the Tian Shan mountains weren't exactly lush, being mostly grass and scrub where the locals weren't tilling their fields. In some ways, it reminded Flanagan of parts of Idaho or Eastern Washington, though it was still early enough in the year that there was snow between the bunches of grass up there on the hilltop.

Going up into the mountains themselves was going to be fun.

Getting down on their bellies, the three men crawled forward until they could just see over the crest of the hill, peering through the grass at the valley below, where the strange helicopter had landed.

There weren't any drones up yet, but Tackett started pulling the camouflage netting out of his pack anyway. Better to be safe than sorry. While he spread it over the three of them, Flanagan pulled out the binoculars they'd gotten from Carter's friend Yuri and started watching the helicopter.

It had landed in a field on the other side of the narrow river that wended its way between Novovoznesenovka and Radzolnoe. The rotors were still turning as two old Ural trucks and a pair of Ford Rangers, all painted in the Kyrgyz Army's camouflage pattern, came trundling down the road from the north. Men in green, gray, and brown camouflage, with very modern equipment, started to get out of the helicopter as the Kyrgyz Army soldiers started piling out of the trucks, the two Rangers setting up on either side of the intersection next to the helicopter's LZ, their mounted DShK machineguns pointing up and down the main road.

Flanagan tried to focus on the shooters that had gotten out of the bird. The Kyrgyz Army was the Kyrgyz Army. Bundled up against the cold, they wore Western Kevlar helmets, though most of them carried AK-74s. They were a known quantity.

It was a long way to focus, though the binoculars weren't little field glass type optics, but bigger, higher powered jobs for OP work. He had no idea where Yuri had gotten them in this forsaken part of the world, but they were good glass. It was *still* a long distance to get a good, steady view.

He didn't recognize the camouflage. It looked a *little* like the PLA's land-based camo, but that wasn't it. This was slightly darker, and the gear was all very Western. High-cut helmets, sleek plate carriers, and while he couldn't be sure, he was fairly certain the rifles they were carrying were Swiss B+T APC-300s. Either that, or CZ Bren-10s, but he was leaning toward the Swiss rifles. The Front tended to like to field the best, and while the Brens were

106

making a good name for themselves, the Swiss weapons seemed more the Front's style.

He had little doubt at this point that it was the Humanity Front they were up against. The tech level alone pointed that way. Unless there was some other group of bad guys out there with near-bottomless pockets and access to just about every country's R&D on the face of the planet, there weren't many other possibilities.

As he watched, the men in the unfamiliar camouflage started directing the Kyrgyz soldiers to set up a checkpoint on the road, while one of them hauled a case out of the helicopter, dragged it some distance away, opened it, and started fiddling with the contents inside. After a few moments, a five-rotor drone rose into the air.

"They're worried." Gomez was watching through his rifle's ACOG. He wouldn't be able to see nearly as much detail as Flanagan, but he could tell that the newcomers were definitely not Kyrgyz, and he had to have seen the drone go up. "Why else would they be setting up checkpoints out here?"

"That just means it's going to get hairier the closer we get." Flanagan kept watching. The Front shooters weren't manning the checkpoint themselves. They were letting the Kyrgyz soldiers do that, and even from that distance, he could see how stiff the interactions were. The Front was paying a lot of money to use the Kyrgyz as their private security force, but that didn't mean the local troops liked it.

They didn't seem thrilled by the two "dog" robots that were unfolded from another couple of cases and sent out to stalk through the brush nearby, either.

"We're going to have to proceed carefully." Flanagan had already lowered the binos and was starting to creep backward. "It looks like they've stepped up their use of drones, so we'll have to hide as best we can on the move."

"They like using drones a lot?" Tackett was still gathering as much information about their opposition as he could.

"You could say that." Flanagan rolled to a sitting position, scanning the hillside below them and the draw they'd climbed up while Tackett re-packed the camouflage netting. "They were thick as flies in Argentina."

Tackett looked up at the sky as they started back down toward the vehicles. "This is going to be a hell of an infil."

"You ain't lyin'." It was a long speech for Gomez, but Flanagan couldn't help but agree.

And if infil was going to be rough, exfil was probably going to be worse.

**

While they kept their eyes mostly on the sky as they descended the hill, keeping to the low part of the draw to conceal their movement from any prying eyes in the village below, though it was impossible to stay completely in cover when there was another farm like the one where they'd met Yuri at the base of the hill, they didn't see the drone rise above the ridgeline, and the helicopter didn't reappear. It seemed that they hadn't been spotted, and that the Front and the Kyrgyz soldiers were primarily hoping to intercept them on the road.

They got to the vehicles, parked under the trees on the bank of the narrow stream that paralleled the road, without incident. The rest of the Blackhearts were on security, though inside the vehicles as much as possible. None of them would necessarily stand out as anything but hikers and tourists. They weren't wearing military fatigues, but regular civilian outdoor gear—except for the plate carriers, chest rigs, and weapons. The concerns about facial recognition were real, though. If the Front was involved, and if they'd been identified via the Kyrgyz CCTV network in Manas and Bishkek, then the odds were good that the Front's surveillance drones—or the system running them—might be using it as well.

It wasn't something they could take chances with.

Brannigan was waiting at the Hunter when the three of them hustled across the fields, using the shrubs along the low stone fence dividing field from field, keeping under the trees as much as possible. So far, they hadn't seen much of any movement from the farm only three hundred yards away, but someone had to have noticed their movement. Villagers in rural, tribal areas notice outsiders. The only question was, who would they tell?

"What did you see?" Brannigan signaled Flanagan to get in the Hunter with him. He clearly wanted to get going.

Flanagan swung into the passenger seat, in front of Carter, as Brannigan put the vehicle in gear and started them moving down the rugged dirt road. "There's a checkpoint just got set up on the road about a mile and a half north, on the other side of the hill. It sure looks like the Front, unless there's somebody else with state-of-the-art gear and weapons, and a helicopter that wasn't supposed to be operational for another five years."

"That sounds like our old friends, all right. They're getting bolder all of a sudden." Flanagan had to nod. While the team that had taken over the Tourmaline Delta had escaped with the help of an old Russian Kilo-class diesel submarine, the Front had used a lot of cutting-edge tech and weapons over the years, up to and including a tailored virus intended to eliminate only certain genetic markers. They'd rarely been so open as to operate this way, though.

"They're in one of the armpits of both Central Asia and the former Soviet Union." Carter had seemingly resigned himself to his position, and was now acting like he was now fully committed to the mission. Flanagan glanced back at him and wondered if they could really trust the Aussie. The man had to have gotten pretty good at being a chameleon to last this long in Central Asia, particularly after the Western military efforts in Afghanistan had ended. "They probably figure that they've paid off anyone who might comment or make an issue out of it."

"Maybe." Brannigan didn't sound entirely convinced, his eyes fixed on the road ahead of them. Flanagan thought he understood.

The Humanity Front had been quiet for several years. While Carter might be right, that they thought this place was remote enough and corrupt enough to hide, the sudden, open presence might also mean that they were getting ready to make a move, and so they didn't give a damn who saw them.

It was a sobering thought, as the handful of mercenaries drove higher into the mountains, as clouds began to gather over the peaks.

CHAPTER 14

The sky was fully overcast, and it was starting to get dark by the time they stopped the vehicles and Brannigan made the decision to leave them behind.

"We've got a long way to go, yeah, but it's going to be a lot easier to hide from drones on foot than in these big hunks of metal." Brannigan was already throwing his ruck on his back, his M4 dangling from its sling around his neck. He looked around the valley, the mountains looming in the gray gloom. They'd passed the snow line an hour before, and it was doubtful that they'd make it far in the vehicles anyway, if they tried to keep going. There was no sign of the road ahead, and if Brannigan was reading the ground right, they might actually have already passed the end of it.

The clouds were getting thicker as the light died. The chill was brutal, and the wind coming off the mountains was getting worse. They should have brought plenty of warming layers, though that had been on each Blackheart.

And on Tackett, he realized. But when he glanced over, he saw the man putting on a mountaineer's jacket over his chest rig. He'd come prepared.

Glancing up at the darkening gray clouds, Brannigan tried to judge the weather. It did look like it was going to snow again. That would be good. Even if the Front's drones could fly in that weather, if it snowed, it might help obscure their movement.

Thermal might still work, but all the same, the falling snow would be a cold thermal veil between a camera and the men on the ground.

Plus, they were heading for some high, rugged country. Not as bad as the Altiplano, but still pretty rough, especially with the snow. He could hope that it would be too high and too rough for the Front to suspect that anyone would be crazy enough to conduct an infiltration that way. From the map, they had at least two ridgelines over twelve thousand feet high to cross.

That alone was going to be enough of a threat. He shook his head and chuckled faintly. There was no humor in the sound. The Front didn't *need* to have drones up there. The terrain alone, along with the weather, might kill them all in the next couple of hours.

The things we do to accomplish the mission.

Another thought came to mind as he looked up at the cloud-wreathed ridgeline above. *This might take a couple of days, and our supplies are going to get mighty thin by the time we get over that. Not to mention how the hell we're going to get out of that valley.*

As Gomez took point, and he followed, the answer came to him.

I guess we're just going to have to kill them all.

***

The first valley wasn't all that bad. While there was plenty of snow on the ground and the air was thin, the terrain was open and relatively flat. The biggest obstacle was simply trudging through ankle to calf deep snow, with their gear, against a slope that was going to bring them up two thousand feet in the next four miles.

Then it was going to get bad.

The snow didn't help, and not all the Blackhearts were acclimated to that kind of altitude. Brannigan, Kirk, Flanagan, and Burgess were doing okay, but the rest were flagging within a mile. They weren't going all that fast, and it was getting dark. But this was going to be a long night.

After the first mile and a half, they had to call a halt. The wind was getting bad, lashing them with frigid air and flying snow. Unfortunately, there wasn't any good shelter at that point.

"We need to halt, John." Santelli was sucking wind, but he'd struggled through the snow to catch up with Brannigan. "If we try to take that ridgeline in the dark, somebody's going to die. And not the bad guys."

Brannigan gritted his teeth as he looked around. It was almost fully dark, and though they had NVGs, he couldn't ignore the possibility that they might start to lose men in the night and the weather, even before the terrain really got bad.

The storm was simultaneously their greatest asset and their greatest liability. It could cover them from drone surveillance—and airstrikes—but all the same, it might well turn out to be fatal in itself.

"We need to push higher before we stop." He looked back at the rest of the team, to see that Curtis and Jenkins had rucksack flopped, and Bianco and Tackett weren't looking too good, either. Gomez had noticeably slowed in front, but he was still stoically ready to keep going. That was Gomez. The man was incapable of showing weariness.

"We're going to have to slow down." Each word was almost a gasp. It had been a while since the Altiplano, and that hadn't been a picnic, either.

Brannigan nodded. This was going to be harder than he'd hoped. The fact that none of them were getting any younger didn't help, either.

"Fine. We'll slow down. But if we're going to halt for the night, we need to get to the top of this valley first."

He could almost see Santelli look up and try to swallow his disappointment.

"You *could* have stayed back, Carlo." He wasn't trying to be a dick about it, but he felt he needed to point it out. Santelli had been their rear-area support man the last time. He'd frankly been surprised that the aging, retired Sergeant Major had insisted that he come along on this mission.

113

"No, sir." Santelli trudged along beside him, his head down, putting one foot in front of the other despite the snow. They were all dressed for the altitude and the weather, but being dressed for it and being acclimated were two different things. "Not after last time. And not if it's the damned Humanity Front."

Brannigan just nodded. He was hurting, too, even if not as badly as Santelli. He lived at a considerably higher altitude than Boston, though still not over nine thousand feet, which was where they now found themselves.

He couldn't just stop here, though. That would mean so much more distance to be covered in daylight, distance that would be more easily surveilled from the air. If they could get high enough, there was a chance—though he couldn't say how slim it really was—that they might get outside the likely target area that the Humanity Front might be looking at.

He hoped.

It got darker as they kept going, while the temperature dropped and the falling snow got thicker. Gomez slowed further, and Brannigan had to force himself to keep his head up and check the rest of the team constantly, occasionally falling back to make sure that one of the lowlanders hadn't fallen too far back, or worse, wandered off.

The entire world closed in to a small green circle in the NVGs, and even through them, visibility dropped steadily. The clouds were too thick to let much illum through, and the snow was thickening. Finally, even before Santelli closed in close to him again, Brannigan knew they had to halt.

"Bring it in." There wasn't much shelter to be had in that valley. It was getting increasingly hard to see, NVGs or not, and while he was pretty sure they were still going the right way based on his compass—not to mention the fact that they were still on reasonably level ground and still going uphill without running into the really steep slopes of the mountain ridges—he couldn't tell at the moment just how far they had come. He was pretty sure they hadn't covered the distance he'd hoped, but right then, as the snow came down harder, swirling around the valley and obscuring the farther Blackhearts, they had to hunker down.

One by one, the Blackhearts moved in closer, Gomez falling back to join Brannigan, taking a knee with his eyes and his muzzle still trained up the mountainside, peering into the snow and the dark despite how poor visibility was getting.

Brannigan let Gomez, Burgess, and each of the other Blackhearts hold security as they joined the perimeter, turning his own attention to maintaining a headcount.

There was Javakhishvili, looking a little ragged but still keeping his head up. Curtis was almost done in. Jenkins wasn't looking too good, either. Santelli wasn't dragging as bad as Curtis, but he was still barely picking his boots up above the top of the snow. Bianco was keeping his head up, but he was shuffling through the snow, weighed down by the ammunition more than the RPK, which was essentially a long-barrel AK.

Kirk was doing okay. Brannigan had been a little worried about the old Special Forces soldier, given the wound he'd taken in Argentina, but he was holding his own. Hank was in good shape. He'd been tramping around the mountains near the cabin for months. Not as high as this part of the Tian Shan, but high enough.

Wade and Flanagan brought up the rear with Tackett. Brannigan took a moment to study Tackett carefully. The fact that the man had fallen back to the rear worried him, but after a moment he decided that their strap hanger wasn't flagging so much as he was trying to find a spot to fit in to hold security. He wasn't a Blackheart, but he was still a warfighter, and while he didn't have a set place in the team, he was still trying to find one. It was admirable, and he'd have to find a way to successfully integrate him before they hit the target.

This was a new problem. He could get used to it, though.

The chill was really setting in now that they'd stopped. The body heat built up on the climb so far was getting dissipated fast, clothing notwithstanding. "Get some shelter up." Knowing the kind of terrain they were probably going to get into, and given

115

the time of year, they'd decided to bring a couple of emergency tents, just in case. It looked like they were going to turn out to be vital gear, after all.

Getting the tents up took some doing. The ground wasn't exactly level, and the wind was kicking. They finally got them up, though, huddled together in a slight fold in the ground that provided just a little shelter from the wind whipping off the mountaintops.

There wasn't time to brief anything before they crawled into the tents. The cold was getting bad, and the longer they were stationary, facing the brunt of the wind and the snow, the worse it was going to get. "Fifty percent, and don't forget to check on security every so often." That was the most Brannigan could shout into the howling wind before they got into shelter and zipped up.

It was a tight fit inside, but being out of the wind had already helped against the cold. None of them could lie down, exactly, but at least they shouldn't freeze to death.

It was going to be a long night.

***

I'm not cut out for this mountaineering shit. Bianco cracked his eyes open. Every part of his body hurt from sitting half bent over in the tent for hours. It was warmer inside than it would be outside, but it was still cold.

He'd spent most of the time he hadn't been on security in a sort of daze, drifting in and out of full consciousness. Now that it seemed to be getting lighter outside the tent, the wind having died down, no longer snapping and whipping the nylon fabric, he couldn't be sure what all had been a dream and what had been real.

He could have sworn that he'd heard footsteps outside the tent at one point, and a hooting cry out in the storm. Or maybe that had just been a dream, his drowsy mind conjuring noises out of the storm that hadn't really been there.

Looking around the tent, he saw that most of the rest weren't in much better shape, except for Gomez, who looked as calm and alert as ever. Bianco could almost swear the man wasn't human.

116

Footsteps really did crunch in the snow outside, and Gomez reached up and unzipped the flap, letting in a blast of cold air. Brannigan crouched down outside. "Let's go. Get the tents torn down and packed up. We've got a long way to go, and I want to be far away from here by the time the weather clears up enough that they can get drone footage of this valley."

CHAPTER 15

Vernon wasn't sure if he was dreaming or not. He had reached the point where he trusted nothing. He *felt* somewhat more lucid than he had in days. Or weeks. There was no way to be sure.

What he was reasonably sure of—though the experience of the last eternity of darkness and visions made him doubt even that—was that he was actually in a cell now. It was small, cold, dark, and uncomfortable, with only a thinly-padded cot, a composting toilet, and nothing else in the bare concrete room. But he was fairly certain that he wasn't in that weird limbo anymore.

Or maybe he was. Or maybe he'd been here the entire time, while his soul passed through whatever that dark and confusing place had been.

The very thought of what he'd seen in the blackness made him want to curl into a ball and cry. Or scream. Or just give up and die.

Get it together, dammit. Think. His head hurt abominably as he tried to recall what had happened, or even who he was. *You're Vernon fucking White. You're a veteran of the US Army and some of the nastiest private-sector warfare in recent memory. You survived being stranded and hunted in the Anambas. You can survive this.*

But what was *this*? Where was he, and what was happening to him? Everything was a fog, colored by a deep and abiding dread that he couldn't even place. He couldn't remember how he'd gotten here. *Think.*

Thinking hurt. It brought horrors to mind that were the stuff of the worst nightmares of his life. Demonic images, monsters in the dark. Pain and terror. *Terror...* He felt it welling up again, surpassing the dread that had dominated his thoughts since regaining consciousness.

Soon he was backed up against the wall, his knees drawn up to his chin, staring at the darkness around him, the fear clawing at his sanity as he looked around with wide eyes, looking for the things in the dark that would come screaming out to eat his soul.

He started again as the door opened with a *click*. Scrabbling at the walls behind him, trying to dig his way into the corner, he stared in horror as the door swung slowly open.

It wasn't a nightmare or a monster that stood in the light spilling through the doorway, though. It was only a man. Fit, clean-shaven, brown haired and wearing camouflage fatigues in an unfamiliar green, gray, and brown pattern, the man watched him impassively for a moment before signaling someone outside, at which point the lights came on, painfully bright.

That momentary hesitation had given Vernon the time he needed, though. Fighting to bring his breathing under control, he focused on the man in the strange cammies and got his mind anchored on the real world again.

I recognize that pattern. Where from? That's right. The shooters in those high-tech helicopters. I remember now.

Kyrgyzstan. Possible Humanity Front operation in an abandoned Soviet base in the mountains. We came up here with Price and the new guy, Travis. Double-crossed and ambushed.

He'd found his equilibrium. He still didn't know exactly where he was or what was being done to him, and he still had to fight that gibbering terror clawing at the back of his brain, but he knew what he was up against now. The team had been captured by the Humanity Front, and this was one of their shooters.

If he'd had more time to prepare, and hadn't been operating in a drug-induced mental fog, he might have managed to maintain the act, appearing terrified and confused as the man closed the door behind him. He was still too actually confused, strung out, and messed up by the drugs and whatever else they'd put him through to manage to play-act. And after a moment, he could see that the man in the strange cammies could see it.

"We've got checkpoints out and drones up, you know." The man folded his arms and leaned back against the wall. "Your friends will be intercepted. We're not amateurs at this."

"I don't know what you're talking about." Vernon shouldn't have been too surprised that his words were slurred, but it still took him aback a little. He didn't sound like himself, or at least, not like he thought he should sound. A little line of saliva dribbled out of the corner of his mouth, and he reached up to wipe it away, another sign that the other man saw immediately as an indicator of his lucidity.

"Oh, I think you do." The man tilted his head as he studied him. "I think you're a lot tougher than Karesinda and her lab-coated psychopaths believe. I think you know exactly who I'm talking about."

Vernon didn't have a witty rejoinder at hand, and didn't trust himself to answer anyway, so he just stared sullenly at the man and kept his mouth shut.

"We're going to find them. Why don't you make it easier for them and for you? Tell me who you called."

Vernon couldn't quite believe his ears for a moment. Was this kid really that naïve? He studied the man, and saw that while he was probably a good five years younger, there was a lot of mileage in those eyes.

A lot of bad stuff.

No, he wasn't naïve. He just wasn't trained for this kind of thing. Neither was Vernon, but as he held onto the lifeline to reality that this man had just provided by his sheer presence, he could still recognize what was happening. He watched his interrogator as he clung to that thread of truth, reaching deep down

121

inside himself, reaching for that core of being that was Vernon White.

Tell him something. Feed him some line of bullshit that will keep him here, keep this conversation going, keep you out of that other place, wherever it is.

Even as he thought it, though, he knew he couldn't maintain. He was too battered, his thoughts too scattered and buffeted by drugs and illusion and terror. He'd slip. That was the problem with trying to lie in an interrogation. You've got to be clear enough to remember the lie, all the threads of it.

So, he just started to laugh.

Even as the sound slipped out, he knew it was over. Knew it was fatal. Especially as the man's face hardened. Knew he was doomed to get dragged back to that other place, that he'd just cut his reprieve short.

"Easier?" His words still came out as a thick, slurred croak. "So you can just drag somebody else into this hell with me? Get fucked."

To his surprise, however, the man didn't storm out. Instead, he shoved off the wall and stepped forward. "You don't get it, do you?" He snorted. "How could you, after what they've done to you?" His voice dropped. Was he pleading? "If I can prove that you've got information that we need for the security of this facility, I can get you out of Karesinda's claws for a while." He almost sighed. "I just need to know who you called."

There was a thread there, something that the man was giving away, but Vernon couldn't quite think straight enough to grasp it. "Wouldn't you like to know?"

It wasn't a great answer. It wasn't even that witty. He was no Jeremiah Denton. To his surprise, however, while the man was clearly frustrated, he didn't fly into a rage or give up.

"I know what you're thinking. And these over-educated morons don't even realize it. But there *is* a point that you can't come back from. Trust me, I've seen it." There was a haunted look in the man's eyes, and for a moment, Vernon's mind cleared enough to wonder just what might have turned a hired gun for the

122

Humanity Front that scared. "I can help you, but you've gotta help me."

The rest of his offer was never to be presented, though. At that very moment, the door clicked open again, and two people in lab coats stood in the doorway, the short, stunningly gorgeous blond glaring daggers at the man in the camouflage, who had straightened and half-turned to face them.

"Mr. Brown, I know you are not questioning one of my research subjects without my supervision?" The woman's voice was icy cold, and Vernon quickly adjusted his assessment of her attractiveness. She *looked* sexy as hell, but that was the voice of a stone-cold, Mengele-esque monster.

The man in camouflage didn't answer. Maybe he knew that there was no right answer.

"This is a highly delicate process, and you are disrupting it by your very *presence* in this cell." She glared at the man in camouflage, utterly ignoring Vernon, as the man behind her stepped inside with a syringe in his hand.

Vernon tensed, ready to fight rather than let that needle sink into him. He was exhausted, strung out, and confused, but he was still a big man, and could do a lot of damage. The lab-coated man noticed, too, and turned to call two armed men wearing the same camouflage as his questioner inside. The man had a decided French accent.

The blond had cornered the man who'd tried interrogating him and was dressing him down. Vernon became too focused on the two burly security men who moved in and reached for his arms to hear much of what she said, but it sounded like she was threatening to add him to the "test subjects."

Vernon waited until the first man leaned in, reaching for him with the bored look of a security guard who'd done this far too many times, and then aimed an elbow strike at the man's head. It was too slow, too sluggish, and his aim was off. The man easily diverted the strike, maneuvering it into an armlock, as the second man grabbed his other arm.

He struggled, but the fight was already foreordained. He was no match for these two in his current condition. In seconds, he was bound up and pinned to the cot, as the man with the syringe brought the needle in toward his neck, bringing oblivion with it.

***

The clouds had thinned, but the overcast hadn't moved off completely. There were still slight flurries of snow falling, but they were in a lot better shape than they had been the night before.

The Blackhearts had reached the bend in the valley barely an hour and a half after stepping off. It had been rough going, and they had to pause at the base of the ridge they were about to have to climb over, but they were making good time, and so far, there had been no sign of drones or other aircraft overhead.

"Everybody hook up." Brannigan was already pulling the climbing rope out. That had been easy enough to get into the country, especially given their cover as tourists and hikers. Each man had enough to tie around himself with enough left over to link in to the next man with a carabiner. "I don't want anyone falling or getting lost if the snow picks up again." He looked up at the steep slope looming above them, dark rocks amid the snow peeking out of the drifting shreds of cloud moving through the slight saddle between peaks to either side.

This was going to be rough.

Flanagan had moved up to take point, while Wade took up rear security. Flanagan was, hands down, the best mountaineer of them all, and while he might be the Blackhearts' second in command, following Roger Hancock's death in Argentina, for a climb like this, he was the best choice for point man.

With his rifle cinched down as tightly across his chest as he could get it, Flanagan waited until everyone was hooked up and ready, one booted foot planted on the steep slope above him. He studied the snow-covered mountainside, and Brannigan could almost see the calculations happening behind the man's eyes.

Looking back, Flanagan saw that the Blackhearts were all ready to move, and he glanced at Brannigan to get the nod. Then he headed up.

It wasn't easy, but Flanagan's route selection was professional and well thought out. He didn't try to take them straight up the slope, but zigzagged his way across, forcing switchbacks as he found good footholds along the way. It still wasn't quick or smooth, as he had to pause several times to search out the next good spot to step to.

About halfway to the overhanging cliff at the top of the ridge—which Brannigan was already eyeing nervously—Flanagan missed a step.

Actually, he didn't so much miss the step as he miscalculated whether or not there was a rock under that mound of snow. His foot slid out from under him as the snow gave way, and for a second, he had nothing beneath his boot but empty space.

Brannigan grabbed the rope and braced himself, knowing that he wasn't in a good spot to hold Flanagan's weight as the man went over the edge.

Flanagan didn't go over the edge, though. Throwing his weight to the side, he flattened himself against the slope, digging into the snow and the rocks with his gloved hands, despite the fact that he'd just buried his rifle in the snow. He slid about two feet, his left boot still planted, as snow and rocks tumbled down the mountainside below him, but he didn't go farther than that.

After he stayed motionless for a moment, clinging to the side of the mountain like a spider, he slowly lifted himself back up, blowing out a deep, relieved breath that smoked in the cold air for a split second before being blown back down the valley.

Brannigan watched him carefully, but he didn't need to worry. Flanagan knew what he was about, and this was probably far from the first time he'd had a close call on a mountainside. Reassessing his route, he started up slightly higher, though he was a little more careful to test each foothold before he put his weight on it.

Step by step, they climbed toward the saddle and the objective beyond it.

***

They got over the first ridgeline without incident. Despite the cold and the blasts of wind coming down off the peaks, Brannigan halted the team for a few minutes to watch the skies for drones or aircraft, as unlikely as it was that they'd be spotted, given the weather. The storm had abated, but the overcast still hung over the peaks. There was enough wind that drones shouldn't survive long, and any aircraft flying higher wouldn't be able to see them.

Still, it made sense to pause to check their security, if only to allow the team a rest after that climb.

Then they were back on their feet and heading down the hanging valley between the peaks again, heading east toward the objective. There was still a long way to go.

CHAPTER 16

Getting to a position from which they could approach the target and actually be able to fight meant going over another twelve-thousand-foot ridge. It wasn't any easier than the first one, and by the time they descended to the valley below, still ankle-deep in snow, they were all smoked. They had to halt for the night, taking shelter in the tents among the short, scrubby spruces clinging to the sides of the fingers that extended down off the ridgeline.

It wasn't a restful night, but it would have to do. As the sun rose, Flanagan and Santelli joined Brannigan up on the top of the finger, under a wind-twisted tree, observing the valley below. It was much like the one where they'd begun their infiltration, if narrower and more steeply sided. The low, rough scrub stopped at the edge of the valley floor, where a stream or river probably flowed once the snow started to melt.

"We're getting close." Flanagan kept his voice pitched low as they joined the Colonel. "And we're low enough again that if they've got drones out, they'll be able to spot us. Do we want to push during daylight, or wait until dark? By the map, we've only got about four miles to go."

Brannigan was thinking about it. Flanagan couldn't blame him. If this was a rescue mission, and the enemy already knew that *somebody* was probably coming, they didn't have a lot of time. Getting to their target was a priority.

All the same, Flanagan would much rather wait until dark. He was sure that the Front probably had night vision, and that it was probably better than the PVS-14s Carter had supplied. But night vision isn't omnipotent, and making an approach to a target in daylight just went against the grain.

"I think we need to close some of the distance." Brannigan grimaced behind his mustache and several days' worth of beard, both encrusted with frost. "Otherwise, the approach alone could end up taking all night, and then we're really going to be up against the wall."

Flanagan glanced over his shoulder. Tackett was helping pack up the tents, and seemed unperturbed, though he was sure the man had to be feeling *something* about how long it was taking to get his friends out of the Front's clutches.

Somehow, Flanagan didn't expect they were getting the best of humane treatment at the Front's hands. It didn't seem their style.

This infil had already taken longer than any of them would have liked, but that was often the case when they were out in the cold, working on a shoestring. And the Blackhearts had been working on a shoestring since Khadarkh. They'd been up against a timeline there, too, as they'd had no idea when the Iranians might have decided to kill their hostages.

"How far are you thinking?" He might have his reservations, but he trusted Brannigan, and this was still *Brannigan's* Blackhearts.

Brannigan had brought out the map. He pointed with his knifepoint. "No farther than here." He was indicating the intersection between their current valley and the next one over, where the old Soviet base itself sat. It didn't seem like the best spot to put a military base, with high ground all around, but trying to put a structure of any kind on the peaks of the Tian Shan mountains was probably not a great idea. The elevation alone was a non-starter. And this was Kyrgyzstan. Unlike Afghanistan, the

Soviets wouldn't have been concerned with insurgents in the mountains.

If the Humanity Front had any such concerns, they probably figured they'd bought off anyone who might present such a threat.

"And if they've got sensors and drones out?" Flanagan felt he had to at least mention the possibility. They'd seen how much tech the Front could leverage before, and those strange, pusher-propeller helicopters weren't anything you could buy on the open market at the moment. "Do we want to take the risk of getting compromised early?"

"If they've got sensors and drones out, they'll probably be able to pick us up after dark, too." Brannigan was scanning the valley and the sky carefully. "We can't hide from thermals in this snow."

"Not up close." Flanagan was well aware of the risks, and just how much open ground they'd have to cross to get to the target. "But if we're in a hide right on their back porch and get spotted…"

"I know. It's a risk. But staying in a hide *anywhere* in these mountains is a risk. And I'd rather have more of the night to make the hit, instead of trying to do it right at sunrise, if anything goes wrong."

Flanagan peered at the clouds. They were still low and gray, and even as he looked, another faint flurry of snowflakes came down. The weather was still somewhat in their favor.

He nodded. It was still Brannigan's call. He'd made his concerns known. He was still worried about the Front's tech advantage, but there was only so much they could do about that.

Trying to stay ahead of the Front's ability to predict where they might be and when they might appear would remain their best option.

Moving back down to join the rest, they rucked up and got ready to move.

***

Torg wasn't looking at Boyd whenever the security team leader glanced over at him, but he was being so studiously nonchalant that it was obvious he'd heard what had happened and didn't want to get too close to whatever blowup was brewing around Boyd. Boyd, for his part, ignored the way Torg was trying to ignore him, and studied the drone feeds.

Nothing. The valley remained as quiet and empty as ever. No vehicles, no hikers, nothing. He chewed his knuckle as he watched, the scowl deepening on his face.

"What if it was a false alarm?" Torg had apparently decided to ditch the awkward silence and try to concentrate on the job, not the fact that Boyd was within a hair's breadth of getting pulled from the team and stuffed in an isolation tank. "I mean, software's been wrong before. What if it just *thought* it saw this 'Person of Interest?'"

Boyd shook his head. "No. If that had been what happened, we would have rolled up some innocent tourist who would have been completely bewildered and wondering just what had happened. We wouldn't have stumbled on a black market safehouse rigged with CS, flashbangs, and self-sealing steel doors." He grimaced at the memory of the argument he'd had with the Kyrgyz police commander after that debacle. "It pinged on this guy, all right. Though I'm damned if I know how he got on the POI list, so don't ask."

Torg might have muttered something under his breath about Karesinda and isolation tanks, but when Boyd looked at him sharply, he was silent, studiously watching the camera feeds.

Boyd turned his own eyes back to the feeds. Whoever had come in country that the Humanity Front considered a security threat, they'd gotten out of Bishkek and promptly disappeared. The Kyrgyz police had found the tunnel they'd used to escape the safehouse, but there was no known connection—aside from the tunnel itself—between the safehouse and the tenement where the tunnel had ended. It had been rented under a different name, and no one around the place remembered seeing anyone there. There was a description of a van, but when they'd finally tracked the van down, it had been abandoned outside Burana.

They've got to be out there somewhere. Yet the empty wilderness seemed to mock him. There was nowhere to hide out there. The woods were neither tall nor thick, and if anyone had been approaching through that valley—which was the only real viable approach, the drones should have spotted them.

What if they're not here for the prisoners at all? What if I've been barking up the wrong tree all this time? He felt a chill and suppressed a shudder at the thought. He'd be joining Price's contractors as a lab rat in short order if that turned out to be the case.

No. There's nothing else besides the usual corruption and terrorism going on in this shithole country. What are the odds that somebody on the client's shit list just so happened *to come in here to go after some rogue Al Qaeda type coming in or out of Afghanistan?*

So, where are they? He reached for the controls.

"What's up?" Torg straightened in his chair a little. Usually, the watchstander handled programming the drone routes and any corrections necessary.

"I'm moving three of the drones south." Boyd was already adjusting patrol routes on the map.

"Why?" Torg sounded genuinely confused. "The dustup was in Bishkek, wasn't it? There's no way anyone got all the way around to come at us from the south since then. Hell, there's no way *to* get all the way around to the south. The mountains cut everything off eventually. There's *no* viable route you can take a vehicle around behind us." He pointed to the drone feed, showing the empty valley to the north. "That's the only way to get here from Bishkek unless you're flying. And we should have picked up on that."

"Maybe." Boyd hit the "execute" button and straightened up. "I'm going to check anyway, just in case.

***

131

Flanagan heard the buzz first. It was so quiet up there in the mountains, especially since the wind had died down, that the sound of drone engines traveled.

He hadn't exactly been doing jumping jacks, but now he went completely still. Curtis looked up from underneath the stunted spruce that formed the center of their hide site. "What is it?"

Flanagan didn't answer except to put his finger to his lips.

"Don't you shush me, Joseph!" Curtis's voice was a low hiss that wouldn't have traveled far, despite his indignation. "If there's a threat out there, we need to know it!"

Very slowly, Flanagan turned to look back at him. "When I have more information, I'll tell you. Until then, stop being a distraction."

"Distraction?" Curtis managed to keep his voice down while simultaneously sounding completely outraged. "I am reminding you of your responsibility to the team and you call it a distraction?"

"Shut up, Kevin." Wade's own hiss was almost as quiet as Curtis's mock outrage. "Not the time or the place." He moved carefully up next to Flanagan. "What have you got?"

"Listen." The buzz had faded somewhat, and he had to strain to hear it again. "There. Hear that?"

Wade nodded, already scanning the slopes to the north through his ACOG. "I can't see shit."

"I don't think they've come around the shoulder of the mountain yet." Flanagan scanned their surroundings and cursed quietly. "We're going to be sitting ducks if they do."

"*When* they do." Brannigan had moved up, too. He looked around their meager concealment, but they were already in the thickest stand of spruce available. He took a deep breath. "If we can knock 'em down with 5.56 fire, let's do it. They'll know that we're here, but they won't know details."

"We'll have to move fast, once that happens." Flanagan kept his eyes trained on the shoulder of the mountain, around which the buzz of drone engines was getting louder.

"Yeah." When Flanagan spared a glance back at the Colonel, he saw the frown. He thought he understood. There was no good, concealed route into that base if they tried to hit it in the daytime, especially if the bad guys were alerted. They'd have to fall back, reset, and come at it a different way. Unfortunately, there weren't many other options. The terrain of the Tian Shan was brutal, and they were already smoked from almost three days humping through those mountains in the snow and ice.

He dismissed the worry as the whine increased in volume, getting down behind his rifle and searching for movement.

There. A dark dot against the snow, on the other side of the valley, about twelve hundred yards away. Finding it in his ACOG, he made out another five-rotor drone, just like the one that had been launched from the checkpoint.

Twelve hundred yards was a long shot with an M4. He'd done it before, though the energy remaining with a 5.56 round out of a 14.5-inch barrel wouldn't be enough even if he could hit the thing. He got lower in the branches and started searching for another drone, hoping that the first one was far enough away not to be able to see through the spruces.

"What the hell?" Wade was squinting through his ACOG. Flanagan lifted his head to try to spot what the big man had seen.

He couldn't see anything different at first. He scanned the hillsides and the clouds, looking for the second drone, or whatever else Wade had seen. Then he noticed it.

The first drone was rapidly winging north again, heading back toward the base. It was moving a lot faster than it had been, and was out of sight in seconds. The buzzing whine of rotors faded almost as quickly.

"I think we might need to move." Wade's face was grim.

"You're probably right. I wonder, though." Flanagan kept watching the valley where the drones had just disappeared.

"What is it, Joe?" Brannigan was studying him carefully.

"Why pull them off? If they'd spotted us, why not orbit to keep an eye on us? Those probably weren't armed, but you don't usually pull ISR off if you've got a target."

133

"Maybe they've got patrols out that didn't like having a flying lawn mower overhead, giving them away." Wade snorted. "I've been there before."

Flanagan pointed toward the slope below them. "We'd have seen them if they were close enough." He looked at Brannigan and shrugged. "I don't know, boss. Something doesn't seem right."

"You think we should move anyway?"

That didn't take long to decide. "Yeah, I do. Just in case."

***

"You've got to be kidding me."

Boyd stared at Dr. Finkelstein, who goggled at him through his Coke bottle glasses. The man looked like the stereotypical nerd. Small, slightly built, with dark hair slightly peaked in the middle of his head and a wispy excuse for a mustache and what might have been a goatee in a different universe, where a few hairs counted as a beard.

Finkelstein was probably utterly oblivious to the drama happening with Karesinda and her psychos. He had a different project he was working on, and from what Boyd had seen, he wasn't really aware that there was a world beyond that project.

"I'm entirely serious. The prototype is ready to be tested, and if you don't want your hardware to get fried, you need to shut it all down." The man didn't even seem to have noticed Boyd's tone, and was acting as if he simply hadn't been heard right.

Boyd snarled as he looked at the drone feeds. He'd been almost sure that they'd just picked up a thermal hit, somewhere there wasn't supposed to be one. But if Finkelstein was about to run his test, and got what he saw as obstructionism from Boyd, word would probably get back to Karesinda. Then he'd really be screwed. If he hadn't tried to interrogate that contractor himself, he might have been able to pull it off. Not now.

"Fine. We'll pull everything in. It's going to take about thirty minutes."

Finkelstein nodded as if nothing had just happened that wasn't supposed to. "That should be sufficient. It will take about

134

that much time to get the generator ready." He turned away and blithely walked out of the command center.

"*Fuck!*" Boyd rounded on Torg. "Call up the QRF. Tell them to meet me here, geared up, in ten minutes." He turned to withdrawing the drones. "As soon as this clown-show is over, we're going out to check on that thermal hit."

CHAPTER 17

The Blackhearts were moving, keeping to the thicker stands of spruces where they could, looking for either a good approach lane or just a better spot to hunker down until dark. Since it was daylight, and they were still together, they really weren't using any electronics, which was why they missed what happened next.

On the old Soviet base, a hatch opened in the roof of the second, larger concrete building, and a mast started to rise into the afternoon sky, topped with a metal sphere. It couldn't hope to rise above the peaks to either side, but it still extended until it stood a good three hundred feet above the compound.

To the naked eye, nothing happened. The mast stayed in place for about an hour, then began to retract back into the building. But as darkness began to fall, still relatively early at this time of year, the lights in the village of Ak-Bulun, north of the base, didn't come on. Nor did they in any other village within a twenty-mile radius.

***

The light began to die, dimmed already by the overcast that had never quite gone away, despite the occasional rent in the clouds during the afternoon. So far, the drones hadn't disappeared, which Brannigan was happy about, though he didn't trust the sudden silence and freedom of movement. Something else was going on, he didn't know what it was, and he was therefore suspicious.

To Carter's credit, the Aussie was clearly just as suspicious. At Wade's suggestion, the team had broken up into ones and twos, spreading out across the valley as they looked for a way into the base. There were trees on the hillsides, and a surprising amount of low ground and microterrain in the valley, which could provide decent cover and concealment on approach, provided the drones stayed off their backs. The longer the sky remained clear, the better their chances, so they'd started their approach already, just as the sun was touching the peaks behind them.

The brief had been quick and simple. The Blackhearts were approaching the base along a sort of crescent, turning into more of an L-shape as they moved out into the wider valley and got a look at their target. That way, they should be able to support each other, provided they could spot a threat before it got too close.

Coming around a short, windswept spruce, Brannigan finally got his first good look at their target.

The base was a simple rectangle, surrounded by a chain link fence topped with triple-strand concertina wire. The dirt road coming down the valley from the north curved out to meet a gate facing the westward mountains. Guard towers stood at all four corners, with two more flanking the gate itself.

Inside the perimeter, the snow-covered ground had been graded flat, providing no cover at all between the fence and the buildings. A helipad had been cleared of snow against the north fence. Three Quonset-shaped hangars or warehouses dominated the rest of the northern half of the compound. All three structures had large rollup doors, all of them currently shut.

The rest of the base was mostly taken up by two rectangular, concrete buildings, set in an L-shape, displaying typical Soviet brutality in their construction. Three-story concrete blocks, they were dingy and run-down, showing cracks in the plaster around the triple row of windows. Both sprouted much newer-looking satellite dishes and antennas from their roofs, and the northernmost one had what looked almost like a cargo container on its roof. Brannigan, knowing what he did about Communist construction, was slightly amazed that the roof hadn't fallen in when that had been put up there.

Right at the moment, there was no one outside. No drones were in the air. Nothing moved on the entire compound. That was strange. Halting where he was, he lifted his M4 and studied the compound through his ACOG, bracing the weapon against the spruce's trunk and "burning" through the branches and needles as best he could. He was sure there were cameras on those towers, and that the men in them—provided they were manned and not automated—had optics that could easily pick up the glare of an objective lens at that distance. He and Carter were less than a thousand yards away at that point.

There were definitely human guards in the towers. They'd been beefed up with what looked like ballistic glass, making any view of the interior dim and unclear, but there were human silhouettes visible, and they were moving, unlike the silhouette targets he'd occasionally seen PMCs put in guard towers to make up for low manning. As he watched, one of them moved to the window, raising a pair of binoculars to his eyes.

They can't see us yet. No reaction, no alert. But they're not just taking naps in the towers, either. As he studied the layout more closely, he thought he could pick out the small, white rectangles of cameras placed on the towers, the gate, and the corners of each building. *They're going to be watching those, too. Son of a bitch. This is not going to be an easy approach.*

He glanced at Carter. The Aussie was watching the compound just as intently as he was. He thought he heard the man curse quietly under his breath.

"We might need to create a diversion." If they'd had time to grab some serious explosives, that diversion wouldn't have been all that difficult. With only two of them, armed only with rifles, it might get a little hairier. Especially given the terrain they had to deal with.

Carter glanced at him, his eyes hooded. It was next to impossible to tell what the former Australian commando was thinking. This wasn't his usual occupation, and hadn't been for a long time. He was even more of a strap-hanger than Tackett. Even more so, he was a generally *unwilling* strap-hanger, as opposed to Tackett.

What would he think about putting his own skin on the line for the sake of an assault he had no stakes in?

Carter turned back to the compound, though, his eyes narrowed. "It would have to be a pretty bloody impressive diversion to get all eyes turned north." He glanced at the sky. "We *could* hope for another snowstorm, but that doesn't look likely."

He started digging in his own load bearing vest, finally coming out with a cell phone. Brannigan's gaze sharpened as he saw it. That thing was a potential security threat for all of them. But it was apparently powered off, and he was trying to power it on. It was debatable just how likely it would be to get a signal that high up... but then Carter was pulling an antenna out of his pack, one of those designed to effectively turn a cell phone into an intermediate-range radio.

Carter frowned, looking down at the phone. The screen hadn't lit up. That alone would have been an issue, if he hadn't been carefully shielding it from the compound with his body, huddled as close under the tree as he could get. He tried again. Nothing. Looking up, he said, "Try your radio."

"If they're remotely on the ball, they'll pick up a radio transmission." The cell phone presented the same problem, but Brannigan was worried about anything that might potentially give the game away at that point.

"I don't think so. Try it."

Gritting his teeth, Brannigan reached up, made sure the earpiece was seated, and tried to key the radio.

Nothing. He frowned, looking down as he pulled the radio out of its pouch in his old, MOLLE LBV.

It was dead as a doornail. He turned it off, turned it back on. Nothing. Fortunately, they had extra batteries, and the Motorola took AAs. Quickly swapping out, he got the same result.

"We've got no comms." Carter sounded a little spooked. Looking down at his own rifle, he reached forward, pointing it at the ground, and tried to turn on his PEQ-15's visible laser.

Nothing.

Carter looked up. "I don't know how they did it, but I think they just fried every bit of electronics we've got."

***

"Do not tell me that half the system was unshielded." Boyd was surprised that he didn't feel the growing panic at what position this might put him in with the client. Instead, he felt a killing rage rising up in his chest. He was a veteran and a killer. He'd had it with being scared of these fucking people.

"Fine. I won't tell you that half the system wasn't shielded." Chance waved at the darkened screens, representing a sizeable chunk of the outer perimeter's camera network. "I won't tell you they were, either."

"*FUCK!*" Boyd stormed out of the command post, stalking toward the team room. He brushed past Brzezinski, one of Karesinda's creatures, ignoring the vaguely androgynous "researcher" as he—or she; Boyd had never been quite sure—bleated something irrelevant after him.

He slammed into the team room. The QRF wasn't geared up, which just made him angrier. They had their gear nearby, but they were playing cards while Animal bitched about not being able to play Xbox.

"Get your shit on and get out to the gate." He glared around at all of them. Animal and Shear stared at him belligerently. After all, *they* weren't the ones on Karesinda's shit list. In fact, if he fell on his face, he was sure that one of those two, as generally lazy and unambitious as they'd been so far, would leap at the opportunity to stick the knife in his ribs and try to take over as the team lead, if only for the extra money.

Not sure that extra money's worth it at this point. But it was far too late for those second thoughts.

He stared them down, his hand resting on the pistol at his side. "I'm not asking."

Torg and Cooker picked up their plate carriers, helmets, and rifles, and started moving toward the door. That seemed to do the trick, and while Animal and Shear still dragged their feet, they got moving.

Grabbing his own gear and his APC-300 out of his cubby, he followed Torg and Cooker outside.

If they couldn't get the cameras up and the drones out fast enough to spot whatever had made that thermal signature out in the trees, he'd do this the old-fashioned way.

***

Kirk halted in another low spot in the snow-choked riverbed, careful to move slowly enough that he didn't overheat and start putting out clouds of steam over his head. That would be a surefire way to attract enemy attention. When he looked up, though, he saw he was getting awfully close to the fence. It was just over three hundred yards away, now.

Still no drones or patrols. What the hell is going on? Kirk knew he was far from the fastest man in a low crawl. He never had been, but being well north of forty, with plenty of scars inside and out from well over two decades in war zones, he was far slower than he once had been.

And yet, either the Front was spectacularly complacent, or there was something really, really weird going on.

Kirk had been in a lot of tight spots over the years. His time in Special Forces had been downright tame compared to some of the stuff he'd gotten into in the private sector, and he'd spent almost four years cumulative in Afghanistan as a Green Beanie. His first real experience with the Humanity Front had been rescuing Sam Childress—whom he'd never met, at the time—from their contractors in the States. The next time, he'd gotten shot in the lung and barely survived.

If anything, that had made him that much more determined to go back out as soon as it had come out that the Front was involved again. He couldn't say he knew as much about their operations as some of the Blackhearts, but getting stove up for months thanks to a sucking chest wound tended to make a man like Kirk hold a bit of a grudge.

Studying the compound ahead of him, ignoring the cold seeping through his clothing as he lifted his head just far enough to peer over the microterrain that was keeping him hidden from the guard towers with one eye, he thought he spotted movement in the nearest tower. No, that was just the guard turning away from the riverbed. Kirk felt a flash of contempt. The man was abandoning his sector, for whatever reason. He told himself not to look a gift horse in the mouth. He could cover some more distance a bit faster while the guy in the tower was looking the other way.

There had been a lot of erosion in that riverbed before the snows had come. The snow itself made it rough going, but the overwhites that they'd found in Yuri's inventory, as old and ill-fitting as they were, gave him an even better chance to stay hidden, provided the bad guys didn't have thermals.

That didn't seem likely, but so far there had been no alert. Which was making the hackles on the back of his neck go up.

As he moved over a lump in the riverbed toward the next rill that should get him within a few yards of the fence, even if it meant getting wet—he couldn't tell if the river was completely dry or frozen over, and he was heading for what looked like the deepest part of the bed when it was flowing—he spotted movement to his right. Wade wasn't far behind him, recognizable only because he looked up at that moment, and Kirk got a glimpse of the man's pale blue eyes.

Kirk was momentarily satisfied with himself that his broken-down old ass had outpaced Wade, if only by a little bit.

He'd just gotten over the high ground when he saw movement in the tower again. He froze, watching carefully and waiting for the alarm to sound. He was close, and he was low, and hopefully the overwhites would make him blend in, the dying light

143

of evening hiding the snail trail he'd made through the snow so far. It wouldn't last forever, but fortunately, there wasn't a CROWS turret on that tower, which meant the man on watch would have to open one of those ballistic windows to shoot at them. And he was pretty sure he could get a bullet in one of those windows without too much difficulty.

As soon as he saw that the man with the binoculars wasn't looking down into the riverbed, but instead out at the spruces and the mountainsides across the river, Kirk got ready to move. Whatever was going on, the guys in the guard towers seemed to think that nobody would be stupid enough to try to cross the open riverbed between the trees and the base, even in the dying light that would have rendered NVGs next to useless.

He froze, instead. Almost a dozen men, dressed in a green, gray, and brown camouflage pattern he didn't recognize—except to remember Flanagan's description of the shooters at the checkpoint north of Novovoznesenovka—were coming out into the courtyard between the two concrete buildings, all geared up and armed to the teeth. Kirk watched them as he stayed as low and as motionless as possible, keeping his breathing shallow to avoid sending up a cloud of steam in the cold.

The react force wasn't looking in his direction as they hustled toward the gate. So far, none of the towers seemed to have noticed the men in white crawling through the snow toward them, either. Kirk decided to take the risk.

Turning slightly to his side, he dug through the snow caked to his chest rig and his overwhites, finding the radio, and keyed it. The radio itself was supposed to be waterproof—they'd made sure of that before leaving the States.

He should have heard a faint chirp as the radio keyed. He heard nothing. Dead silence. "This is Lumberjack. I have eyes on a react force, approximately ten to twelve foot mobiles, leaving the compound to the west."

No reply. No indication that it had even gone out. He slowly turned to look back at Wade. The bigger man was close enough that he should have heard.

Wade shook his head. He hadn't heard anything. The radio was dead.

Kirk watched the react force slog out into the snow of the riverbed, coincidentally moving into the deeper part and out of sight for the moment. He started moving forward again.

This was bad.

***

Brannigan could see the same thing Kirk saw, only from a different angle. Still up in the trees, he watched the Front's QRF come out of the northern concrete building, obviously cussing at being out in the cold, led by a man who appeared far more determined than any of the rest. He was Caucasian. Brannigan could tell that much in the dying light, but little more. And that was going to remain the case as night fell. A quick check, still sheltered in the trees, had confirmed that not only the radios and the PEQs were dead. Their PVS-14s hadn't survived, either.

It was almost like an EMP had hit, but those shooters out there didn't seem like they'd suffered the same effects. *What could create a targeted EMP, especially if they don't know for sure we're out here?* He had to assume that they'd been compromised, which meant things were going to get really kinetic, really quickly.

As he watched the shooters come out of the gate and start down into the riverbed, though, he had to revise his assessment. They weren't acting like men who knew exactly where their targets were. They were preparing for a sweep of the surrounding area. Brannigan knew what a security patrol looked like. He'd commanded enough of them, and he'd sent Marines out to conduct easily as many.

What the hell is going on here? He didn't know, but the Blackhearts, as spread out and uncoordinated as they were at the moment, couldn't afford for him to sit there in the trees and try to puzzle it out. Whatever was going on, they were currently about evenly matched with the opposition on the ground, if they could move fast enough.

He grabbed Carter by the sleeve, putting his mouth within a couple inches of the Aussie's ear. "Joe and Dan should be down below us and about fifty yards south. Stay in the trees and keep your movement slow. Follow me."

Though he couldn't see exactly where Flanagan and Tackett were, Brannigan got to his feet, careful to keep the tree between him and the enemy, and started down the hill. He hoped he could make linkup without a radio or IR, without alerting the bad guys who even then were starting to fan out across the riverbed.

CHAPTER 18

Flanagan wasn't far from where Brannigan and Carter were watching the react force come out of the central concrete building. Tackett was down in the dirt behind another spruce only a few feet away, also watching the compound through his ACOG.

Tackett got up carefully and moved up next to Flanagan, moving so quietly that if Flanagan hadn't been completely still, breathing through his mouth to stay even quieter—nose breathing, even if it wasn't audible at any distance, was still going to be louder inside his own head—he might not have even heard Tackett's boots crunching in the snow. "I don't see any drones yet, but they're coming right out into the riverbed. Those guys crawling up toward the south side are going to get compromised."

"I know." Flanagan reached down and checked his radio before transmitting. It was a habit he'd formed after a guy he'd known had accidentally sent a call on the wrong channel, in the middle of a life-or-death situation. The mistake had been caught and corrected in time, but it had been a lesson learned that Flanagan had taken away ever since.

He frowned. Even in the low light, he should have been able to see the channel numbers on the little LCD screen on the radio's face. It was blank, though.

He turned the radio off, then back on. He'd changed the batteries in the last hide site, so he knew they should be good. Nothing. The radio was dead. "Is your radio up?"

Tackett checked his own, his frown increasingly hard to see as the light faded. "No. It's dead. Why is it dead?"

With a sudden sinking sensation in his chest, Flanagan reached up and lowered his NVGs, turning them on. Or, perhaps more accurately, trying to turn them on. The switch turned and clicked into place, but the tube remained dark.

"Everything's dead." He flipped the PVS-14s back up out of the way. "I don't know how they did it, but they just fried all of our electronics."

Tackett flipped his own NVGs down to check. He nodded. "You're right. Great. Now what?"

"We need to link up with whoever we can and deal with that bunch while we can still see." Flanagan chewed his lip. Putting his eye back to his ACOG, he saw that the oncoming react force had their NVGs down. So, their gear was working, while the Blackhearts were back to Vietnam-era night fighting. Except they didn't have any flares.

This was about to get interesting. Especially since they didn't have suppressors for any of their weapons.

"Friendlies!" The whisper was just loud enough to carry from the trees just above and off to the left. Flanagan turned toward the dark figures, barely visible in the foliage but still standing out just enough against the snow, despite their overwhites, to partially identify Brannigan and Carter.

"Come ahead." This was going to get hairy, fast. Without comms, scattered across a line that probably totaled more than fifteen hundred yards, they couldn't coordinate, at least not without exposing themselves to the react force and the guards in the towers. Not to mention whatever other technological surprises the Humanity Front might have hiding inside that compound.

Brannigan catfooted it down to their position, the big man still managing to stay surprisingly quiet, even despite the snow. Carter was a little louder, but they couldn't necessarily expect the facilitator to be a ninja in the bush, not after all his time away from the commandos.

"Comms are down," Brannigan whispered as he knelt beside Flanagan.

"We know. I just tried to get on the radio." Flanagan watched as the react force started to spread out across the riverbank, thinking. "What are we gonna do now? Half the team's out low-crawling through the snow out there. They're gonna get spotted."

"If we can push far enough north, fast enough, we might hit them from outside their cordon and draw them off." Tackett hadn't been asked, and he hadn't taken his eyes off the compound, but he was comfortable enough at that point to venture an opinion. And it was one that Flanagan couldn't necessarily argue with. "We had to do some creative stuff like that on the island."

That's right. Tackett's been in far worse situations than this. Flanagan looked at Brannigan and shrugged slightly. He didn't have a better idea.

Brannigan nodded. "Have you got eyes on Curtis or Jenkins?" They were the next ones down the line to Tackett's right.

"No, but I've heard them several times." Flanagan loved Curtis like a brother, but the man was hardly a ghost in the bush. "They're only about fifty yards back."

Brannigan looked toward the riverbank again. It was getting dark, but without artificial light effecting their night adaptation, it wasn't as hard to see as it might have been. The snow helped too, in addition to the fact that the Front's shooters were arrogant enough—or simply hadn't considered the fieldcraft factor enough—that they weren't wearing overwhites. Their green, gray, and brown camouflage stood out in the white-blanketed riverbed as glaringly as if they'd been wearing black. "Go get 'em, but make it fast. We don't have much time to get into position and draw them off before they walk on Herc or Hank."

***

149

Jenkins was cussing silently, a continuous stream of profanity echoing in his head. *This isn't happening.* Sure, the Blackhearts had operated on a shoestring for a long time, but this was something else. No comms, no night vision, no lasers, and without suppressors. They were screwed.

George Jenkins had been a SEAL, and that alone had led to some conflict with his teammates. He'd figured that he'd made it among the best of the best, and that had formed his identity for a long time. That he hadn't been quite as good at certain aspects of warfare as some of the men who'd come from what he'd always thought were "lesser" units had come as a nasty surprise, and it had taken a long time to get over that.

Now he was facing one more thing he really hadn't been mentally prepared for. Despite his years with the Blackhearts, out in the wind with whatever gear they could scrounge to accomplish the mission, a part of him still hadn't gotten over that feeling that as Americans, they always had the edge. He'd had the best gear and support that SOCOM could provide as a SEAL, and even though things hadn't been that good on this job, they'd always generally been able to rely on their equipment, and been able to talk and adjust as the situation changed.

Now, they were completely cut off, and they couldn't even use the darkness to its full potential because the NVGs weren't working.

Jenkins had never really trained all the way low-tech. Even when they'd run drills with little more than a couple of walkie-talkies and Brannigan's arsenal of rifles, he'd always mentally thought of that kind of Luddite warfare as just notional. *We'll have the gear in the real world.*

Now they didn't, and he was having to fight off the panic. *You're a SEAL. Fucking act like it.*

He slowed his breathing down, hoping that Curtis, only about two yards away and watching the react force coming out of the compound over his RPK, hadn't noticed his loss of bearing. Curtis could be a clown at times, but he got deadly serious when the situation called for it, and he wouldn't stand for a freak out in the bush.

Neither should you.

Jenkins forced himself to calm down. *The situation is what it is. You can either lose it, run away and leave the team behind, or deal with it, adapt, and make shit happen despite the setback.*

There'd been a time when he might have seriously considered the second option. That had been when he'd considered mercenary work somehow different from the brotherhood of arms he'd mostly embraced in Naval Special Warfare. That had been another time, and while the Blackhearts—especially Santelli—had given him a rough time sometimes, this was the team, and this was the mission.

He *wanted* to run for it. He wouldn't, though. If only to prove to Santelli, and Wade, and all the rest who'd been angry or disappointed with him over the years that they were wrong. That he was a Blackheart, and that he was every bit as good as they were.

A footstep creaked in the snow behind him. "Friendlies." He turned his head, his muzzle still trained on the enemy, realizing that he was precisely in a *Jurassic Park* "Clever girl" position, to see what had to be Flanagan partly obscured by the next tree behind him, watching him.

Gulping as he lifted his muzzle slightly, realizing that he'd just been caught off guard again when he shouldn't have, Jenkins whispered back, "Bring it in."

Flanagan slipped between the trees without any sound but the snow compressing beneath his boots. "We're pushing up north, to try to get behind them. We need to move fast. We'll get behind their sweep, hit them from the rear, then bound north along the valley to draw them off the main infiltration team."

"That's gonna make noise." Curtis hadn't moved, his breath smoking as he spoke. "Don't get me wrong, I'm all about moving a little faster. My extremities are starting to freeze off, including the most important one, if you know what I mean."

151

Flanagan ignored the quip. "We'll have to chance it. They're getting way too close to Herc's route."

Jenkins frowned as he scanned the riverbed below again. There was so little light—and the ACOG's glass cut down on more of it—that he really had to search to find Javakhishvili, even from up above.

Shit. There he was, low crawling carefully up a shallow indentation in the riverbed, eroded by snowmelt sometime during a warmer part of the year, barely two hundred yards from the skirmish line of Front shooters spread out across the bed. They were starting their sweep, moving down toward the south along the line of the river.

"Let's go. Stay in the thicker trees but step it out." Flanagan got up and started to move.

***

I hate low crawling. It wasn't the first time Javakhishvili had thought that since they'd started their infiltration. *I should have gone up onto one of the support positions.*

It was too late, now, of course, and he knew he was bitching primarily to try to take his mind off the cold seeping into his limbs as he crept along the riverbed, shoving a little berm of snow up in front of himself to hide a little bit more from the watchers in the towers, dragging his rifle through the snow with the barrel hooked up over his shoulder to keep it out of the snow and the dirt beneath it. His knees and elbows ached, and he was becoming increasingly aware that he wasn't a young man anymore.

He paused as the riverbed got a little deeper, and when the ice creaked underneath him he realized he was on top of an iced-over pool. There was a little rise just next to him, however, which provided a little bit of extra cover, so he stayed in place.

It was uncomfortable, and his mental bitching didn't stop, but he knew that the discomfort was a necessary price to pay. He shuffled closer to the cut in the wash, then peered up and over.

He already knew his NVGs were dead. He'd tried to drop them just before he'd started his crawl, only to find they weren't working. He'd dismissed the issue as dead batteries and driven on. It wouldn't have been the first time he'd had to operate in the dark without NVGs. He could haze himself later for failing to maintain his gear sufficiently. There wasn't time to fiddle with them, so he'd just driven on.

It was a good thing that the old base was blacked out. Apparently, the Front didn't want to attract any attention, so they weren't turning on the lights at night. That could be an advantage, with no NVGs. His night adaptation could take over completely.

So, he could actually see fairly clearly, if not as far as he might have wanted, when he lifted his head to peer over the top of the little rise in the riverbed. Clearly enough to see the line of nearly a dozen men less than a hundred yards away, walking toward him across the open ground.

He dropped, immediately burrowing deeper into drifted the snow, trying to brush more of it over himself. This was bad.

Looking back, he couldn't tell just how visible the track he'd left through the snow was, but he knew that it was visible enough. It was possible—and he could still hope—that the illum was low enough that the bad guys wouldn't make out the contrast in their NVGs, but he knew he couldn't necessarily bank on that. Especially since the moon had already peeked out from gaps in the clouds once already.

All the same, if they walked on him, he was done. From what he'd seen, he might just be far enough between two of them as they passed that they might walk by him without spotting him, especially if he was dug deeply enough into the snowdrift.

For a moment, he considered just going for it, crawling the rest of the way toward the fence as fast as he could. But he knew that while they were moving toward him, looking in his direction, he'd be screwed if he tried that.

Patience. See if you can evade. Then see about fighting. He took some comfort in the fact that the rest of the Blackhearts were out there, and sooner or later, one of them would see the fix he was in. He wasn't alone. He set in to wait, his rifle held close to his chest, ready to engage if he got the chance.

Boyd almost missed it. He stepped down, scanning the trees that covered the hillside above as he moved along the edge of the riverbed. About half the team was still down in the riverbed itself, despite the fact that he'd been pretty clear that they needed to get up into the rougher terrain and the woods, since that was where any infiltrators were probably going to be. It was easier going down in the riverbed, though, so that was where the lazier contractors were walking, ostensibly watching the trees as they went. They did have NVGs and IR lasers, so they should be able to engage anyone in the scrubby forest.

It still annoyed the hell out of him, but he was on thin enough ice that he didn't dare push some of these guys very far, or the knives would come out. There were enough of them who might well welcome his demotion to lab rat that he had to tread carefully.

His foot slipped slightly, and he looked down, then frowned behind his GPNVGs.

He couldn't be sure. Even with the quality of the panoramic night vision, the illum was low enough right at the moment that he couldn't be sure of what he was looking at. But the snow was far more compressed than it should have been. Almost as if it was a trail.

Instinctively, he looked to the right, following the faint line of compressed snow toward the compound.

He pivoted, bringing his weapon up. He couldn't be entirely sure, but that lump of snow in the low ground about twenty yards away looked wrong. He stepped forward.

The man with the rifle started to move, bringing his own weapon around as Torg walked past, closer to the compound fence. Boyd leveled his weapon, his finger on the trigger. "Freeze!"

He didn't know for sure why he said that, instead of just shooting the man. But this was the first of the infiltrators they'd actually spotted, and there was no way the man in overwhites was going to be able to bring that carbine around fast enough to shoot him before he killed him.

Boyd wanted to know what they were up against. And since Finkelstein had completely borked the surveillance systems with his weapons test, interrogating this unknown gunman might work.

Cooker and Justus closed in on the man, weapons leveled. Boyd waited, his finger on the trigger, watching the look in the man's eyes as he calculated his odds.

***

They weren't good, and Javakhishvili knew it. The fact that none of the other Blackhearts had opened fire yet told him a couple of things. For one, they were out of position, and couldn't be sure that enough of them had shots on the bad guys to get them all before he got killed. Also, without comms, coordinating that kind of shot would be next to impossible with comms down.

"*Ar isrolo*." He doubted that any of these men spoke Georgian, but he might use that to his advantage. If they couldn't understand him, but wanted to hold him and interrogate him, it might buy the others time.

He unclipped the sling and let the M4 down to the snowy ground. *As long as I'm not dead, I can still work this problem.*

The men in strange camouflage and high-end NVGs closed in on him, reaching down to haul him quickly to his feet.

CHAPTER 19

"Oh, hell." Brannigan had looked back just in time to see Javakhishvili get rolled up. It was hard to see exactly what was going on, but he could see enough, see the silhouettes of the Front's shooters against the snow as they gathered around what had to be Javakhishvili's position, to figure out what was going on. He was surprised that nobody had opened fire yet, but for the moment, he had to take that as a good thing. It meant Herc was still alive.

He turned back to Flanagan, who was right behind him. Brannigan had, contrary to the team's SOP, taken point, mainly out of a sense of urgency. "I think they just rolled up Herc."

Flanagan peered through the nearby branches at the riverbed below and the cluster of figures down there. "I think you're right. What do we do now?"

Brannigan thought about it, his mind working as he watched the situation unfold. This was going to slow them down, and put them farther away from their target when things went loud. That wasn't good. But they couldn't just leave Javakhishvili to his fate. Especially not if he was in the hands of the Humanity Front.

They all remembered far too well what had happened to Sam Childress when the Front had taken him prisoner.

"Our diversion just became a hostage rescue." He knew that this was going to put their primary targets at further risk. Who knew what the Front was going to do to the hostages they already had, once they figured out that someone was right at their back door with guns? They were a terrorist organization under the "humanitarian" façade, after all.

One problem at a time.

Must be nice, only having to worry about one problem at a time.

Flanagan, for his part, didn't question it. Herc was one of theirs, and had been since Transnistria. Without a word, Flanagan turned and headed downhill and through the trees, making for the riverbank closest to where the Front's shooters had grabbed Javakhishvili. The next few minutes were going to get dicey.

***

"Back to the base?" Cooker had the captured shooter, who didn't seem to speak English, on his knees, his hands zip-tied behind his back.

Boyd looked up toward the darkened bricks that were the two main buildings and gritted his teeth. He *should* take the prisoner back to a secured position for processing and interrogation. They had the towers manned, and the cameras *should* be back up, though he hadn't heard any drones redeploy yet. Maybe that system was borked, too.

If I take him back in there, though, Karesinda's going to get involved. He suppressed a shudder, trying to pass it off as a shiver in the increasingly biting cold. He seriously doubted he'd get the information he wanted if the client stuck their grubby paws into his interrogation. Sure, he wasn't entirely certain just what language the long-haired man in combat gear, overwhites, and carrying an M4 was speaking, but it sounded Eastern European to him. Maybe Romanian? They did have a Romanian on the team, though Dumitru was probably asleep right then, and he was a sullen, contentious man who questioned every order and was even lazier than Animal or Shear, if that was possible.

158

Screw it. If he doesn't want to come out, I'll go back in and get him. I'm not turning this over to Karesinda, and letting her get in another dig at my usefulness. He pointed toward the trees. "Get him up there and set security." He keyed his radio. "Base, this is Static. Need you to send Lugosi out." Dumitru hated that callsign, which had only cemented its use among the team.

"Roger. Any reason why?" Chance was probing, probably because either Karesinda or one of her creatures was at his elbow, trying to figure out what was going on.

"Just send him out here." Boyd wasn't interested in explaining himself. Fortunately, he'd made it pretty clear to Dumitru early on that he wasn't going to put up with insubordination within the team. It was still possible that their sullen, often drunk Romanian had caught wind enough of how Boyd was on the outs with the client that he'd try to play Animal's and Shear's game, but Boyd would make damned good and sure that he paid for it.

Chance's reply took a moment. Boyd felt his eyes narrow and his fists clench as he imagined Karesinda grilling Chance on just what was happening. He found he was hoping that the cameras *weren't* all the way up yet, so that she couldn't zoom in and study him.

"Copy that. Might take a couple of minutes."

Boyd didn't bother to answer, but turned and followed the little diamond formation of his security team, the captured shooter in between the center two, hustling up toward the bank and the woods beyond.

***

Wade had finally gotten his feet under him, though they were now in the water under the cracked ice that had broken under his weight as he'd leaned into the steeper bank at the base of the fence. He looked up past where Kirk was crouched in the same puddle, his M4 aimed in at the tower looming over the nearest corner. The whole place was still blacked out, which was a problem and an advantage all at the same time. He could see farther in what natural illum was still afforded by the last light in

159

the western sky over the peaks of the Tian Shan, and the rising moon behind the clouds to the east, but he couldn't see *as* far as he might have been able to if the old floodlights had been lit.

Kirk reached a boot back and nudged Wade as he checked on Gomez, Bianco, Burgess, and Santelli, who were also crouched in that little bit of dead space beneath the fence, partially obscured from both of the nearest towers. When Wade carefully moved up next to him, trying to keep an eye on that tower, still amazed that they hadn't been made yet, he whispered, without taking his eyes or his sights off the corner tower, "Something's wrong. I think one of ours just got snatched up."

Wade peered into the darkness, but all he could see was vague figures moving, dark against the snow. It was impossible to tell for sure what was going on, but he did know that there were a fair number of Blackhearts up there in the trees. Whatever was happening, it wasn't good.

He looked up at the towers, just in time to see one of the ballistic windows on the eastern corner tower slide open.

He didn't think. He just reacted. The only reason for one of those windows to open would be that they'd been spotted, and were about to take fire.

Snapping his rifle to his shoulder, he leaned around Bianco's shoulder, put the faint, red chevron in the ACOG, still illuminated despite the fact that the optic was so old that the tritium had to be half depleted already, on that dark rectangle in the top of the tower, flipping the weapon to "semi" and squeezing the trigger as soon as the chevron settled.

The M4 thundered in the otherwise quiet night, spitting flame in the dark as Bianco flinched away from the muzzle blast. Wade leaned into the rifle, dumping four more rounds into the opening even as Kirk opened fire on the other tower, if only to cover Wade's back.

They were committed, now.

Gomez and Santelli lunged forward, wire cutters already in hand, and went to work on the fence. The cutters were well-built and had been picked out carefully to go through a cyclone

160

fence as fast as possible. They were a lot faster than tinsnips, and it took the two men only a handful of seconds to cut enough wire to bend it out of the way, pulling the fencing aside far enough for one man to crawl through with gear and weapon.

Kirk was still hammering away at the other tower, though the guard hadn't been stupid enough to open the ballistic window while Kirk was slamming round after round into the laminate. Wade wasn't sure he'd killed the guy in the other tower, but he ceased fire and threw himself up over the lip of the bank, quickly wriggling through the hole in the fence, sure he was jamming more snow into his mag pouches as he went.

Rolling to one side, he shoved himself out of the way as Gomez followed. Keeping his muzzle trained on the open window, he got to his feet, driving forward as Gomez got up and joined him. The others were coming through, but they needed to secure these towers quickly.

Wade knew that they were on the clock now. They'd just opened the ball with that gunfire, and the enemy would be reacting quickly. But trying to bypass the towers would only invite a shot in the back. He wished, with every fiber of his being, that Carter's cache had included RPGs, but it hadn't. They were going to have to do this the hard way.

Kirk had ceased fire. Wade sprinted for the far tower, Gomez right beside him, as the others kept coming through the hole in the fence. Somewhere, an alarm started to wail.

It apparently wasn't enough to get the bad guys to secure the door at the base of the tower, however. It had a cipher lock, but it came open easily when Wade grabbed the door handle and pulled. Gomez went through, rifle up and tracking up the steps.

This wasn't any leftover from the Soviets during the Cold War. This tower was every bit the ballistic, concrete monstrosity that Wade had seen on many a FOB and airfield during the GWOT. The Front might be hiding in an abandoned Soviet base in the mountains, but they'd upgraded it. *Probably why they don't want any up-to-date imagery getting out.*

Gomez led the way up the staircase that led to the trap door in the steel floor of the actual watchtower. The door was shut, and if it was barred or otherwise locked, this might get real interesting, real fast.

Tucking his carbine under his arm, Gomez reached up and pushed on the trap, keeping his muzzle pointed at the seam. It moved, rising a little bit, so it wasn't locked, but it wasn't opening easily, either.

Wade moved up, adding his own strength to Gomez's. It was an awkward angle, pushing the trap door open overhead, and it felt like there was a dead weight on top of it. Maybe he'd killed the guard in the tower, after all.

They got the trap door open a few inches before they stalled out and had to let it down again with a *clang*. They stepped a little higher, braced themselves, and heaved.

It still didn't open all the way, but it opened enough that Gomez could shove his way up the rest of the steps, bracing his shoulder against the inside of the door. Wade held the door open as best he could, though he took more of the weight for a moment as Gomez squeezed himself into the main room of the watchtower. Then Gomez dragged something out of the way, and the weight was gone from the hatch. Wade heaved it the rest of the way open, driving up the steps and into the cramped compartment.

Blood was splashed across the chair that was now leaning against the wall, as well as the wall itself, the ballistic glass on the rear windows, and the steel roof. Wade's marksmanship had been on point, despite the fact that he'd basically been pumping barely-aimed rounds through the only opening that might have given him a shot. The guard was crumpled on the floor, shoved against the table where the radio was squawking with demands—in English—for status updates.

They turned at the sound of muted gunfire echoing through a concrete tube. Wade saw flashes through the ballistic windows of the other tower. They blinked three or four times, then went silent.

The gunfight up there was over. Who had won they couldn't tell, not without comms.

It didn't matter. They had to keep pushing, using speed and violence of action to keep ahead of the enemy's OODA loop. Without a word, Wade started back down the stairs, M4 up and ready to engage.

He'd slow down when he was dead, or everyone in his way was a rapidly cooling corpse.

CHAPTER 20

Cooker and Animal threw the detainee onto his knees in the trees. They'd found a narrow draw that afforded some cover to north and south, and after a moment, Boyd had directed the rest of the QRF to take security on the high ground. It wasn't an ideal defensive position, but it was the best he was going to get.

At least, it was the best he was going to get while staying far away from the flagpole.

As he turned toward the man with his hands zip-tied behind his back, he almost laughed. The Humanity Front was probably the last organization that would approve of calling their headquarters "The Flagpole." They disdained any national loyalties or symbols, after all. *All while coming up with their own and somehow thinking that's different.*

He stepped around to face the man, who was staring at the snow at his feet. "Look at me."

The man didn't move, didn't respond. He just stayed in place, his head bent, staring at the ground.

Boyd felt a flash of irritation. He didn't have time for this. Didn't have time to play games. He realized, even as he stepped closer and gave the man a short kick, that he may have shot himself in the foot already. Interrogation wasn't something that could be rushed. Even battlefield interrogations had rules—not so much that anyone who worked for the Humanity Front, himself included, gave much of a damn about the Laws of Land Warfare, but that there were certain ways of doing things that were effective and others that really weren't—and they took time. Time that he didn't have.

Not to mention that he had very little actual training in this beyond brutalizing the prisoner until he talked. He wasn't so squeamish that he'd balk at that, but the realization that he was in over his head was coming down on him like a ton of bricks even as he kept going with the only course of action he saw open to him.

"I'm talking to you." He squatted down in front of the man, his APC 300 angled to the left, across his knees. "You've got a choice. You can talk to me, or things can get real ugly, real fast."

"*Ar mesmis.*" The man still didn't look up at him. Boyd had no idea what he'd just said, but he recognized the tone of, "I don't understand," well enough.

He didn't believe it. The man had been carrying an M4, and while there hadn't been time to go through any pocket litter he might have been carrying, Boyd seriously doubted that someone speaking Romanian or whatever in Kyrgyzstan, trying to infiltrate a Humanity Front base, was just some dumb gun for hire from Eastern Europe who didn't speak a word of English. The guy was stalling him, and the more he felt time slip away, knowing there had to be more of them out there, the angrier Boyd got about it.

Standing up again, he stepped in closer and grabbed the man by the hair. It was long enough he could do it easily, especially since they'd taken the man's helmet, along with the old PVS-14s mounted on it.

"Listen to me, motherfucker. I know you understand me. I don't have time for this shit. You're going to tell me what you're doing here, how many you brought with you, and where they are, or I'm going to skin you alive on this mountainside." Even as the words came out through clenched teeth, Boyd wondered if he'd really be willing to do that. He'd done some messed up stuff over the years, but, surprisingly, torture hadn't been one of them.

Yeah. Yeah, at this point, I totally would. What's the alternative? Let this play out and get demoted and turned over to Karesinda's freaks for experimentation? He was determined not to let that happen.

The man looked up at him then, though he didn't have much of a choice with Boyd's gloved hand wrapped in his longish hair and twisting his head back and up. The light wasn't great under the trees, and even the advanced GPNVGs needed *some* illum to work right, but he could still just about make out the lean, hatchet-faced man's expression.

Maybe he was reading more into the dim image cast in shades of green than was really there, but he saw a sort of laid-back contempt in the man's eyes. As if he'd seen far scarier men than Boyd, and he wasn't impressed.

He felt a surge of rage at the expression. *I'm a lot scarier than you think, cocksucker.* With a snarl, he yanked on the man's hair and shoved him onto his back in the snow. The man twisted as he fell, so he didn't land directly on his bound hands.

He's been through something like this before. Boyd ignored the warning in the back of his mind. He was the man in control, but it sure didn't feel like it. He felt cornered and hunted, and he knew that it was affecting his planning and his reactions, but he didn't have the time or the maneuvering room to worry about it.

"You're going to talk. Whether it's now, or after I've peeled your legs from your ankles to your crotch, you'll talk. Don't give me this *ne ponimaioo* shit, either. I know you understand me." He slung his rifle to his back and drew his knife.

"Boyd, quit fucking around, do the guy, and let's finish the sweep." Cooker had come down to join him, his voice pitched low so that the others shouldn't be able to hear. "He's not going to talk. This is just wasting time, and if there are more—and I'm sure there are—they're getting into position while we screw around with this guy."

Boyd looked down at their prisoner, who was still looking up at him with that infuriating calm. Boyd knew that Cooker was right. This was a waste of time. But he knew nothing about their opposition, and it bothered him. Whoever they were, they'd showed up in Bishkek, then vanished like smoke only to reappear up here in the mountains. And he had *no* idea where they'd come from. They'd had eyes on the valley to the north the entire time.

Who were these bastards, and what kind of resources did they have?

He was about to go to town on their detainee when the thunder of gunfire echoed across the valley from the base.

***

Tackett was a little surprised as well as a little gratified at how well he was still able to hang with these guys. The Blackhearts were pros, and they'd been keeping sharper than he had been lately, but he was still able to keep up without making as much noise as a charging elephant through the bush. In fact, if he could trust his own perceptions, he was actually moving more quietly than some of them, especially Jenkins.

He paused behind a tree, reassessing his position, not only on the terrain, but relative to the rest of the team. He was just a little higher than Flanagan, who was at the point of the rough wedge they'd formed as they moved toward where they'd seen the Front shooters disappear into the woods with Javakhishvili. Jenkins, Carter, and the younger Brannigan—who hadn't gotten nearly as far into the riverbed as had been expected—were above him and to his right. Brannigan himself, along with Curtis, the loudmouthed machinegunner, were below Flanagan, closer to the riverbank.

The Front shooters and their prisoner were out of sight, but if he was navigating correctly, they weren't far away. Maybe another two hundred yards, on the other side of the next finger coming down off the ridge.

Tackett was scanning that finger when gunfire echoed across the valley from somewhere near the base. That was how he saw the movement when two of the Front's shooters turned to look at where the noise was coming from.

Once they'd moved, he had them. It was dark, and he had no NVGs, but their camouflage showed up almost black against the snow.

He had his ACOG's chevron on the nearest one, his finger resting lightly on the trigger, but he paused.

The Blackhearts were pros, and he wasn't one of them. If he blew the movement, if he was the first one to open fire, before the rest were in position, this could go very badly. Especially if it got Javakhishvili killed.

All the same, those guys had NVGs, and he didn't. At least, he was pretty sure they did. Which made it a borderline miracle that they hadn't spotted the Blackhearts already, given how close they were. If he could see them in the dark, with just his natural night adaptation, they had to be able to see him.

Then one of them turned back, and unless Tackett's imagination was getting away with him, the man started a little as he saw one of the Blackhearts. Maybe even Tackett himself.

There was nothing for it. He put his chevron on the man's head and squeezed the trigger. The rifle barked thunderously in the mountain quiet, spitting fire as the bullet punched right through the quad-tube NVGs and out the back of the Front shooter's skull.

***

Boyd's head snapped toward the ridge. That shot hadn't come from the base. That became even more evident when Scofield tumbled down the slope, his limbs flopping limply, trailing dark fluid behind him. A moment later, half a dozen more shots thundered along the north of the perimeter, including what sounded an awful lot like an AK on full auto.

Cooker didn't hesitate, even as two more bodies dropped, and Boyd roared, "Contact, north!" The former Legionnaire lowered his APC 300, put the muzzle against the prisoner's head, and fired.

169

Blood and brains splashed as the man's head bounced, and Boyd unconsciously jumped back to avoid the splatter as he looked down at the ruin of the intruder's skull, then back up at Cooker. Cooker just shrugged. "Should have done that from the get-go."

Then they were running up the hill, as more gunfire lashed the northern edge of the perimeter.

***

Brannigan heard the first shot, and just for a moment, he thought that either Tackett or Carter had jumped the gun and they were made. He had no targets ahead of him, but a moment later, he heard more gunfire, and saw Flanagan open fire. So, at least Flanagan had a target. So did several others up the line. He started to push forward, leaning into the slope, weaving between the trees and searching for more targets.

The snow made footing treacherous, but he kept his rifle up and quickly compensated when his boots started to slip. He came around yet another tree and came almost face to face with another shooter, his camouflage looking dark against the snow, the faint green glow from his NVGs lighting up his face beneath his helmet.

The man was looking just barely the wrong direction as Brannigan came through the spruce branches, looking up toward where Curtis was laying into the top of the finger, his RPK spitting fire as he raked the trees with green tracers. Brannigan barely bothered to get much of a sight picture, keeping his off eye open and just putting the unfocused red blob of the ACOG's chevron on the man's torso as he cranked off a hammer pair, the reports blending together into a single roll of thunder.

The impacts forced the man back a step, but he was apparently wearing body armor, so Brannigan lifted the rifle as he moved forward, and put two more rounds into the dark blob that was the man's head. The first must have hit the helmet, jerking the Front shooter's head back, and the second went in under his chin a moment later. The man dropped like a puppet with its strings cut.

Driving forward faster, Brannigan kept pace with the rest of the line, as the enemy fire died down to nothing.

***

Wade paused just before starting back down. The guard's helmet was bathed in blood and brains, and was probably cracked from the bullet that had punched through the man's skull. But it was intact enough to hold the GPNVGs that were still on the mount and still working, so Wade, ignoring the gore, picked it up, let his rifle hang for a moment while he pulled the helmet on and dropped the panoramic NVGs in front of his face, and turned toward the trap door.

Then he cursed, ripped the helmet off, and let it fall on the floor.

Gomez was halfway down the steps already, and looked up with a frown.

"I don't have a laser, and I can't get a sight picture with those damned things." Wade started toward the trap door again, though he had to wait for Gomez to get clear of the steps.

"So, grab his rifle and his mags. He won't need 'em anymore."

Wade shook his head. "No time. Let's go."

Gomez just shrugged, turning and hurrying down the stairs without another word as more gunfire echoed through the night below.

Wade took a glance out of the windows just before he started down, trying to see what was happening before he went running into the middle of it.

Muzzle flash strobed from the rear windows of the other guard tower, and Bianco was down at the base, pouring full auto RPK fire toward the corner of the closest building. So, whoever had stormed that guard tower must have come out on top, and now they were trading fire with more guards coming out of the building.

As he and Gomez reached the base of the tower, Wade came out the door and turned to the right, checking the other corner of the building. Just in time, too, as four more dark figures with weapons came around the corner.

Dropping to a knee, partially barricaded on the still-open door, Wade opened fire, using the ACOG's chevron as the next best thing to a red dot, dragging the muzzle back and forth across the group as he dumped half the mag into them.

The lead man staggered, then dropped, keening, gripping a leg that was suddenly spurting blood, and then the two immediately behind him fell flat, one limp, one thrashing in pain. The one man still standing turned and ran back to the corner, leaving the other three to their fate.

Wade slowed down and slammed another round apiece into each of the men down on the ground. The first one, who was even then trying to put a RAT tourniquet on his leg, shuddered and went still. The other one that was still moving let out an even longer scream as the bullet tore into him.

The last one didn't move.

He saw the fourth man start to peek around the corner, shifted aim, and fired. The lighting was bad enough, and trying to use the ACOG awkward enough in that low light, that he hit the corner and just spat fragments of concrete into the man's face.

"Turn and go!" Gomez was back at the other guard tower, next to Kirk, who was covering the far corner while Bianco sent the odd burst at the guards who had taken shelter behind it.

Wade sprinted toward the rest. Every fiber of his being wanted to push the other corner and kill that last shooter, but he knew that if he got too separated from the rest of the team, he was dead.

Skidding to a halt, he dropped to a knee and checked the far corner. He couldn't see as well, but he could see that that fourth shooter hadn't reappeared.

Bianco lowered his RPK. The corner opposite was chewed up and pockmarked by bullet impacts. None of the windows had opened, and Wade suddenly suspected that they couldn't open. It was a Soviet building, after all.

"We need to push." Wade had to raise his voice as Santelli opened fire from above again. "We don't know the layout, so we're going to have to clear each building as we go."

"I'm not sure we've got enough zip-ties to secure everybody, and half the team's still up there." Kirk waved toward the far side of the riverbed, where muzzle flashes flickered, and more gunfire echoed across the mountainsides.

"So, we'll take some of the heat off." Wade got to his feet and got ready to sprint to the side of the building. "I doubt the Front's cronies will be all that happy about having their security out there while we're kicking their door in."

CHAPTER 21

Curtis cussed to himself as he struggled up the snowy slope. *Stupid snow. Stupid mountains. Mama Curtis' baby boy was not meant to go mountaineering in the winter. Give me the desert any damned day. Even the jungle. This snow shit sucks.* Despite his clothing, Curtis was wet, cold, and miserable, and having to rely on his night eyes in the dark because none of their NVGs were working wasn't helping anything.

He had to force himself to look up, even as he slipped again, for probably the fiftieth time that day. *How does Joe like this crap?*

It was a good thing he'd craned his neck to look up, because he saw movement just then, as he came around a spruce. A dark figure was turning back toward him, leveling a rifle. There might have been a faint, red glow at the weapon's top rail, which would be the IR laser. *Holy crap, I can see that.*

Throwing himself prone, Curtis mashed the RPK's trigger, hardly bothering to put the bipods on the ground. He walked the green tracers across the figure, just about cutting him in half. The man fell, his screams of agony drowned out by the rattling roar of the light machinegun.

He held his position for a moment, panting hard. Not only was it cold and miserable, but the air up there was *thin.*

Intellectually, Curtis knew it wasn't as bad as the Altiplano had been, but it sure *felt* every bit as bad.

Flanagan passed him, appearing out of the trees, his M4 up and scanning. With another quiet curse, Curtis hauled himself to his feet, keeping the RPK's muzzle out of the snow, and kept struggling up the slope.

He reached the top right behind another tree and threw himself flat, searching for targets. More fire was roaring out across the narrow draw, and a bullet *snap*ped past Curtis head even as he hit the ground, clipping a branch off the tree above him and dropping it on his back.

He'd spotted the muzzle flash, even though all of the bad guys seemed to be running suppressors. It had been faint, but his eyes were adjusted enough—and he'd just happened to be looking straight at it—that he'd picked it up.

Still, he hesitated. If Herc was up there, he didn't want to cut their teammate in half.

Then he glanced down below.

There were bodies in the snow. He could see the dark shapes against the white, even in the dim light as the moon peeked out through a rent in the clouds overhead. Most of them looked right.

That one didn't.

It took him a second to realize that the man lying on his side in the snow had his hands tied behind his back.

Even looking at that, as the image burned itself into his brain, Curtis didn't put the pieces together all at once. But only one person could be lying there with his hands tied.

They'd killed Herc.

"You motherfuckers!" He shifted the RPK back toward where he'd seen that muzzle flash and pinned the trigger, leaning into the bipods as he dug them into the hillside.

***

Boyd just about buried himself in the snow as bullets chewed into the tree just above his head. The volume of incoming fire was ferocious, and when half his react force had just been cut to dog treats in a handful of seconds, he didn't have the guns to respond accordingly.

Shots cracked off to his left, as Animal shot back, only to get hammered back behind cover by a storm of fire. *How many of these bastards are there? And why are they so effective when the EMP generator should have fried everything they've got?*

Movement caught his eye, and he shifted to fire over Animal's head at the figure dashing between trees up at the top of the draw. He couldn't tell if he'd hit him or not. The laser was bouncing and flickering off tree limbs. He'd discovered that the GPNVGs weren't that useful for passive night vision aiming, so they were limited to the lasers. And those had some serious limitations in dense timber.

Another laser tracked toward where he'd fired, and more rounds tore through the spruces, only to be answered by more muzzle flashes and a roar of gunfire. The laser jerked and dropped, going still as it shone scattered through branches and needles.

Whoever these guys were, they were serious, and they weren't deterred by the fact that the Front's react force had night vision and suppressors, and they didn't. At least, they weren't using IR lasers to aim, and they'd managed to hit several of his guys who were running suppressed.

He also still had no idea how many there were. Despite their muzzle flashes, by the time a laser moved toward one, it was gone, and they didn't seem to be hitting anything.

Something had gone very badly. And it was about to get worse.

"Static, Static, this is Chance." He almost didn't hear the radio over the roar and crackle of gunfire. He was down to five or six of his original twelve, and they were huddled on the south side of the next finger, leaving several of their own—and their detainee—lying in the snow, rapidly cooling as the night temperature dropped. He ducked back down as another burst of machinegun fire flayed the top of the finger. That belt-fed was killing them.

"This is Static. Kind of dealing with a problem here."

"We've got one here, too." Chance sounded a lot more wound up than usual. "We've got shooters in the wire, and the perimeter security hasn't been able to stop them. We believe they've penetrated Building Two. We need all hands back here."

Boyd was sure that Finkelstein or Karesinda was currently in the CP, standing over Chance and swearing at him in panic. His voice had just the right combination of urgency and tight control. There was no way Chance was going to flip out in front of the client.

"We are pinned down here!" He realized he was raising his voice and shouting into the radio, and forced himself to calm down, even as he ducked beneath another stream of green tracers that rained bits of needles, bark, and branches down on him. "If we try to cross that riverbed, we're fucked!" Decades of proper radio procedure went out the window, facing this nightmare situation.

He gulped and huddled in the meager cover behind a spruce and a couple of boulders sticking up out of the snow. *Calm down. Think.*

Taking a deep breath, he keyed the radio again. "Get the drones out."

"The copters?" Chance wasn't getting it.

"No, damn it! The walkers. The gun dogs. Get them out here and get me some fucking fire support, if you want us back there to save your worthless asses!" Flipping back over onto his belly, he tried to peer through the branches, afraid to trigger his IR laser until he was *sure* he had a target.

More fire hammered at them from higher up the mountain, and he glanced toward the base. If they didn't get those drones out soon, he was going to die.

And he was far more afraid of that eventuality than he'd ever thought he could be.

***

Brannigan didn't know exactly what prompted him to look across the river toward the base just then. Maybe it was just the long-established habit of checking his surroundings even during a fight, making sure that he wasn't getting sucked into the immediate threat to the point he missed the one that was coming around on their flank. Maybe it was just some sixth sense, his mind picking up a clue he hadn't noticed consciously.

Either way, he spotted the threat coming, though he couldn't quite tell what it was at first.

Those weren't men bounding across the snowy riverbank, and even as he squinted through the gloom at them, he saw one of the vaguely doglike shapes slip and stumble, correct, and keep coming.

From the motion, they were running on all fours, but they weren't moving like dogs. He got a sudden very bad feeling.

"Hit the dirt!" Brannigan suited actions to words as he threw himself flat, putting a slight fold in the ground and a fallen spruce between him and the advancing threat.

A moment later, full auto fire raked the hillside, smashing through tree limbs and trunks and kicking up geysers of snow. Brannigan felt more than heard the round that went by his head with a *snap* and spat snow and frozen dirt into his face.

He wormed backward, getting down behind the finger and deeper into a fold in the ground. Dirt makes for some of the best cover against bullets, and there were a lot of bullets incoming as those dog-shaped things sprayed down the hillside. More fire was coming from the Front's shooters on the other side of the draw, too, showering more needles and splintered branches down on the Blackhearts as they did their damnedest to become one with the ground.

Twisting over on his side, he got as much of his body behind a tree and another rise in the ground as he could, peering through his ACOG for a target. The things firing on them weren't suppressed, so the muzzle flash was easy to spot.

He frowned as he put his chevron on the shape. He'd seen pictures of concepts for these drones, but never seen one in the wild. Four-legged, all four limbs bent forward like a dog's hind legs, the boxy main body was topped by a faceted turret with a shrouded machinegun muzzle protruding from the angular front.

That muzzle was currently flickering with muzzle flash as it blazed away at the Blackhearts on the hillside.

There wasn't time to check that none of his boys had gotten hit. He had to deal with this threat first.

The drone wasn't moving at the moment, but was just standing in the riverbank and sending burst after burst into the trees. Maybe it was more stable that way. Maybe the operator needed that stability to try to see what he was shooting at. It didn't matter. It gave Brannigan a shot.

Staying as low as he could, his M4 flipped on its side to reduce his signature still further, laid across the lowest branch of the spruce, he squeezed off a shot just as the chevron, sideways in his vision, settled just above that muzzle flash.

That angle wasn't perfect. The ACOG's Bullet Drop Compensator was designed for shooting straight up and down, not sideways, and the sight's height over bore meant that the bullet was going to hit to the right of wherever he was shooting. But it was going to have to be good enough.

The first round sparked off the facet of the turret beside the weapon muzzle. The thing might have swayed slightly, but then Brannigan had to duck even lower as a new burst all but shredded the tree above his head.

These things weren't going to go down to 5.56 except by a lucky shot. And meanwhile, provided the Blackhearts were all still alive, they were pinned down.

This fight had just gone badly sideways, and as Brannigan started to low crawl backward down the little fold in the ground, he hoped that the rest could figure out that their only chance of survival was to get out of the kill zone.

**

A burst from the riverbed raked his position again, and Boyd ducked as he was showered with shattered bark. "Shift fire, *shift fucking fire!*" he screamed into the radio. "Shift north!"

The drones weren't going to do his team—what was left of it—any good if they just hosed down any thermal signature on the hillside. The drone operators had to have client personnel in

180

their business, too, screaming at them to kill whatever they could see.

Letting them have access to the security spaces was proving to be more of a liability than even he'd expected.

Fortunately, the fire shifted, and he found that they were in the clear. They were no longer taking fire from their unknown adversaries across the draw, as the intruders were pinned down— and hopefully getting shot to ribbons—by the drones' massed machinegun fire.

He got up. "Let's go." He had to reach down and grab Animal, hauling the other man to his feet. "We've got to get back to the compound and clear out the active shooters there. We can worry about these bastards later."

It took a moment to get everyone up. Despite the training and the background that was supposed to be required for this job, it had presumably been a long time since any of the Front's contractors—at least among this bunch—had been under that kind of fire. And losing half the team in a few seconds hadn't been good, either. They were all rattled.

Finally, though, he got them all up and moving down the hillside toward the riverbed. The drones were spread out in a sort of echelon formation, though it was ragged enough that Boyd was pretty sure it wasn't intentional. Each drone operator was just trying to get a better shot at the targets, and their field of view through the drones' cameras couldn't be that good.

Boyd was running, hardly waiting for the rest to catch up. They could worry about retrieving the bodies later. Not that he had a great deal of affinity for any of them. There wasn't the kind of brotherhood among this team that he'd seen elsewhere.

He hadn't been very tight with any of the rest of those teams he'd been on, either. Which had made him that much better a fit for this operation.

He wasn't thinking about that. He was barely thinking about the bodies left behind. The one thing that was seriously on his mind was what was going to happen to him if the shooters who had penetrated the compound captured or killed any of the researchers.

It seemed like a strange thing to think about while he tried to sprint across the snowy, uneven ground of the riverbed. Gunfire echoed behind him, and a bullet *snap*ped past his head, too high to worry about but still close enough to make him duck as his boot slipped and he stumbled. Somebody up there wasn't so completely suppressed that they couldn't spot him and take a shot. He could see flashes through the windows of Karesinda's Building One, as the intruders engaged with the guards he'd left behind. There were a lot of immediate tactical problems to focus on, but he couldn't help but think about his own future, and how the next few minutes could affect it.

There was more than just his paycheck on the line here. If he'd been working for any other NGO, or even a Western government, and one of his principals got killed or captured, he'd probably be fired, his clearance yanked if he was working for a governmental agency. Working for the Front, though, in this place and with these researchers involved, he wouldn't just get fired. He'd disappear. If he was lucky, he'd be shot or strangled, his body rendered down by chemicals and poured out in an obscure ditch somewhere.

If he was unlucky...

He didn't want to think about that.

Reaching the gate first, about twenty yards in front of Animal, he ignored the body lying next to the guardhouse at the entrance. The guardhouse hadn't been built with rifle ports, so the poor, dumb bastard had gotten out to try to engage the intruders as they breached the fence, and had been gunned down as they pushed deeper into the compound.

He ran across the yard toward Building One, already hearing muted gunfire from inside.

CHAPTER 22

Wade came around the corner and almost ran into a man in camouflage and a plate carrier, crouched back in the doorway at the end of the blocky structure. Both men snapped their rifles up at almost the same time, but Wade was just a little bit faster and a lot more aggressive.

His M4 thundered and roared, spitting fire as he hammered six rounds into the man. A couple probably hit the plates, but the others tore through flesh, bone, and vital organs. The Front's security contractor slumped back in the doorway, dark fluid spattered against the concrete, another dark smear showing on the plaster as the man slid down to lie still on the steps.

Wade put a single round into each of the other forms slumped down on the snowy ground in front of the entrance, just in case. Brannigan, Santelli, and Flanagan might have their reasons to object, but Wade wasn't taking chances. Especially not with these bastards.

He held back just before the doorway, waiting for another Blackheart to join him. Gomez was at his shoulder a moment later, giving his tricep a painful squeeze, as Santelli set up to cover the far corner and the yard beyond. Wade took a breath, momentarily glad there was a door on the end so that he didn't have to go out into that yard to find an entrance, then turned into the recessed doorway, driving up the steps and toward the door itself.

True to Soviet architecture, the door set into the crumbling plaster of the doorway was windowless steel, the paint peeling off. If it was locked, this could slow them down a lot. There were windows on ground level that they could breach, but it would take time, and it would be a lot more awkward—making the first man in vulnerable—than going through the door.

Tucking his M4 under his arm, he tested the door. It was locked. Probably mag-locked as an add on by the Front after they'd occupied the base. He swore sulphurously as he wished they had some breaching charges, but while Carter had had some explosives in his cache, there hadn't been time or facilities to really prep charges the way they needed.

"Get to a window." He turned back toward the outside, in time to see Santelli flatten himself against the inside of the recessed doorway. He turned his eyes toward the outside fence, craning his neck to look toward the yard around the corner, in time to see what looked like four or five mechanical dogs running out through the gate.

Drones. That was bad.

Fortunately, the four-legged gun drones didn't turn to right or left, but kept going out the gate and into the riverbed. That wasn't good, either, as Wade was pretty sure they were heading for the other Blackhearts on the far side, in the trees. It gave him a little bit of breathing room, but only a little. He grabbed Gomez by the shoulder and propelled him toward the outside. "We need to move."

Gomez didn't need much prodding. He was already turning toward the nearest window, his muzzle high, and brought it down sharply, shattering the glass before raking the barrel around the window frame to clear any remaining fragments that could cut a man climbing through. They didn't have a blanket or tarp to put over it, so they were probably going to get some cuts and scrapes anyway, but time was pressing.

With Wade covering him, while Kirk, Bianco, and Santelli covered the corners and the fence line, Gomez grabbed the windowsill with one hand, his M4 held muzzle high in the other, and started to haul himself up.

The room was dark, and Wade saw no movement as he covered the interior. The Front's guard force didn't seem to have thought in terms of manning the outer windows. Which was a good thing, but Wade hadn't lived as long as he had by assuming that the enemy would be lazy or incompetent.

Gomez got over the windowsill easily, dropping to the floor with his weapon already in both hands, up and ready to engage.

He moved aside, and Wade followed him in with somewhat more difficulty. Wade was a rather larger man than Gomez, and with his gear on it got a little harder to get through. But he made it without falling on his face, kept his muzzle pointed at the door in the corner of the room, and as soon as he was set, both men started moving toward that door.

The room they had entered appeared to be someone's office, with a laptop closed on the desk that faced the door, back to the windows. Stacks of papers littered the desk, disorganized and scattered. Wade thought for about half a second that there might be some intel value in the papers, but there wasn't time. If they cleared the compound, they could come back later. If they didn't, they'd have more important things to worry about.

And this *was* a hostage rescue mission, so they were on the clock.

Gomez cracked the door open, peering out into the hallway, which was well-lit, unlike the office itself. Then he pulled it the rest of the way open and went out, while Wade button-hooked through behind him, checking that there wasn't another shooter crouched just inside the entry door, waiting to shoot them in the back.

Clear. He swung back and joined Gomez as he moved down the hall, gliding catlike over the concrete floor.

They seemed to be in an office section of the building, currently unoccupied. As they passed several more doors, checking each one and finding a darkened office or storage room

185

in each case, they got closer and closer to the main entryway, which appeared to open up onto a much larger central room. A stout steel door stood at the far end, apparently secured with a cipher lock.

Gomez spotted the man in green, gray, and brown cammies first, as he came clattering down the staircase at the near end of that large foyer. The M4's report was deafeningly loud in the concrete corridor, and the man spun aside and fell on his face, leaking red out onto the cement floor.

A moment later, to Wade's astonishment, that cipher-locked steel door opened, and two men in the same camouflage, plate carriers, and carrying those boxy carbines, came out, driving toward their position, guns up.

Wade shot the first one through the eye a split second later, snapping his head back with a spray of red and sending him crashing to the floor. The second man stutter-stepped, and Wade got a bullet into him a half second behind Gomez, who'd just shot him through the throat.

Then a storm of fire came tearing out of the portal behind the dead men, and both Blackhearts had to split to either side of the hallway to avoid the bullets that sprayed through the opening. One chipped fragments off the ceiling, another tore a groove in the floor, and Wade felt one tug at his sleeve as he flattened himself against the wall, looking for any cover at all. Both he and Gomez were shooting back, the entire structure ringing with the thunder of their reports.

He kicked an office door open, hastily cleared the inside as he ducked out of the hallway, only then realizing that Santelli and Bianco had followed him in, and then found he was blocked from the doorway as Bianco barricaded on the wall, braced the RPK against the doorframe, and opened fire, the thunder of the machinegun physically painful as it reverberated through the concrete.

There was no other door to let them out, only the window, which would mean going in the main doors. That might or might not be a good idea. Wade moved to the window to check the

186

outside, seeing no other shooters in the yard. When he moved to check out the gate, though, he saw the drones pouring fire into the trees on the other side of the riverbed, while small figures ran back toward the base.

They'd pulled some of the heat off the others, but it might not have been enough.

And if he didn't do something quick, they were going to be cut off, trying to defend this room as a strongpoint, instead of taking the fight to the bad guys.

***

Gomez kicked the opposite door open, doing much the same thing that Wade had on the other side of the corridor. A lot of CQB training was based on owning the hallway and getting into the room fast, though he'd had some urban combat experience that felt disturbingly similar to this, where the jihadis had barricaded a machinegun at the end of a hallway. The only way they'd managed to get that guy had been to get up on the roof, knock a hole in it, and toss a frag down. He didn't think this was an option here, and not just because he didn't have any frags.

Kirk had flowed into the room with him, and now they had some cover, but they were still stuck. Gomez was starting to eye the exterior window, much the same way Wade was doing on the other side, when Bianco opened fire down the hallway and across the foyer with that RPK.

The incoming fire suddenly slackened to nothing, and Gomez stuck his head out just far enough into the hallway to confirm it. Then, tapping Kirk on the shoulder with a fist, he was moving out into the hallway, heading for the stairs where he'd shot the first man they'd encountered in the building.

Bianco was going to be out shortly, even as he hammered a stream of green tracers into that hallway, so he moved fast, going around the corner without pausing to check it, his weapon up and ready to fire as soon as he had a target. He stepped over the corpse at the base of the steps and started up, twisting to cover the landing overhead as he went. Kirk was right behind him, and didn't seem that bothered by the fact that they'd just potentially run out into a kill zone, not to mention the fact that Bianco's stream of machinegun fire had just crackled a bare few inches past their shoulders.

The two men hurried up the steps, keeping close together and making sure they covered each other as they moved. Kirk might have been out of the game for a few missions, but he'd trained back up to his usual standard, and the two men burst out onto the landing quickly, both M4s roaring as they engaged the pair of camouflage-clad security guards sitting just outside the door just a few yards down the hall. Both men had been holding their weapons semi-ready, and the first one had managed to level his just as Gomez had drawn a bead and shot him through the teeth. Kirk dumped the other with a fast pair. The first bullet tore along his rifle, mangling his off hand, the second punched through his forehead, dropping him like a rock.

They moved up quickly, Gomez taking point while Kirk checked their six then moved to catch up. With only two of them in that hallway, they could get caught and murdered very quickly if they didn't watch every angle, every chance they got.

Closing in on the door, Gomez kicked the weapons away from the two men's hands. He might have shot each one once more, just to be on the safe side, but they were both obviously dead. Unless the Front had started working on tech to turn dead men into zombies, anyway.

He wouldn't put it past them. Gomez had grown up with stories of *brujas*, after all. But neither corpse moved, and he turned his attention to the door while Kirk held security.

The door was cipher locked, but while he might not admit it in polite company, Gomez wasn't that bothered by trying to get through locks. Just about any kind of locks. He'd started learning in the Marine Corps, and has his military career had turned into more of a private military career, he'd continued to study.

Cipher locks were considerably more difficult in many ways than ordinary mechanical locks, but Gomez had figured them out a while back. While Kirk held security, he started to manipulate the lock, feeling his way through the combination.

"Shouldn't we be finding a way down, get behind those bastards while Vinnie still has some ammo left?" Kirk was busy checking either direction, making sure they didn't get blindsided.

"This might be a command center." Gomez got the last digit and kicked the door open, dropping his muzzle level as he started moving through. He didn't finish the thought as he went, and he heard Kirk curse as the other man turned to follow him in.

It was a command center, just not the one he'd been looking for. Three men sat at laptops, their backs to the door. At first glance, he might have thought they were playing shooter games, but after a split second he recognized what he was looking at.

Drone operators. And the drones they were running currently had the rest of the Blackhearts under fire.

Gomez didn't hesitate. He shot all three in as many seconds, double tapping each as he dragged his muzzle across the room. Blood splashed across the tables and the laptops, and one monitor shattered, turning to a weird amalgam of black and fractured color as the bullet passed through the operator and smashed the screen.

Double checking that the room was clear, he turned back toward the door. They hadn't found their flanking maneuver yet, but at least they'd taken some of the heat off Brannigan and the others.

Flowing back out into the hallway, he and Kirk continued toward the far end of the building.

CHAPTER 23

Bianco ceased fire and dropped back into the room, stripping out the empty 75-round drum. Santelli stepped back in to replace him, as Wade wracked his brain to determine their course of action.

From where he stood, he could take the gateway under fire, halting the reinforcements coming back across the riverbed. But that meant strongpointing this room and holding it, while the Front did who knows what around behind their backs.

Not knowing even vaguely what kind of strength they had in this place was messing with his decision making.

Hey, at least they haven't brought one of those steroid-head freaks out to play this time. Those guys had been a nasty surprise in Argentina, taking far too many rounds to drop. So far, everyone they'd faced here was normal, which meant they died decently when you shot them, provided you got around their body armor.

The gunfire from the hallway had fallen silent. Santelli wasn't shooting as Bianco reloaded. Wade looked over at him. "What's the deal?"

"Got no targets." The former sergeant major's Boston accent was thicker than ever, especially since he was breathing pretty hard. It did still seem to be just from the exertion and the altitude, which was good. Whatever issues the man had needed to work through over the last couple of jobs, he'd apparently taken care of them. "I think Vinnie killed whoever was back there shooting at us."

Wade glanced out the window again. The figures crossing the riverbed were getting closer, the man in the lead almost to the gate. He put his sights on him, his finger on the trigger. He could smoke the dude right there—provided the glass didn't divert the round too much.

But they had an opening. And the drones had just ceased fire.

He decided. "Let's push. Get across that foyer fast, and let's see what they were guarding back there." Rolling away from the window, he crossed to join Bianco and Santelli at the door. "With you."

Santelli moved, stepping out and darting into the hallway, and Bianco, with the RPK, took the rear, crossing behind him and clearing the hallway they'd come up, pointing the long barrel down toward the entrance. Wade fell in behind Santelli, giving Bianco a thump to the shoulder as he went, and the two of them moved into the foyer, fast, guns up and tracking toward the corners.

Clearing each corner—which in Wade's case meant clearing the bottom flight of the stairs that Gomez had gone up not long before—they turned and dashed across the foyer to the open steel door on the far side. Wade kept his muzzle about halfway between the door and the small desk at the back wall, just in case, but nobody popped out from behind it before they reached the open door.

With Santelli in the lead, they made entry, finding that Bianco had indeed caught the third shooter with a burst. The full burst, from the looks of it. Rifle and man alike were pretty mangled.

They were in a short entryway, with another security checkpoint off to the right. It appeared that the third man, the one Bianco had killed, had come out of that checkpoint. The door was open, leading into a small room lined with CCTV monitors.

While Santelli covered down the hallway, which was lined with more blank steel doors, instead of the hollow-core office doors in the corridor they'd just come from, and Bianco held on the main door, Wade stepped inside to see what they were dealing with.

He felt his fists clench and his face stiffen into a snarl of rage. John Wade considered himself a hardened, jaded man. His sense of humor was usually what most people would consider dark. Very dark. He could look at carnage that would have a lot of people staring in shocked horror and grin. Especially if he thought that whoever had just been turned into hamburger had it coming.

Wade figured a whole lot of people had it coming.

But this was different.

He was looking at surveillance footage of small, cramped, barren cells. The only furniture in each of them was a military cot and a composting toilet. It appeared that a great deal of modification to the original Soviet structure had been made to render these cells secure.

It wasn't the state of the cells that tripped Wade's "murder button," though. It was the state of the men in them.

Most of them appeared to be locals, Kyrgyz farmers or even soldiers, and those guys he couldn't care less about. But he recognized at least two of the Westerners, and a third looked familiar, too. He'd met them in Chad, and while they weren't Blackhearts, they'd been pretty good dudes.

The big black dude would be Vernon. He was currently on the cot, curled into the fetal position, shaking. And not with cold.

Wade almost didn't recognize Max. The man had lost weight—something he'd insisted was next to impossible when they'd met in Chad—though he was every bit as pale as he had been before. He was staring at the wall, his arms wrapped around himself, flinching at every sound.

Even the ones that weren't real.

He didn't remember the name of the skinny guy, but he was just sitting against the wall, his knees hauled up to his chin, staring at the door. Not moving.

Whatever the Front was up to, they'd put these guys through the wringer. And while Wade might not have any moral hangups about torturing jihadis, Communists, pirates, narcos, or any other bad guys, seeing it done to guys like that pissed him off. A lot.

He started looking around for keys or cell door controls, when Bianco opened fire with that RPK from the doorway.

***

Boyd heard the drones go silent as he passed the gate, pushing toward the main entrance to Building One. He swore as he saw more flashes through the windows. Things were going from bad to worse.

He sprinted across the yard, slipping on the snow and falling on his face, just in time to avoid getting his head taken off by a bullet from across the riverbed. The drones had pinned the intruders down for a bit, but now that the drones had gone silent, they were getting right at it again.

Did they run out of ammo? Did those stupid bastards only load one belt apiece? He had no way of knowing, and he honestly didn't know for sure how much the drones could even carry, but right then, with the enemy trying to blow his brains out from two directions, he didn't care. All that mattered was that the fancy machines had failed.

They should have been able to kill all of them with those fancy thermals and everything. He scrambled to his feet and ran to the front entrance. He'd torn out his earpiece for the moment, just because the net was a mess of screaming and yelling, as every client retard with a radio hollered for the security contractors who they held in such contempt to come save them.

Only long experience prompted him to halt at the edge of the entryway and wait for Animal and the rest to join him. So far, no one else had come out of Building Two, despite the fact that Chance had to have seen him coming on the cameras. Judging by the bodies sprawled at the corner, he figured that anyone left in there just didn't want to be the first one to stick their necks out, given the buzzsaw that was running through the place.

He got his breathing and heart rate under control as Animal and Torg caught up. He'd been sure that he'd seen Torg go down, but he'd lost track of just who was still up and who was dead in the confusion. With the two of them on his heels, and refusing to wait for the others, he drove in through the main doors.

And was immediately forced back by full-auto fire from the cell block. Bullets chewed into the concrete and punched holes in the steel door. Boyd threw himself flat, barely avoiding getting his head taken off, and then rapidly crawled back out the doorway, even as the man with the machinegun in the cell block started to shift fire toward him. He felt a savage blow as a bullet clipped his helmet just before he got out of the doorway.

Flattening himself against the outside wall, he panted, his heart racing, his breath smoking in the frigid air. That had been way too close.

The fire from inside had ceased, but Boyd didn't think for a second that that meant the threat was any less immediate. The man in there just had good fire discipline.

The rest of what remained of the QRF was stacked up beside him, and he took stock quickly. He had Animal, Torg, Shear, Freight, and Couteau. Hardly enough, when he considered where they stood.

We need reinforcements. If I can get this under control, even if it means using the backup force at Manas, then I can still salvage this nightmare.

He pointed toward Building Two, which seemed to still be secure. "Get to Building Two. Now." Without waiting for an acknowledgement, he surged to his feet and ran across the yard toward the doors.

Fortunately, the rest of the team kept up. Apparently, none of them were all that eager to assault a barricaded machinegun. At least in the case of Animal and Shear, that came as no surprise to Boyd.

"Hold here and cover the front of that building." He pointed at Torg and Couteau. "Nobody comes out." He turned and charged into the main doors, immediately heading for the command post.

Bursting through the door with a *bang*, he scanned the cameras. It looked like several of them were *still* out, probably fried by the EMP test, despite the fact that they were *supposed* to be shielded. "Have we got comms up with Manas?"

Chance looked over at the computer, hooked to the satcom radio that was supposed to have constant contact with the team at Manas. It hadn't taken a huge amount of money to get the Kyrgyz to turn the former Coalition airbase over to another of the Front's quiet affiliate companies. It had been a good amount to the Kyrgyz government, but it was peanuts to the Humanity Front.

"I think so." He quickly rolled his office chair across the concrete floor to the laptop and started typing. After a moment, he frowned and craned his neck to peer at the radio. "We're linked, but there's no reply yet."

Boyd fumed. Of course those lazy bastards weren't paying attention to the comms. They were probably watching porn or just drunk. It wasn't as if anyone would possibly dare to come after the Front in the middle of the Tian Shan, even if they'd guessed what was going on. "Keep trying. We need immediate support. And if it helps, tell that fuckhead Scorch that I'll shoot him myself if this goes completely sideways. In the nuts."

"It's going to take at least forty minutes, even if they leave right now." Chance was trying not to sound nervous, but he was failing.

"I know." Boyd turned back to the door. "Tell me everybody is up."

"Everybody. Even Janson." Chance turned back to the cameras.

For a moment, Boyd considered telling him to gear up and come with him. The cameras were next to useless at this point. But he shook his head and headed back toward the barracks. The cameras might not help, but he still needed Chance on comms.

196

The ready room was packed with the rest of the security team. He looked around, realizing just how many had already gotten burned down. They were just over half strength.

"Okay, Building One's been penetrated. We need to lock that building down, then move in and clear it. If they're trying to free the prisoners..." He paused, hesitating ever so slightly. He could see this next order going badly for him, but he could still defend it to the client if he had to. "If you see them bringing the prisoners out, don't hesitate to dump the prisoners too."

There was no way in hell the client wanted anything about this program getting out, and he was sure he could explain that if it came up later, and enough of the client personnel would agree with him that it would divert Karesinda's wrath.

He hoped.

"Let's move. We can still salvage this."

CHAPTER 25

Bianco ceased fire again. "We've got bad guys trying to force the front entrance!" He didn't take his eyes or muzzle off the doorway, but turned his head just far enough to yell over his shoulder. "Tell me we've got something!"

"We've got something." Wade had found the controls for the cell doors. They were on a tab on the laptop, instead of actual physical switches, which he found somewhat annoying. Fortunately, the laptop's security program was all in English. Given some of what he'd seen from the Humanity Front, he'd been half expecting it to be in French, or something.

It took him a few seconds to match the cell to the button. He didn't want to let all the locals out. He didn't know what had been going on here, and he didn't give a damn about them, anyway. They were there for Price's guys, and he was sure about three of them.

"Carlo!" He leaned out the door. "I'm about to open the first door on your right. His name's Vernon. We worked with him in Chad." Even though they were on a time crunch and under fire, given what he was seeing on the monitors, Wade really did not think that just pushing all the doors open without taking precautions was a good idea. These guys were messed up, and trying to just push in and grab them might cause more problems than it solved.

Wade might take a perverse pride in being considered a blunt instrument—some buddies of his had joked about giving him the callsign "Belt-Fed" some years before—but he was a lot more of a thinker than he generally let people see.

As soon as Santelli was set up on the cell door, Wade reached down and opened it.

***

The door unlatched with a *click* that he could hear in the quiet now that the shooting had died down for the moment. Keeping his weapon muzzle high but ready to drop it quickly and go to work, Santelli reached out and pushed the door open slowly.

The man on the cot was in rough shape. His hair and beard had grown out, he was emaciated, and more importantly, the vacant look in his eyes and the lack expression on his face weren't right. The man the others had described meeting in Chad had been a professional, collected and ready for action at any time. This man was a wreck, and the look in his eyes reminded Santelli of a few stoners he'd met.

No, there was something more to it than that. Santelli had seen a lot over his nearly fifty years of life, almost thirty of them in the US Marine Corps. He'd seen profoundly broken men, both on the other end of his rifle, and standing tall in front of his desk. He'd seen what serious drug use could do to a man. He'd also seen what serious trauma could do to a man.

He was seeing all of that mirrored in Vernon White's eyes, as the man looked up, squinting in the light coming through the doorway, shrinking back against the wall as he tried to assess the new threat coming after him.

Hoo, boy. This is gonna suck. Santelli didn't know what all Vernon had been put through, but it was obvious that the man was confused, scared, and right at the knife edge between fight or flight. And he was still a big enough guy that if he freaked out and tried to fight, Santelli was probably going to have to shoot him.

"Easy, Vernon." He decided to take the risk and slung his rifle around on his back, holding up his hands to show that he wasn't a threat. "My name's Carlo. I came here with Dan Tackett. We're here to get you out."

He took a step forward, but stopped as the big man flinched, still squinting at him suspiciously. *Hell. He's all the way out in left field. We don't have time for this.*

He was already trying to plan how to handle this situation without just choking the man out and fireman's carrying him away. They had at least two more to get out, anyway, so that wasn't going to be a great idea.

Santelli just wasn't sure what else to do. He was no counselor. Or so he thought. If he'd thought about it, he'd probably talked more Marines down off the ledge than he could count. He just wasn't thinking about it right then.

He was thinking about how to get this man out in a controlled manner, before the Front's security came down and killed them all.

***

Vernon squinted at the squat, barrel chested man in chest rig, helmet, and overwhites as the man slung his rifle behind him, trying to get his sluggish brain to process the thick Boston accent and figure out whether this was a trick or not.

He mentally cursed the fog in his mind and the gibbering terror welling up involuntarily, even as the man…Carlo? Was that the name? He couldn't remember, even though he'd just heard it a moment ago. Carlo…Carl…something like that…had both his hands up, speaking softly and gently, assuring him he wasn't there to hurt him, but that they had to go.

This is a fucked up new angle they're trying. The thought came unbidden, but after the last time he'd gotten a friendly visit, he couldn't trust anything in this place. The nightmare that had followed the previous man's entrance had made all the horrors that had come before pale by comparison. The small kernel of his mind that was still his knew that was probably deliberate.

That knowledge, coming to the forefront of his mind now that he was faced with a similar situation, proved to be the key. While his lizard brain screeched and gibbered at him that this was

201

a trick, that it would be followed by pain and terror even worse than before, he forced himself to grab hold of that spark of lucid thought.

They want you to be scared. That way they can control you. They can trigger you to respond the way they want. He'd never made a serious study of the kind of conditioning he'd been put through, but he'd held on tightly enough to that little core of himself through it all—as hard as the drugs had made it—that during the quiet times, when the drugs had worn off some, and he'd faked intoxication well enough to avoid getting dosed again, he'd been able to analyze things a little. It had been hard, and it still was, but he'd managed it, if only in a vague sort of way.

But it meant that he could force himself to calm down, though his heart was still jackhammering so fast that he thought it might explode. "Dan's here?" His voice was a dry croak, and his throat felt like a desert.

"He's here." The man named Carlo stepped closer. "He's trying to keep these Front bastards off our back right now, but he's here." He kept his hands out at his sides and his voice low and even. "I figured he was crazy, trying to come along, but he's held his own."

Vernon tried to laugh, then thought better of it. It might just sound cracked and crazy right then. And while the growing dread in his thoughts just *knew* this was a trick, another vicious, sadistic mind game to get just the right reaction out of him, he was still clinging desperately to the hope that this was real. "That would be Dan. The man's a machine."

He forced his aching body to move as he got his feet on the ground. He was in a coverall and barefoot, which could be an issue if he really was being rescued. But he was moving, and he was keeping the screaming terror quashed down where it couldn't overwhelm him.

Another figure loomed behind the man named Carlo. He looked vaguely familiar, but right then Vernon couldn't trust his own memory. At least he was dressed the same, in overwhites, helmet, old-style load bearing vest, and carrying a thoroughly beat-up M4.

"We're running out of time. I just opened the next cell." The man's voice sounded familiar, too.

Chad. That had to be it. His brain was catching up, despite the drug-induced fog. *These are Brannigan's guys. Got to be.*

Unless I'm hallucinating all of this, and the electrodes are going to kick in any second.

But no shocks came. No weird visions loomed out of the dark as the lights went out. The door was still open, the men with guns were still there, and while they were watchful, they weren't hauling him away or turning on him with needles and a blindfold.

Carlo stayed with him, as the big man moved to the next cell over. As he hobbled out into the blindingly bright hallway, Vernon saw yet another man, dressed and geared out the same, bigger than either of the others, kneeling at the doorway at the end of the hall, with an RPK braced against the doorframe. That guy looked vaguely familiar too, and he was pretty sure they'd met in Chad.

The big man got the next door open and stepped inside. A few moments later—it might have been seconds or hours; Vernon was too messed up to be able to tell at the moment—he came out with Max, wasted away and haggard, hanging onto his shoulder.

"Vernon." Max sounded about as bad as Vernon felt, but he *looked* like he was a bit more together. "You okay, buddy?"

"No." Vernon felt like hammered shit, and he was aware enough to know that. He was far from fighting shape, and he had no idea if he'd even get back there again. "But I will be. If we can get out of here."

"We're getting out of here." The big man was moving across the hallway. "Don't worry about that. If we've got to kill every son of a bitch on this compound, we're getting out of here." There was a simmering, cold rage in the big man's voice and his icy blue eyes that would have been daunting if Vernon had thought it was aimed at him.

Boy, they really did mess you up, didn't they? You never would have been intimidated before all this.

Wade. That was the big man's name. The memory of Chad had come back suddenly, and Vernon started to hope that maybe, just maybe, he might recover.

***

Wade pushed the last door open. The man inside hadn't moved when Wade had unlocked the door, which had prompted him to go ahead and get Max out first.

The door swung open slowly. It was solid steel and pretty heavy. There was no sound from inside.

He knew what he was going to find, though. He'd smelled death before.

The lean, surly man named Sam hadn't been dead for very long. He was still warm as Wade checked his pulse, but cool enough that he was rapidly assuming room temperature. What had killed him wasn't obvious, but Wade suspected it had something to do with the needle tracks in his arm, marks that both of the other two men shared.

He turned to where Max was leaning against the doorframe. "What the hell were they doing to you guys?"

"I'm not sure," Max answered. He looked half dead. "There didn't seem to be much point to it. Drugs, sensory deprivation, noise, electroshock. They didn't even ask any questions, really."

"I think it was conditioning." Vernon was looking a little more stable, but as Wade studied him, he wasn't sure how far the man was going to get on foot. They needed to get both hostages some boots, at least. "It's some sick stuff, but there are techniques using drugs and trauma to condition certain responses into subjects. I don't know what they were trying to condition us for, but it can't have been good."

Santelli looked from one to the other. "Wait. You mean like mind control? MK Ultra stuff?"

"Something like that."

Santelli was eyeing both men carefully. "So, what? They got you wired to do some Manchurian Candidate thing? Assassinate somebody?"

"I don't know that it works that way." Max just sounded tired. "And I don't think they got to either of us as much as they wanted to." He looked over at Vernon, who looked shaky but was still on his feet and looking increasingly lucid—and pissed. "Still, probably not a good idea to give us weapons yet. No telling what kind of time bombs they *did* manage to plant. We might not become threats, but we could become a liability."

Wade nodded. It made sense. He wasn't sure that he would have given these guys guns in the shape they were in, anyway, even if there hadn't been the possible brainwashing issue. They were strung out and could barely walk. They wouldn't be an asset in a fight.

"I didn't see Price on any of the monitors. Any ideas?" He knew it was probably futile. There was no way these guys would know much of anything about the base operations, unless they'd been able to resist the drugs that were getting pumped into them to a truly heroic degree.

"No idea." Max shook his head. "Haven't seen anyone but the Front's psychos since we were taken."

"Figured as much." Wade took stock. "Stick between me and Carlo. Vinnie! Any sign of Mario or Kirk yet?"

"They're coming down the…" Bianco suddenly stopped talking as he got behind the RPK and sent a long, withering burst toward the main entrance. They were out of time.

CHAPTER 26

Gomez was halfway down the stairs when Bianco opened fire.

Trying to find a back way into the secure area had been a non-starter. While it appeared that most of the upper floors were barracks—and partially defended, at least by the residents; they'd left two men in civilian clothes dead in the hall when they'd taken fire—there was no other entrance into the secure section of the building. They'd had to backtrack, hearing Bianco's machinegun fire echo through the structure, and now they were going to have to deconflict to get back together with the others.

Gomez slowed as he descended toward the last landing, crouching down behind his M4 as he tried to see what Bianco was shooting at. He could see the younger man, barricaded on the secure doorway, leaning into the RPK as he directed another burst at the main entrance, then pivoted to shoot down the hallway they'd entered through. Apparently, the Front was trying to retake the part of the building they'd cleared.

Dropping into a side prone on the landing, Gomez searched for targets. The twin steel doors at the main entrance were ajar, but only partly, and he had no shot on anyone outside. The paint was pockmarked and blasted apart by bullet holes.

Shifting his weight, he pivoted around toward the hallway, but even as Bianco sent another thunderous burst down toward the side entrance, he couldn't see anyone there, either.

What to do? Linking up with Bianco might be the best option, as it would put the bulk of the element together, but at the same time, they'd all be boxed up in the same hallway. That was not what Gomez considered an ideal situation.

Right at the moment, with Bianco holding down that hallway, he could take a few seconds to think and judge the angles. In many ways, CQB is a game of angles. Get the angles right, you get the drop on the bad guys and live to see another day. Get them wrong, and you're a corpse.

He decided. Getting to his feet, making sure that Kirk was with him, though the older man was still covering up the stairs, he started down, keeping his muzzle trained on the front door as he passed it. No one moved out there, and he took no fire, so he turned his attention to the hallway, as Bianco spotted him and ceased fire.

A moment later, as he felt Kirk reach him, backing into him boot-first, he whispered, "High, low."

"High, low." Kirk didn't need elaboration. "I'll go high."

It was what made sense, but Gomez still hated being the low man. Still, he dropped to a knee. "Three, two, one."

At the same moment, both men leaned out into the hallway, little showing around the corner except rifles, ACOGs, and single eyeballs.

They'd popped the corner at just the right moment. Gomez shot a man coming out of the nearest office through the pelvis, mainly because that was most immediate target, less than ten feet away. The man doubled over, and Gomez shot him again, this time smashing through his clavicle and into his chest cavity. He fell on his face, aspirating blood onto the floor.

Kirk fired three fast shots into the man coming out of the opposite door, smashing him back against the doorframe. Then a small canister flew out of another doorway, and both men ducked back just before the flashbang went off, eyes squeezed shut though they couldn't do anything about the concussion.

Kirk backed up, dragging Gomez by the back of the load bearing vest with him, just as Bianco opened fire again from across the foyer. The big man was going to run out of ammunition soon.

That burst of machinegun fire seemed to have decided the Front's security men, though. A moment later, Gomez though he heard raised voices, then a pair of canisters clattered out into the hallway.

He and Kirk flattened themselves into the corner, sure they were about to get up close and personal with a couple of frags. But the earsplitting detonations and flensing shrapnel didn't follow. Instead, a couple of *pop*s were followed by a loud *hiss*, though not so loud that it could really be heard over the roar and rattle of Bianco's RPK. The billows of white smoke that drifted out of the hallway, though, told the story.

The bad guys had popped smoke and fled, possibly even low-crawling out through the hallway.

At least, that was what Gomez rather hoped had happened. He couldn't be sure, so he got himself turned around and aimed in at the hallway, even as the HC smoke drifted in, barely reacting to Bianco's bullets, the harsh chemical fumes starting to bite at the back of his throat.

But no assaulters came out of the smoke. Bianco ceased fire a moment later, rather than waste his dwindling supply of ammo spraying it at targets that might not be there.

Keeping guns up, Gomez and Kirk started to work their way back around the room toward the cell block, careful to re-clear the stairs as they passed. "Friendlies." Gomez had to suppress a cough as he called out, raising his voice to make sure Bianco—who had to be just about stone deaf after letting rip with that 7.62x39 machinegun in a concrete hallway—heard him. The smoke was getting thicker, and it wasn't necessarily good for human lungs.

"Come ahead." Bianco had gotten down in the prone behind the RPK, the bipods deployed and resting on the floor. It was far from perfect, since he couldn't exactly load the bipods on slick concrete, but it was better than nothing.

"We need to get the hell out of here while we still can." Gomez took in the sight of Wade and Santelli with their haggard, emaciated charges. Both men had put bloodied Front camouflage on over their coveralls, their feet in the dead men's boots. The big black guy was too big for the boots, so they were unlaced, but that was probably better than going barefoot in the snow in the mountains.

He also noticed that neither of them was armed.

"Where's Price?" He didn't know exactly how many they were there for, but he knew that neither of these guys was Mitchell Price.

"Don't know. He's not in this cell block." Wade was standing over Bianco, watching the doors to the outside. "These guys don't know, either."

A glance at both of them and Gomez could believe it. They both looked like they'd been through hell.

"Okay." He turned toward the foyer, then looked at Wade. "Out the side door, the way we came?"

Wade nodded, glanced back at the two hostages, then turned toward the foyer, his rifle at high ready. "Let's move."

***

Flanagan waited next to Curtis, down in the prone, watching the guard towers on the north side of the base. Curtis was cussing quietly, probably about the lack of NVGs or other night optics. He'd be able to shoot at a muzzle flash and not much else. Flanagan had a better view, though the ACOG dimmed the light even more than he would have liked.

The rest of the Blackhearts—Brannigan, Jenkins, and Hank, with Tackett and Carter following—were sprinting across the riverbed. Flanagan and Curtis were waiting for the guard force to try to stop them.

He might have seen movement. His M4 was already on "semi," his finger on the trigger, and he squinted through the ACOG, trying to determine if he could really see what he thought he could see. The Blackhearts' overwhites were doing their job, making it harder for the enemy to see them against the snow, but the darkness was doing the same thing for them, since none of them had functioning NVGs. One of the ballistic windows might have just opened.

Lifting his head from the scope, he tried to spot the rest of the team. It was hard, in the dark and with most of their clothing being white on white. But after a moment, he decided that they couldn't risk waiting any longer. Stealth was blown, anyway.

"Let 'er rip, Kev."

Curtis didn't need to be told twice. Leaning into the RPK, keeping the stock clamped into his shoulder pocket as tightly as he could, loading the bipods where they were dug into the snowy, frozen ground, he pinned the trigger and sent a stream of tracers at the top of the tower.

Despite the low visibility, made worse by the RPK's muzzle flash, Curtis was on point. He'd put the sights right on the guard tower before he'd opened fire, and he was a master at keeping a belt fed under control. When Flanagan gave him a slight correction, following the tracers as they arced across the riverbed, he made it easily, then maintained fire on the tower, leaning into the gun as he sent five-to-eight-round burst after five-to-eight-round burst into the ballistic glass and steel.

It might not get the man in the tower, but it would keep him bottled up for a while. Hopefully, just long enough for the rest of the Blackhearts to get on the base and deal with him.

***

Tackett followed Brannigan, Jenkins, the younger Brannigan, and the Aussie named Carter across the riverbed. He wasn't having a good time of it; the snow and ice underfoot slowed him down and he stumbled a couple of times. Passing one of the inert drones, he got a good look at it, and then diverted to kick it over. It crashed to the ground, its legs sticking out and its muzzle buried in the snow.

It wasn't a gesture of pettiness. He didn't think, judging by what he could see, that that thing would be able to get back up once it was on its side. Knocking it over rendered it less of a threat, just in case the enemy managed to fix whatever had stopped the drones in the first place.

A shot *snap*ped past his head just then, and he ducked as he scrambled to catch up with the rest, who were making good time toward the gate. He hadn't seen the muzzle flash, but a moment later Curtis opened fire, and a stream of green tracers hammered into the northwest guard tower. Panting in the thin air, struggling against the snow and the uneven ground, he ran to join the team at the guardhouse. Brannigan had led the sprint, outpacing even his kid, and was currently down on a knee, trading fire with the Front guard force at the entrance to the big concrete building directly across from the gate.

Carter pushed out a little farther into the gateway, dropping prone as he sent burst after burst at the building. "Shift left! Get some cover!" He was giving them a corridor to move around the gatehouse and toward the guard tower that Curtis was keeping suppressed, while beating back the shooters in the building.

The geometries weren't great. There was too much open ground to cover, between the helipad and the open yard semi-enclosed by the L-shape of the two main buildings. They were shielded from the northeast tower by the hangars to the north, but they had a long way to go to reach that northwest tower, and Curtis was going to have to reload soon.

More machinegun fire erupted from the entrance to the southernmost building, directed toward the same shooters that Carter was trying to suppress. The incoming fire slackened, and Tackett saw their opening.

So did Brannigan. The big man got up and grabbed Jenkins, thrusting him toward the north. "We need to clear that tower!"

Keeping a tight formation, the five of them got up and sprinted toward the north, even as Curtis's fire went silent. Carter was reloading, and Tackett was momentarily thankful that the Blackhearts in the southern building were still up and kicking. They'd be screwed otherwise.

They hit the base of the tower just as the guard started shooting, his aim slightly too high and too late. Unfortunately, that also put them in line with the last tower, and a split second later, bullets chipped away at the concrete over their heads, and they had to shift around to the west side to take cover.

Jenkins leaned out and dumped an entire mag at the other tower. He was shooting too fast to be all that accurate, but the incoming fire was suppressed just enough that Brannigan and Carter made their move, circling around the north side, opposite Jenkins, and pushing toward the door at the base of the structure.

"Come on!" Hank didn't have quite his father's presence, but he was clearly no green rookie, either. Sending a burst of his own at the second tower, even as gunfire echoed and thundered from inside the first one, he sprinted toward the corner of the northernmost hangar.

Tackett followed, if only because he couldn't let the kid charge another guard tower on his own. Plus, they were going to start taking fire again as soon as the other half of the Blackhearts had to move or change mags, and there was still open ground with no cover between them and the main building.

Hank hit the corner of the hangar, barely slowing down and skidding a little on the snow as he slammed his shoulder into the wall, catching his breath for a moment while he waited for Tackett to catch up. Tackett was feeling every foot of elevation and every day, week, and month since the Anambas when he hadn't trained, hadn't pushed himself. He slammed into the wall behind Hank, hitting more heavily than the younger man, his breath burning in his throat and lungs.

Shouldn't have assumed I could stay out. Should have listened to that little voice that told you to stay ready. He knew that some of that had simply been the natural reaction to what they'd gone through in the jungle. No one can ever quite turn it off, once they've been in a life-or-death struggle like that. There was good reason why many veterans got home to immediately arm themselves and get ready for the next fight, even when they were supposed to be done. That fighting instinct, that need to be ready at all times, gets burned into a man's neural pathways. He can try to suppress it, try to convince himself that he'll never need it again, right up until the time when reality comes calling.

Fighting to get his breathing under control, fighting the wobbly feeling in his legs, he reached over and gave Hank's shoulder a squeeze, just as Jenkins reached them, and either Brannigan or Carter took the last tower under fire. At almost the same moment, more machinegun fire erupted from the gateway, hammering at the central building and further suppressing the enemy inside.

The two of them went around the corner, sprinting toward the door. Tackett had barely gotten halfway there, though, when an arm and a rifle fell out of the open ballistic window up top, the arm dangling against the concrete, the weapon falling with a clatter to the snow-covered ground.

The door was locked. But when Hank looked up, as the other two Blackhearts ceased fire, he shook his head. "Unless there's a number two man up there, I think they got him."

Jenkins joined them, gasping for breath. "Now what?"

Hank kept looking up, chewing his lip. Tackett held security on the back side of the hangars, just in case. His instinct would be to push the fight at the main building, take the heat off the guys in the southern structure. But while he might have been, officially, the client, he wasn't in charge. He was a strap-hanger and he knew it.

Brannigan and Carter were sprinting across the northern edge of the helipad. "Let's go!" Brannigan's bellow echoed, still not drowned out by the crackle of gunfire from the southern half of the compound, as he ran past them toward the eastern corner of the hangar. "We need to get to that second building!"

Leaving the dead man in the tower undisturbed, they followed.

CHAPTER 27

They hustled down the line of hangars, guns up and clearing each gap between buildings as they passed. More full-auto fire was being poured into that big cement block of a building, now from both the secondary barracks—or whatever it was—and the gate. Flanagan and Curtis had made record time getting across that riverbed.

Reaching the corner of the last hangar, Brannigan slowed and took stock. There was a blank steel door at the end of the building, flanked by two windows. He'd half expected the bad guys to have shooters coming out this side, trying to flank, but right at the moment it looked like all they had left was holding the front entrance.

He wasn't sure if he believed that they'd gone through the Front's guard force that thoroughly, but if the bad guys were trying to maintain something of a low profile in Kyrgyzstan, it was possible. They hadn't won yet, though.

No movement showed in the windows. Like the rest of the base, they were dark and dead. Checking down the length of the building, he saw no movement there, either.

They had to move. The gunfight out front wasn't calming down much, and they didn't have the ammo to hold position and trade fire indefinitely. He left the cover of the hangar and sprinted toward the closed door.

It was locked, as he'd more than halfway expected. The windows to either side, however, appeared to be ordinary glass, not ballistic glass. Pivoting away from the door, he brought his muzzle down and, mirroring Gomez's earlier action, smashed the left-hand window open.

Carter was covering over his shoulder as he cleared the windowsill and clambered inside. His boot, clogged with packed snow, slipped on the sill and he dropped to the concrete floor with a clatter, his weapon hitting the concrete just before Carter fired twice, the bullets going over his head with a pair of painful *crack*s. He looked up to see a man fall behind the massive machine that filled most of the large room.

The entire north wing of the building appeared to have been hollowed out, and what looked at first glance like a stack of containers or diesel generators, with a thick cylinder extending from the top to the ceiling, took up the majority of the floor. The man Carter had shot lay just between the massive machinery and the nearest window looking out on the yard, still twitching as he rattled out his last breaths in a slowly spreading pool of red.

Carter followed him through as he got to his feet, with Tackett and Jenkins not far behind. Tackett got through, checked the room, then pivoted to cover the window they'd just entered through. The man was clearly tired and out of condition, but he was keeping his head on a swivel and his mind in the game. His skill, after as much time as he'd said he'd been out of the business, was impressive.

They spread out to either side, clearing the room. Brannigan took the long wall, clearing the side of the machinery where the dead man had finally gone still. He was somewhat relieved to see a pistol on the floor next to the man's limp hand. Carter wasn't one of his, but he was still gratified that the dead man had actually been a threat, and that they didn't have a contact who was so trigger happy that he'd double-tap anyone in front of him. The moral dimension aside, without comms or night vision, they were running some serious risks when it came to linking the team back up, and they'd have to be *very* careful of their targets going forward.

Thick cables ran from the stack of machinery out the back wall. Currently, the entire room was quiet, except for the reverberating reports of gunfire coming from the front of the building, but Brannigan could imagine the machine pulsing with power. Power to do what, he wasn't sure.

He came around the corner of the machine to come face to face with a skinny, pale man in a lab coat, his hair slightly greasy, a faint mustache and a wisp of hair on his chin, staring at him through thick glasses. The man had a Glock in his hands, but as he stared down Brannigan's muzzle, he dropped the weapon with what might have been a squeak.

Carter pushed past to the door, Tackett behind him. "Jenkins! Collapse in!" Brannigan didn't take his eyes—or his weapon off the guy in the lab coat. "Who the hell are you?"

The man gulped. "I'm Dr. Finkelstein." He had a high-pitched, nasal voice with a bit of a Midwestern accent and a healthy portion of arrogance. "If you turn around and leave right now, I'm sure it will work out much better for you."

Brannigan just looked at him for a second, then stepped in close as he slung his rifle to his back, kicked the man's feet out from under him, and slammed him on his face.

"I'll take that under advisement." After the exertion, the cold, and the altitude, Brannigan's voice was a harsh rasp. He pulled a loop of 550 cord out of his vest and quickly tied Finkelstein's hands behind him.

"What do you think you're doing?" The Humanity Front toady sounded genuinely outraged. "Do you have any idea what you are interfering with?"

"Enlighten me." Brannigan stepped back, flipped the man over with a boot, and swung his M4 around to the front, pointing the muzzle at the lab-coated man's forehead.

Finkelstein's eyes crossed as he stared at the dark hole at the end of the barrel, suddenly rethinking his position. "It's an EMP generator. It stands to revolutionize strategic warfare. A target can be completely neutralized without requiring a nuclear explosion or even a missile launch." He looked up at the stack of machinery. "We still need to do some miniaturization, but it works. When we're done, this could be put in a cargo container and delivered to a target by truck." He actually sounded proud of himself.

Maybe he was. Maybe this was all just a technical problem to be solved to him. Brannigan had run into people like that before, often working for decidedly evil bastards. Once a man—or a woman—put their curiosity over any moral or ethical concerns, and eagerly accepted work from anyone who would finance their pet projects, they tended to go down some dark, dark roads.

And this was a big one. He glanced up at the machine. If this guy was right, and they could shrink it down to the point they could load one on a truck, the Front could cripple entire cities. Then probably come in with their "humanitarian" aid in the aftermath, shaping the new society the way they wanted.

Given what they'd learned about the Front's idea of what that new society should look like in Chad, based on the careful genetic targeting of their bioweapon, what came out the other side was going to be ugly as hell.

He started toward the door, where Carter and Tackett were stacked up. Jenkins was barricaded on the machine itself, watching back the way they'd come in. "We're going to need to find some explosives. Or just a bunch of diesel." He looked back at Finkelstein. "Where are your records?"

"No!" The man in the lab coat struggled to get to his feet, his hands still tied behind his back. "You can't do that! There are *years* of research tied up in this prototype!"

Brannigan turned and pointed his M4 at the man. "I couldn't care less. Where are the plans and the notes?"

The pencil-necked researcher gulped. "The office just outside the test chamber. But you can't..."

Jenkins turned, slung his weapon, and wrapped the man up in a triangle choke. "Night, night." Finkelstein struggled for a couple seconds, then went limp. Jenkins let him fall. "Sorry, Colonel. Couldn't take any more of that whiny-ass voice."

"Let's go. We need to get the heat off the others, and then destroy that thing."

Carter led the way through the door, Tackett right on his heels, and Brannigan winced a little. The local contact and the client were now on point. He needed to get in front of both of them, if only for form's sake. But it was CQB, and the Number One slot tended to rotate fluidly. It was inevitable.

They found themselves in a short hallway, another steel door at the end, with stairs going up on one side and what looked like another office on the other. Carter held the stairs and the door while Tackett went in the office, Brannigan on his heels.

Computer monitors glowed under bright lights, notes and technical drawings scattered across the handful of desks. No one was in the room.

Brannigan glanced out the door, but Carter and Jenkins had the angles covered. "We need to pull the drives."

He was slightly surprised that Tackett didn't object that this wasn't the objective. The man was keener and more adaptive than he'd thought. He was here to rescue his friends, but he recognized the threat this tech posed. "Shouldn't we just smash the computers?"

Brannigan shook his head. "I don't want to run the risk that they might reconstruct the data. Pull the drives. I don't give a damn if they get damaged, I just don't want to leave them anything."

"If we were really being serious about it, we'd make sure we wiped 'Doctor Finkelstein's' memory with a bullet." Carter was still watching his sector, but had raised his voice enough to make himself heard.

Brannigan actually seriously thought about it for a moment. The threat posed by this tech—and he had no doubt that Finkelstein would go right back to work on it after they left—was significant.

But murdering the researcher wouldn't put the genie back in the bottle. The tech existed. Someone, somewhere, could reconstruct it, eventually. Even if Finkelstein and everyone he'd ever talked to about it was dead.

"Even if he's got it all in his head, it will take a long time to reproduce." He didn't want to just kill an unarmed man with his hands tied behind his back. He'd seen that done too many times in hellholes around the world. He wasn't going down that route.

Wade might not have a problem with it. Neither would Jenkins. Maybe not Gomez. Javakhishvili…he had to thrust the memory of their slain teammate aside. Time to mourn the dead later.

Tackett was already yanking hard drives out of their ports, both portable and internal. Several monitors flickered, then went dark as he went. He wasn't being careful about it, either, which was fine.

The last one was pulled, and Brannigan led the way out, giving Carter the nudge to move toward the door. Jenkins fell in behind Tackett, who was still shoving the last of the hard drives into cargo pockets.

Carter paused just at the door, which was still shut. They could hear the ringing reports of gunfire on the other side. If Brannigan had the geometries of the place right, they were probably right at the main foyer, which was probably where the gunmen were trying to keep the rest of his boys pinned down.

The next few seconds could get really, really hairy. Especially if the other Blackhearts were still keeping the main entrance to the building under fire.

None of them wanted to be the subject of a friendly fire incident.

Still, they could hang out in the hallway until the rest of the team ran out of ammo, or they could move. Brannigan reached around Carter, put his hand on the door handle as Carter faced it, M4 up and ready, and gave him the nod.

He yanked the door open, and they went through almost as one.

If the timing had been even minutely off, they might have jammed up in the doorway, they were that close to going through side by side. As it was, they burst into the foyer, facing a tableau of four men in the Front's distinctive camouflage, all shooting through the partially open front doors, though one ducked back as another stream of green tracers punched through the opening to smack bits of concrete and dust off the back wall.

As he did so, he saw the two men in overwhites coming in the door. He was still out of position when Carter shot him.

Brannigan cleared the stairwell immediately to his left, then pivoted and dumped the next man, even as the last two sprinted for the stairs, one of them yelling at the top of his lungs as he fired back, missing but spitting frag and spall off the wall just above Brannigan's head.

Then the fire died down, as the Blackhearts outside had nothing to shoot at anymore.

***

Boyd didn't slow down or pause to let Animal catch up as he sprinted up the stairs toward the command post. It wasn't just the CP he was heading for, either. That section of the top floor had been hardened into the "Alamo," where they could hold out indefinitely until relief arrived. The client really didn't like that term, but it had stuck with the security team.

He burst through the heavy security door, and Animal had to sprint hard to get through before he closed it. Two more of the team, probably among the last ones standing at this point, were just inside, their APC 300s half-raised as Boyd came through the opening and started pushing the door shut. "Get this door secured and get the Alamo locked down, both buildings!"

Even as he said it, he felt a momentary flash of relief that he was in Building Two. Karesinda and her band of sadists and freaks were in Building One. Provided the intruders hadn't killed them all.

It might not be a bad thing if they had.

Slowing down, knowing that he couldn't appear to be as panicked as he felt, he stalked toward the CP. Sure enough, several of the client supervisors were in there, clustered around Chance, making all kinds of noise.

His blood ran cold when he saw that Karesinda was one of them. She'd crossed to Building Two before things had gotten really sporty.

Boyd shouldered through the press, ignoring the questions, especially Karesinda's shrill demands to know what he was doing about this. He grabbed the radio from Chance. "Skulker Five One, this is Static. Request ETA?"

The reply, when it came, was broken and staticky. "Static, this is Skulker Five One. We are running into some weather over the lake, and have to divert. Going to be another twenty to thirty minutes."

He didn't bother to respond. Twenty to thirty minutes. A lot could happen in twenty to thirty minutes.

But they were in the Alamo. Unless the intruders had brought a lot of explosives, or some serious cutting torches, they weren't getting in.

They could hold until the reinforcements got there from Manas.

They had to.

CHAPTER 28

Brannigan pulled a chemlight off one of the dead men's vests, cracked it, and tossed it out into the snow. "Collapse on me!" His voice sounded hoarse, and his throat stung in the dry, cold, thin air.

The front door of the southern building cracked open, and Wade, Gomez, Kirk, Santelli, Bianco, and two men in Front camouflage but without weapons came out and moved quickly across the lawn. The Blackhearts kept their muzzles up and covering every angle or window they could see, moving fast, while the other two just tried to keep up.

Flanagan and Curtis waited until the rest of the team had fallen back into the northern building before getting up and sprinting across the lawn. Flanagan reached the doorway a couple yards ahead of Curtis, who was puffing and swearing as his shorter legs pumped furiously to get him across the open ground.

"Where's Price?" Brannigan recognized Vernon and Max, though barely. Both men had clearly been through hell.

Max shrugged and spread his hands. "We haven't seen him since we got snatched up."

"He's not in the cell block back there." Wade broke off to join Brannigan next to the stairwell as the rest took up security positions on every entry and exit from the foyer. It wasn't an ideal defensive position, but it would have to do for the moment. "We couldn't clear the entire building, but unless he's hanging out in the Front's barracks, I'm pretty sure he's not over there."

Brannigan glanced back at Tackett, then at Vernon and Max. "So, these guys are it?"

Wade didn't even blink. "Not quite. That skinny guy, Sam, is dead. Not that long, either. They must have overdosed him."

"Travis, the new guy, got smoked on first contact." Vernon's voice was a croak, a far cry from the dynamic, confident presence he'd shown in Chad. "It was just the five of us." He looked down at the floor for a moment. "If we can find Mitchell, we need to. He's got his issues, but I'm sure he wouldn't be working for these bastards."

"We need to find something to blow that EMP generator up, anyway," Tackett pointed out. "We can search the rest of the building, see if he's in here." He looked over at Vernon and Max. "Good to see you guys, by the way. Sorry about Sam."

"You are a sight for sore eyes, Dan." Max didn't sound that great himself, but he gave a wan grin.

"Okay." Brannigan looked around the foyer. "I'll take Tackett, Jenkins, Carter, and Santelli. We'll go upstairs and see if we can find some explosives to wreck that EMP generator. Joe, pick somebody to hold this foyer, and then search the rest of this floor, see if you can find Price." He turned and headed up the stairs, muzzle up to cover the landing.

They didn't have much time.

**

Flanagan took the lead on the search, while Wade held their exit. Flanagan couldn't be sure, but he thought that Wade was keeping an extra close eye on Vernon and Max. He didn't know why, but he trusted Wade, and if the big man figured there was something off, Flanagan would follow his lead until the situation changed.

With Kirk and Gomez following, Flanagan headed into the far hallway. That part of the building seemed to be mostly administrative offices, with each door leading into an office with

226

two or more desks, computers and papers stacked on top of them, the monitors dark. It seemed that the Front had called it a night a while before.

At the end of the hall, however, things got different.

The other rooms had had normal office doors, hollow-core wood, easily opened. The last two doors, set farther from the exit on the end of the building, were noticeably heavier, and each sported another cipher lock instead of the regular door handle on the rest.

"That look a little off to you?" Flanagan was holding on the door, against the wall where he could cover that door, the end of the hall, and the two regular doors across from it.

"It does." Gomez stepped forward. "Cover me."

Flanagan didn't see what Gomez did to the lock, but a moment later it clicked open. Gomez stepped back, pulling the door open with his M4 leveled. "What, no Mexican jokes?"

"Wouldn't dream of it." Kirk went around Gomez and into the doorway, Flanagan covering them until he could flow in after them.

They were in a well-appointed suite, the only signs that it was a prison cell being the reinforced door and the ballistic glass in the window at the back. A bed, a couch, a desk, a TV, and even a refrigerator furnished the room, and there was what looked like a full bathroom with a shower just off to one side.

Mitchell Price, unshaven, gaunt, and grim, stood at the bed, in a fighting crouch, ready to sell himself dearly.

It took him a second to realize that the three men who'd just rushed into the room and had momentarily pointed guns at him weren't with the Front.

"Who the hell?" He squinted at them, especially Flanagan and Gomez. "You're Brannigan's guys."

"We are. We've got two of yours outside. They didn't want to leave without you." Flanagan really wasn't sure whether or not to trust Price very far. There were a lot of stories about the guy, not all of them pointing to the heights of honor and integrity.

Price's shoulders slumped, apparently with relief. Then he looked up sharply. "Wait. Two? There were three still alive when we got taken."

"Sam's dead." Flanagan's voice was flat and matter of fact, as he lowered his muzzle while Gomez and Kirk covered the door. "Wade said something about overdosing. I don't know what they were doing to them, but they're in bad shape."

Price took a deep breath and nodded. "We should get going, then. They'll have reinforcements coming. They suborned my whole operation here." He started toward the door, though he stopped to wait for the Blackhearts before going out. "How did you guys know to come out here?"

"Vernon called Dan Tackett and he got in touch with us. It was a bit of a chore after that." Kirk hadn't been in Chad—he'd been a part of the stay-behind team who had rescued Sam Childress—but he knew who Price was. And from the tone of his voice, Flanagan suspected he had the same split opinion on Price that the rest of them did.

Flanagan led the way out, still clearing as they went, though he soon lowered his weapon and sped up as he spotted Wade standing in the foyer, covering the stairwells. With Price in the middle, they hustled down the hallway and joined the rest of the Blackhearts.

"Any change?" Flanagan didn't trust the quiet. He knew for a fact they hadn't killed everybody, and the longer this lull in the fight went on, the more he suspected that the bad guys were cooking up a particularly nasty surprise.

"Nothing." Wade was still watching the stairs. Bianco and Curtis were covering down on the entryway, spread out across the room so that they could cover the most ground outside as possible. "They got real quiet all of a sudden." He glanced at Price.

The PMC magnate shrugged. "I never got a good enough look at how many they had on site. They kept me locked up in there, with only a couple of visitors. Their head of security came to see me once, I'm guessing when you boys got on the ground. They knew you were here, but he didn't know who you were, and while he suspected that you were coming for us, he didn't know what your source of information and support was." He snarled silently. "That told me all I needed to know about my support network here."

"You think they've got your company penetrated?" Flanagan asked, as he found a sector to cover.

Price looked both disgusted and more than a little perturbed. "I'm sure of it." His mouth thinned as he bent over one of the dead men in the foyer and began taking his weapon, armor, and ammo. "I've got a serious security audit to do when we get back."

"Hold on a second." Wade stepped closer to loom over Price, his hands on his weapon. "I'm not sure we can trust you with a weapon just yet."

Price looked up at him, his brow furrowed. "You think *I* arranged this?" His voice began to rise as he stood up and faced the big former Ranger. "You think I sold my own team out, for what? So they could lock me up in a cell for the last couple of weeks?"

Flanagan was trying to watch the overall security situation and Wade at the same time. He half expected the big man to go off like a nuke. Wade's callsign wasn't "Angry Ragnar" for nothing.

But Wade was calm and composed, if totally unyielding. "There are some rumors out there. And if I believed 'em entirely, then I wouldn't put it past you. But I don't think so. No, the concern here is what they were doing to your boys." He nodded at Vernon and Max, both of whom were sitting on the floor, their backs to the wall. "They've been telling us a little bit about what they can remember. Drugs. Sensory deprivation. Torture. What sounds a lot to my dumb ass like hypnosis. Neither one of them thinks they can be entirely trusted yet. They've got a lot of shit to work through, to figure out what kind of nasty surprises might have been programmed into them." He turned his baleful, icy stare on Price. "Can you guarantee they didn't do something like that to you?"

229

Price looked like he was going to explode, but he glanced over at his two operators and visibly forced himself to calm down. When he finally spoke, his voice was low and even. "Guarantee so that you'll believe me? No. I can't. But consider this. I was a SEAL, once upon a time. I got all the same training these men did. If they'd gotten to me, they would have had to put me through all of that for just as long. Instead, you found me in that gilded cage back there." He looked over at Flanagan. "Did that look like where they'd stash a test subject?"

Flanagan didn't think so, but even after Chad, there was only so far that he'd trust Price. He shrugged. "Depends on the tests. I don't know."

Price looked awfully frustrated at that answer, but he turned back to Wade. "They wanted me for something else. I didn't know what they were doing to my guys." He looked over at Vernon and Max, and his eyes were genuinely haunted. Turning back to Wade, he spread his hands in supplication. "I don't know why they wanted me intact, but I can only guess that they wanted my organization. That kind of trauma-based conditioning wouldn't serve them well, if that was their objective. They probably planned on blackmail or even just trying to buy me out."

"Wade." Vernon shoved himself to his feet, swayed for a moment, then steadied. "I know you don't necessarily trust Mitchell." Wade's cold, unimpressed stare didn't change, and only confirmed Vernon's assessment. "But we know him. We've worked for him for years. He wouldn't fold, not if they tried the kind of shit on him that they did to us. If he's himself—and he is—then you can trust him. At least while we get out of here." He looked around for a moment. "I think we're going to need every gun we can get."

Flanagan nodded grimly. "Especially since we lost Herc."

Wade's eyes snapped over to him. So did Bianco's and Kirk's. "Wait. Herc's down?" Flanagan had forgotten, in all the confusion, that the rest of the team, that had already penetrated the compound, wouldn't have seen Javakhishvili's murder.

Curtis's voice was a little thick. "Yeah. They nabbed him halfway across the riverbed, tried to interrogate him, then killed him when we tried to get him out."

"Motherfuckers." Wade was already pissed, but that news definitely tripped his murder button. The look he shot up the stairs suggested that he was seriously considering just going up there and killing everyone in the building who wasn't a Blackheart.

"I'm sorry." Vernon hadn't heard it, either, and he wouldn't have known Javakhishvili from Adam, since the Georgian medic had stayed back to rescue Sam Childress when the Blackhearts had last crossed paths with Price's Special Projects team, but from what Flanagan had heard about the mission Tackett had been on, the man had to know what it was like to lose a teammate. He looked Wade in the eye. "It's one more thing. Mitchell's not on their side. *Trust me* on that. We've gone after their operations a couple times since Chad, and they know it."

Wade looked over at Flanagan and raised his eyebrows. Wade might have been the senior man in the military, having retired from the Army as an E8, but Flanagan was the Blackhearts' second in command. It was his call, until Brannigan came downstairs.

"Take a weapon, Price. But if you so much as twitch wrong, Wade's going to blow your brains out." It wasn't a threat. It was just a warning.

Price seemed to accept that. "I wouldn't expect anything less." He bent to pick up the blocky B+T rifle. When he was armed and kitted up, as Brannigan started to come down the stairs, he straightened and looked first Wade, then Flanagan in the eye. "You won't regret this. And if you're willing to stay on for a bit of a bonus, after we get out of these mountains, I've got a reckoning to reap with these bastards."

"We'll see." Flanagan turned to Brannigan. "We ready to go?"

"Not quite." Brannigan took in the sight of Price, wearing a plate carrier and carrying a rifle, then seemed to nod slightly and accept it. "We've got some demolition to do, first."

CHAPTER 29

Santelli huffed under the load on his back. They'd swept the entirety of the upper two floors, at least as much as they could access. The Front appeared to have an "Alamo" built into the building, about half the top floor that was sealed off and locked down. Without some serious breaching charges, they weren't getting through that, and they had neither the explosives nor the time.

From the way Gomez looked at that locked ballistic door, Santelli suspected that their quiet, half-Apache teammate wasn't too happy about that. He wasn't either. From what he'd seen already, Santelli was sure that killing every single living soul that wasn't a prisoner or a Blackheart on that facility would be a long-overdue act of justice.

What they hadn't expected was to find that the security team had been storing extra weapons and munitions outside that "safe floor," the next level down. It had been mostly cleared out, but not entirely. And there was still a substantial cache of explosives in crates under the weapons racks and the cases of extra gear.

They'd grabbed up as much of those explosives as they could carry. Santelli knew that Brannigan was planning on blowing up the EMP generator, but if he had his way, they'd drop both these buildings, too.

He didn't know if they'd have enough time, but if he could bury whatever they'd been doing to Price's operators, along with the researchers, he'd do it.

Holy shit, I'm turning into Wade.

There was a problem with that plan, though, and Santelli realized it as he turned to cover their six as they approached the stairs leading down toward the foyer.

What to do with the locals they were using as guinea pigs?

They couldn't very well take all twenty or so with them, though there was a part of Santelli's mind that was telling him, aggravatingly, that they needed to, one way or another. They couldn't just leave those poor bastards in the Front's hands.

The problem being, in addition to the timeline, that they simply couldn't trust any of them. What would they do if and when one of them hit a trigger implanted through the Front's use of drugs, torture, and psychological manipulation?

Santelli had actually seen that sort of thing before. It wasn't something he talked about much. Technically, he'd been violating regulations at the time, since he'd been a Gunny when he'd gone with several of his junior NCOs to go retrieve a young sergeant's girlfriend from a local cult. It was something they were supposed to talk to the cops about, or even the FBI. They'd been hot-headed young Marines, though, and when Sergeant Easton had told Gunny Santelli what he'd seen and heard, and what he suspected, the then Company Gunny had seen red.

They'd gotten the girl out. They'd even managed to do it without killing anyone. A few might have ended up in the hospital, but he'd seen nothing on the news about it, so he'd always suspected that the cult hadn't wanted any attention, either. Given what he'd seen, they'd had good reason for trying to avoid law enforcement scrutiny. Or any public scrutiny at all.

Things had gone bad a couple of days later. Something Sergeant Easton had said or done had apparently triggered a psychotic episode, and his girlfriend, whom he'd risked his life and his career to rescue, had tried to stab him.

That relationship hadn't lasted, unfortunately. Santelli still didn't know what had happened to the girl. Sergeant Easton had gotten out the next year and promptly dropped off the map.

So, Santelli had some experience with what this kind of treatment could do to a person. They might well have their hands full with Vernon and Max, never mind twenty or so Kyrgyz, who didn't speak the same language, and had presumably been subjected to the torture, drugs, and mind games for a lot longer.

Can't save everybody. It was a bitter pill to swallow, though, and it brought back some really bad memories. So, even as he brought the explosives down to the foyer, where Brannigan and Wade were already building charges, he was still trying to think about how to get those prisoners out.

He didn't have any answers as he put the explosives down, looked around to see that the others had security set and covered, and knelt to start building charges along with Brannigan and Wade. He knew what he *wanted* to do, but without the practicalities being sorted out in his head, he wasn't sure how to say it. So, he concentrated on the task at hand.

***

Tackett, where he stood at the bottom of the stairwell, covering the way up in case any of the Front's security decided to get froggy and come down after them, was close enough to talk to Max and Vernon for the first time since they'd linked the whole team up.

"You guys look like hell." It had been years since they'd been in this sort of situation together, but somehow it didn't seem like that long at all. "Hell, you looked better when we got of the island."

Max chuckled painfully. "You have no idea dude."

"What were they doing to you guys in there? I mean, I heard something about drugs and torture, but it's been a little hectic." This seemed like a weird place to have this conversation, but with the charges being built and no security coming for them, they had a moment. He had no idea if they were going to get another.

"Something like that." Vernon sounded worse than he looked. "It's hard to say. I can't remember a lot of it. Drugs will do that to you. There's…" He hesitated, staring at the floor for a moment. "There's a lot of subconscious stuff going on. Feelings. Impressions. That sort of thing." He looked up at Tackett, who met his eyes for a moment and saw a degree of horror that none of the carnage they'd gone through on the Anambas, hunted by pirates and Chinese commandos alike, had elicited. "I don't know what all they did, Dan, and that scares me more than what I can remember."

Max looked up and around at the Blackhearts, all either holding security or working on building charges, then looked up at Tackett with some new urgency. "There were other cells. Other cells around ours, I mean. Sam wasn't the only other one. We didn't see in—and we sure as hell never saw anyone else but the security guys who held us down while they drugged us—but there had to be other subjects." He gulped and lowered his voice, as if he was afraid that if the Blackhearts heard him, they might take exception to what he was about to say. "If there are others, we *have* to get them out. We can't leave them to these monsters."

Tackett looked over at Brannigan, who had lifted his head and was watching them. Max hadn't been quite as quiet as he'd thought. "What do you think, Colonel? I don't know how many there are, or what kind of condition they might be in."

"There are about twenty, and if they're still alive, they're in no condition to travel." Wade hadn't looked up from the explosives. "We can't trust them, anyway. Two is one thing. One or two guys freaking out we can handle. Twenty-two? Forget it."

Brannigan turned cold eyes on his teammate. Tackett knew he was supposed to be watching the stairs, but he found he was riveted, wondering which way this was going to go. Vernon had clearly trusted these guys, and they'd been absolute professionals so far, but if Brannigan took Wade's unilateral decision badly…

This was hardly the time or the place for an inter-team fight.

Brannigan apparently thought so, too. His initial hardened expression softened as he looked thoughtful, then nodded. "I get it, John, but we have to try." He jerked a head at Tackett. "Joe, take Gomez, Jenkins, and Tackett, here. See if you can find a truck and get them out and loaded up."

"Trucks should be in the closest hangar." Jenkins pointed to the north, on the other side of the EMP generator. "I saw a couple in there when we went past."

"Good. We'll need 'em, one way or another." Brannigan looked up at Tackett and Flanagan. "Get moving. We'll need a few minutes to get these charges set, anyway."

Tackett looked over at Flanagan, who waved him toward the hall. They could exit through the door on the end of the building and avoid crossing that open lawn, at least for most of the distance.

The four men hustled down the hallway and out into the cold. Tackett had barely noticed just how much warmer it was inside, until he'd been stationary for a while, letting his core temperature drop. The cold hit him like a brick wall, almost snatching the breath out of his lungs. He didn't dare stop, though, as the four of them exploded through the door, spreading out as if they were clearing a room, just to make sure they weren't about to run into bad guys or any bad guys' field of fire.

The compound was still dark and quiet. It really felt like the enemy had just given up and disappeared as soon as they'd taken the entryway to the northernmost building, but Dan had been through enough that he didn't trust the quiet.

Skirting the lawn, they hurried toward the main entrance to the southern building, pausing just long enough at the partially open doors to make sure everyone was ready to make entry. Tackett tilted his head, listening, as Flanagan got up behind him, muzzle pointed past his ear, ready to go.

Are those voices? He couldn't be entirely sure, as the sounds were muffled enough by the doors that he couldn't quite hear over his own beating heart and the rasp of his own breath. He wasn't planning on sauntering in like nothing was wrong, but now he was even more on edge as he launched himself through the opening.

He cleared the area directly in front of him as he went through the doorway, kicking the door behind him as he rotated around it, digging his corner before sweeping back around to put a pair of shots into the man in foreign camouflage and carrying an advanced carbine in his hands. His M4 thundered at the same time that the other three Blackhearts' rifles roared, smashing the man off his feet at the same moment that Tackett registered that his own rounds had been stopped by the man's front plate. One of the other three had just double-tapped the guy in the face, though, and his head snapped back with a spray of red as he collapsed limply to the floor.

Another Front shooter came out blazing, but he wasn't exactly aiming. It looked to Tackett, even as Flanagan shot the man through the throat and nose, almost like some of the videos he'd seen of Russian CQB tactics. Just spray through the door as you go. It hadn't worked out for this guy.

Weapons still up, eyes just above sights, the four men converged on the cell block, Tackett and Flanagan focused on the door and the dead bodies while Gomez and Jenkins watched the other openings around the foyer.

Movement inside the doorway. Tackett snapped his weapon up just as the flash filled his vision, and he was sure he was dead.

The bullet, however, went past his ear with a harsh *crack*, smacking plaster and concrete off the ceiling behind him. His return shot was better, in small part because the chevron in his ACOG was completely covering the man's nose when he fired.

That was actually a little low. He'd forgotten about the sight's height over the barrel's bore. The bullet smashed through the man's teeth and blew out the side of his face. The Front shooter started to howl, but he barely got a fraction of the sound out before Flanagan's shot silenced him. His head bounced under the impact and he slumped onto the floor.

The man had thrown himself down on his side behind the two dead operatives, half in and half out of the armored security post for the cell block. The cameras were still on, and Tackett could see some of the surveillance of the inside the cells from outside.

He already knew what he was going to find as he stepped on the dead man and into the little booth. He'd seen enough already. But he had to check.

Every kidnapped Kyrgyz or other local in those cells was dead. A couple were still twitching, but they were gone. Foaming spittle came from several of their mouths, and they were all frozen in attitudes of violent, painful death.

"Nerve gas." He'd never actually seen it used before, but he'd been trained enough on it that he recognized the symptoms. The Front, those psychotic cowards, had flooded the cells—which were presumably airtight—with a nerve agent, the chemical poison getting into each man's nervous system and completely locking them up as it stopped their hearts and lungs. "Those bastards."

"I guess that solves this problem." Flanagan's voice was grim, fury in his eyes as his jaw worked beneath his black beard. "Too bad we didn't bring any charges over here." He glanced up at the ceiling, where the monsters who had ordered this atrocity were presumably still hiding out. "And we don't have the time to go through and make a clean sweep of it."

Tackett found he was clenching his own teeth. "Don't we? They haven't exactly budged to come at us for the last half hour. Just had to come down here and murder these poor slobs."

"No, we don't have the time at all." Jenkins was looking out the main door, his eye to his ACOG. "We've got two helicopters incoming."

CHAPTER 30

Wade was sharing Flanagan's frustration at the moment, though in a somewhat more generalized way. He'd always been a man quick to anger and entirely willing to visit terrible violence on anyone he figured deserved it. Only the prospect of jail had kept him from racking up a considerably higher body count than he had, over the years. He'd developed a powerful hatred for the Humanity Front, some of it starting on general principles as soon as he'd heard some of their rhetoric, before he'd even known they were a terrorist organization. Knowing what he knew now, he'd be more than happy to strangle anyone affiliated with that pretentious, evil bunch of assholes.

If he could blow them into tiny pieces or bury them under a mountainside, that was fine with him, too.

They just didn't have time, though. As much as he was prepared to fight to hold the position, provided they could kill everyone on site, he knew that they'd already been on the X for far too long. They needed to move. Just staying in place long enough to blow up the EMP generator was running a hell of a risk.

He got the charge inside the inspection plate, pulled the igniter, sniffed to make sure the fuse was burning, then put the inspection plate back. He didn't need to, not really. As he glanced down at it, he frowned. *Why the hell did I do that? It's not like we're trying to hide the fact that we sabotaged their little toy.*

He knew why. They'd been up, moving and fighting, for hours, and he was getting tired and strung out. *Not in my twenties anymore.* Picking up the stack of charges he had left, he went looking for another good spot to place one.

Pulling off another panel, he made sure to just leave it on the floor as he looked in and spotted what looked like a big coil of copper wire. "That looks important." He started wedging two of the charges in place, above and below it. *P for Plenty* was a truism, and while Wade hadn't been a dedicated breacher, he knew enough about explosives to put them to good use.

He'd just gotten the top charge wedged into place when Curtis yelled from the doorway. "Helos inbound! We gotta go!"

Wade cocked his head and listened, but the helicopters must still be some distance away. He hastily pulled the igniters on the first two charges, looked down at what he had left, and swore. There was no time to set them for maximum damage, so he'd just have to settle for blowing up as much of this side of the generator as he could. He started placing charges and popping smoke as fast as he could.

***

Without the other hostages in tow, Flanagan, Tackett, Jenkins, and Gomez could move faster, sprinting across the eastern edge of the lawn, along the front of the northern building. "Friendlies coming through!" Flanagan bellowed as they neared the doorway.

He slowed as he got closer to the doorway itself. It was possible that the others hadn't seen the incoming birds. "We've got helos incoming! We are out of time!" He stuck his head in the door, seeing Bianco, Curtis, Max, and Vernon. The others must all be placing charges. "We need to get on the vehicles and get moving. Now."

Curtis stood up. "Everybody else is in there." He jerked a thumb toward the EMP generator room. "I'll pass the word and meet you outside." The banter, the wisecracks, the general goofing around that was part and parcel of Curtis's personality were all gone under pressure. That was why he was a Blackheart. The man was a professional, behind the big mouth and the off-duty shenanigans.

Tackett hurried inside to help Max and Vernon. Flanagan held up, along with Jenkins and Gomez, and waited for them. The two former prisoners might need some extra help, but if they had to fight their way out, they needed every gun up they could get.

Tackett came out with his two old teammates. They were doing their best, and both of them were on their feet and somewhat steadier than they had been, but they weren't going to be moving fast anytime soon, particularly not in these mountains.

That presented some problems, and Flanagan realized he needed to start thinking about them. If there were checkpoints on the road to the north—which appeared to be the only good way out—particularly around Ak-Bulun, they might have a real fight on their hands.

The alternative was hiking over the mountains again, with two men who were strung out, malnourished, and traumatized. That was going to be a hell of a hump.

They didn't have any other options, though. Even if they grabbed one of those fancy, advanced helicopters—if you could call something with wings and two pusher props a helicopter—none of them were trained pilots. It was possible that Price could fly one, but they had too many bodies for just one bird.

It was trucks, or leather Cadillacs through the snow and the mountains.

He hoped they could make the trucks work.

Looking to the north, he could just see the lights of the advancing helos. They weren't running blacked out, which was odd. Maybe they were just that overconfident.

Still, since he could see them, it meant they had ten minutes, max.

With Tackett and Price practically dragging Vernon and Max, they ran toward the hangars. Ducking through the small entry door, Flanagan found the button to open the big rollup, as Gomez moved in to see what they had for vehicles.

The trucks weren't the beat-up old Soviet GAZ or Korean Kia trucks he might have expected to find in Kyrgyzstan. It was apparent that the Front hadn't been quite as concerned about keeping a low profile in-country as they might have been. They were trying to hide this base from outside observers, but they were only willing to sacrifice so much of their technological toys to camouflage.

These things were massive, faceted, eight-wheeled monstrosities that looked like slightly sleeker and lighter MRAPs. Their tires were huge, and it looked like they could easily handle any terrain aside from climbing right up the mountains themselves. Maybe even that.

Gomez was already climbing into one. "Looks like we can take eight each."

"Load up." Flanagan ran to a second truck, yanking the door open and clambering up inside. There was a single driver's seat, center line, with bucket seats behind, side by side. The whole thing looked brand new and was probably comfortable as hell. It still reminded him of an MRAP, right down to the hatch right where the machinegun turret would go. He sat down in the driver's seat, gratified to find the keys already in the ignition.

"Hell. Everything's in Russian." He could read some of it, but only some. "Dammit Herc, why'd you have to go and get yourself killed?" The thought stung, but he put the truck in neutral and started it up with a thunderous rumble.

More Blackhearts piled in behind him. He couldn't count everyone in, since a couple piled in through the door in the back, but a moment later, Brannigan was pulling the door shut. "We've got everybody. Let's go."

The other truck was already pulling out, heading for the gate. Flanagan fell in behind, keeping close for the moment. The vehicle, for all its impressive size and eight massive wheels, didn't feel like it had a huge amount of power. At least, it didn't have a lot of acceleration. It probably had torque to burn.

Then again, it was Russian. He wasn't going to trust it all that far.

The two massive Avtoros Shamans roared out the gate and onto the narrow dirt road running down the eastern bank of the currently dry riverbed, heading north as two big, black helicopters came in low and circled to land.

***

Boyd was fuming. Comms with the birds had gone completely to shit in the last ten minutes. It happened sometimes, but that didn't help anything. Especially as he watched on the still-functioning camera feeds as the intruders ran out the gate in their own Shaman all-terrain vehicles, and the helicopters kept coming in to land on the helipad, apparently oblivious as to the fact that the enemy—and possibly at least three high-value detainees—were fleeing at that very moment.

One burst from a door gunner would have ended it all, right then and there. But comms were down and he couldn't tell them to burn down the vehicles.

He couldn't have even if he'd had comms. Price was in one of those trucks.

With an incendiary curse, he grabbed his weapon and headed for the door. He'd open the Alamo before the compound was cleared, but he was watching his entire life flash before his eyes. If this went all the way south...

"Where are you going, Mr. Boyd?!" Auguste Boivin wasn't one of the researchers. He was an admin type, but he sure acted as if he was in charge most of the time. Given the fact that he could screw with their pay and deployment times, in a way he was, but that didn't endear him to anyone. "The compound is *not* yet secure! You cannot open that door!"

Boyd had just about had it. Boivin could cause all sorts of havoc, but if he lost the enemy and those prisoners, he was screwed and he knew it. If he got them back—and possibly added more test subjects to Karesinda's sick project—then Boivin wouldn't be able to touch him.

So, he pointed his rifle at the fat, pasty Frenchman, and watched the man gape like a fish, his eyes bugging out like a frog's, as he turned an even whiter shade of pale.

"Get out of my way, Boivin."

The fat administrator scrambled to clear the doorway, and Boyd stepped up, punched his access code into the door lock, and the heavy, ballistic door opened with a *click*.

He hauled it open and then he was sprinting down the short stretch of hallway toward the stairs, throwing himself down the steps, not even bothering to check to make sure the intruders hadn't left any nasty surprises behind. His own sense of immediate self-preservation was warring with a much more long-term priority of survival.

The foyer was clear as he pelted down the last flight of steps and toward the doors. He'd just reached them when Finkelstein's wing of the building blew up.

He threw himself flat as glass shattered and the entire structure shook, flame, smoke, and debris boiling out of every opening in the half of the old Soviet barracks building that had been hollowed out for the EMP research. Smoke kept pouring out of the windows as he turned to stare at the place for a moment, along with the flickering light of what had to be multiple fires, some with the actinic glare of electrical blazes.

The lead helicopter had been descending toward the helipad as the rippling series of explosions rocked the compound. Now it pulled away, just as its rotor wash started to kick up clouds of snow from the night before. Boyd heard a tinny, small voice in his earpiece, and frantically stuffed it back in as he keyed his radio.

"Skulker Five One, Skulker Five One, this is Static." He couldn't tell what the pilot had been saying, but comms were back.

"Static, this is Skulker Five One. What the hell is going on down there?"

"Intruders have just escaped in two Shaman all terrains." He was up and running toward the helipad. The rest of the team could worry about securing the compound. "Get me on board and then we need to pursue."

"Static, this is Brimstone." Boyd felt his blood go cold. He knew Brimstone, but he didn't know what he was doing in

Kyrgyzstan. Last he'd heard, the man had been working with one of Winter's teams. "We got instructions that we needed to secure the compound. Are you telling me the compound itself, and all personnel, are secure?" There was a brief pause, but Brimstone came back over the radio before Boyd could answer. "Because it sure doesn't look like it."

"The intruders left charges behind." He was winging it, and he knew it. He had no way of knowing for sure that they hadn't left anyone behind to cause more mischief, but in his gut, he was sure that they'd all headed out in those two Shamans. Even though he still didn't have a solid number of just how many bad guys there had been. "They are escaping to the north with a minimum of three high value detainees. We need to go *now*."

The helicopter was settling toward the helipad once again, blowing up a white cloud with its rotors. He needed it to land so he could board, but he watched the second bird still circling with a growing, desperate rage. They were both going to land and sweep the compound first. Especially if Brimstone thought he was off base.

The helo, a black-painted S-92, settled to the helipad, the rotors still beating the air, and Boyd had to lean into the wind as he surged toward the bird. The side door was closed, which meant the mounted minigun wasn't deployed, though it slid open as the bird landed. Probably too cold for the crew to be comfortable at altitude, but it meant that they might not have been able to engage the fleeing Shamans anyway.

The ramp lowered, and the hulking figure in plate carrier, helmet, and rifle stepped out, recognizable by size and demeanor as Brimstone. A former SAS commando, the man scared the hell out of Boyd, and he was generally the kind of man who scared *other* people.

"What the fuck is going on here, Boyd?" Apparently, Brimstone knew his current alias, which was more than he could say about himself. He'd never known any other name for the man but Brimstone.

"There's no time to go into all of it." He was somewhat grateful for the roar of the S-92's engines, since it meant they both had to shout to be heard, and it helped him keep the nervousness out of his voice when he was bellowing at full volume. "We got hit by a professional team of shooters, and if we don't move fast to intercept them, they're going to get away with three of our high-value individuals, including Mitchell Price."

That seemed to get Brimstone's attention. "You're bloody shitting me. You had Price on this facility? Why wasn't that sent up to the Board?"

"Not my call." And it hadn't been. That had been Karesinda's decision, and while she wasn't technically the installation's coordinator, she pulled enough weight—Boyd *really* didn't want to know the gory details of that bit of backdoor maneuvering—that she'd been able to prevail on the entire staff to keep Price's presence quiet, for the time being. "But they're getting farther away by the second."

Brimstone stared at him for a moment, and Boyd could almost see the gears turning behind the man's GPNVGs. Brimstone was a proven murderer, and had been drummed out of the 22nd SAS for just that reason. Which was, naturally, why the Board had snatched him up as soon as they'd been able to maneuver him out of prison.

"I'll deal with you later." He turned back to the ramp, ignoring the half-dozen operators who'd already sprinted past them toward the open doors of Building Two. "Let's go."

The two of them ran toward the helo, Brimstone already on the radio to the Dash Two bird, telling them not to land.

Two minutes later, the S-92 was pulling for altitude, struggling in the thin mountain air, while the Dash Two helo was already nose-down, arrowing north along the valley toward Ak-Bulun. Boyd hung onto a strap next to the door gunner, staring out into the darkness, green-tinged in his GPNVGs, feeling a little bit of relief for the first time that night.

You can't outrun us this time, you sons of bitches.

CHAPTER 31

The Shamans did have a lot of power, but they weren't fast. Big, heavy, and plenty stable on the uneven ground, they could probably have powered along the riverbed itself at just about the same speed they were making on the road, but that was still limited to maybe forty-five miles an hour.

They were never going to outrun helicopters at that speed.

Of course, Flanagan reflected as he stared into the dark, trying not to drive off a cliff in the dim moonlight since the vehicles were both blacked out, there never had been any hope of outrunning helicopters on the ground, anyway. That just wasn't happening.

"They're coming after us." Price was in the very back, peering through the rear door's small window with the GPNVGs that he'd picked up before they'd left. Flanagan thought he probably should have done the same, given the fact that he was driving, but there simply hadn't been time. "The first bird just lifted off, and the second didn't land. They're turning around and coming up the valley."

"What do you want to do, Colonel?" Flanagan glanced in the rear-view mirror out his left side, and saw the white cone of a searchlight stabbing down toward the riverbed from one of the S-92s. It was coming toward them, all right.

Brannigan was in the seat right behind and to his right, craning his neck to try to see through the right-hand rear-view mirror. "Find us a draw where we can bail out and head up into the mountains." He paused, and Flanagan saw him look back over his shoulder. "It's going to be rough on Max and Vernon, but we might be able to hide from helos in the trees. There's no way we can evade in these things."

"Gonna be a long hump back to anywhere." Bianco wasn't complaining. He was just pointing out.

"Yeah. Let's hope Mr. Carter's contacts are extensive enough that he can get us some support as soon as he can get to a functioning phone." Even as Brannigan said it, Flanagan wondered how far they were going to have to go to accomplish that.

How far did that EMP reach?

It was fortunate that the hangars—and possibly the vehicles themselves—had been hardened against the EMP, because otherwise they would have really been up the proverbial creek without a paddle.

There. The narrow valley opened up a bit up ahead, with wide draws coming down out of the mountains to either side, lined with the darker swathes of trees. There might be a chance to hide there, or even get moving up over the mountains themselves, provided Max and Vernon could make it. "Thirty seconds!"

He might have driven all the way to the confluence of draws, but that might also tell the bad guys exactly where they were going. He'd rather leave that a little murky, even as he knew they were going to have a very limited window to get the hell away from the massive vehicles and into some cover.

Instead of stomping on the brakes, he coasted to a stop, just in case the brake lights might light up. He was pretty sure he'd hit the vehicle's blackout switch, but he'd been burned before, so he was going to play it careful. "Get out, get out, get out!"

The doors slammed open, and the Blackhearts were piling out before the vehicle had even come to a dead stop. Behind, the second vehicle was doing the same, still lined up on Flanagan's truck.

Flanagan, as he piled out, catching his breath against the sharp chill of the night after the relatively warm interior of the vehicle, wasn't actually sure which way they were going to go, after all. Brannigan hadn't said.

"Mario, get us going up there." Brannigan pointed to the wider, U-shaped valley to their left, heading west into the mountains. The trees thinned out fast, but they'd provide some concealment, at least for a while. "Step it out. We have zero time."

Gomez didn't say anything. Didn't even nod. He just turned and started off across the riverbed, making as good time as he could on the snow and ice.

Flanagan fell in at the rear with Wade, as the rest straggled across the valley and the helicopters closed in.

We're moving faster without the weight, but somehow, I expect we're going to miss our rucks in a real short time.

There was nothing for it, though. They could make their escape, or they could end up cornered back in that hanging valley where they'd left the rucksacks before they'd begun their approach to the target, with nowhere to go but up, where their "packages" couldn't necessarily go in their current condition.

We might still end up in that position. But they had to make do with what they had. So, they hustled through the snow and up into the spruces, as the helicopters roared in close.

***

"There!" Brimstone was pointing. "Two vehicles, on the road. Take us down!"

Boyd hauled himself across the passenger compartment to join the former SAS commando at the other door gunner's station. The doors were still closed, but they could be opened quickly and the miniguns swung into position.

"Why are they stopped?" He wasn't plugged into the bird's intercom, so he still had to yell.

"Doesn't matter, does it?" The door gunner was leaning out over his minigun, the barrels pointed down at the vehicles. "I can burn 'em down easy enough."

"Hold your bloody fire." Brimstone's roar was loud enough that he could be clearly heard over the thunder of the rotors. "Price is a Priority Gamma asset. He is to be taken alive. The rest might be expendable, but the Board wants Price in one piece." The bird was already starting to flare, the nose coming up as the pilot slowed them, the lead helo already settling toward the road ahead of the lead vehicle. Brimstone turned back to the rest of the shooters on the benches to either side of the compartment. "Ten seconds! Identify your targets before you engage!"

The bird touched down on the road just behind the rear vehicle and the ramp came down a moment later. Boyd chewed the inside of his lip as he watched it lower. He would have already had the ramp down before they'd passed fifty feet. They were burning time.

He pushed forward and ran out, ducking his head as he carefully turned to the left to avoid the spinning tail rotor. That could have ended his troubles real quick, but he didn't want to go that way. His APC 300 up in his shoulder, he closed in on the trail vehicle quickly, only realizing as he slowed and approached the rear door that Brimstone was right there with him.

The doors were shut and the engine was off. He frowned as he watched the window, but the interior lights were off and he could see no movement, not even with his NVGs.

Something made him scan the surrounding hills as he halted at the rear of the vehicle. Brimstone ignored him, already reaching for the door handle.

Was that movement? He could have sworn he'd seen what might have been a human silhouette for a split second, up in the trees on the other side of the river. But then Brimstone was pulling the door open, and he dropped his muzzle to cover the inside next to the other operative.

The vehicle was empty. A moment later, the same report came from the team at the front. They'd ditched the vehicles.

Boyd suddenly felt his blood go cold as he realized what they'd just walked into.

Then the machineguns opened fire from the other side of the riverbed.

**

Green tracers arced lazily across the valley and hammered into the figures dimly lit by the helicopters' running lights. Three men fell in the first few seconds.

"Shift fire to the helos!" Brannigan had to shout the command to be heard over the gunfire. "Try to disable them, or at least hit the pilots or gunners!"

He was down behind his own M4, peering through the ACOG, trying to get a good shot at one of the door gunners. Some solid hits to the engines could do some serious damage—helicopters can be awfully fragile, especially when they're on the ground—but those miniguns were a major threat. They could mow through the trees and kill every Blackheart on the mountainside.

At that distance, and in the poor light, he had to settle for volume over pinpoint accuracy. Not that the M4 was anything more than a four-minute-of-angle gun under the best of conditions, but since he couldn't see more than dim shapes through the scope, he had to dump about a third of the magazine into the side of the S-92. He was rewarded with a sudden violent movement that he *thought* was the minigun swinging skyward as the gunner slumped.

The shooters on the ground had reacted fast, diving to cover behind the Shamans and the low ground on the other side of the road. Return fire was starting to sail across the riverbed, slicing through the air overhead with harsh, supersonic *crack*s.

One of the machinegunners had done his work well. The lead bird, down on the road facing the front Shaman, was smoking and shaking, sparks flying from the cowling as the damaged turbine shook itself apart. Brannigan hadn't been sure that a 7.62x39 could do enough damage, but as with most things, it was where the bullet hit that counted.

253

More machinegun fire raked the vehicles before smashing against the hindmost helicopter, just as the bird started to haul itself aloft. The thin air was helping the Blackhearts. It was harder for the rotors to gain lift, and it was a strain to get the helo off the ground.

Bullets chewed into the rotor and the engine cowling before tracking down through the fuselage. Smoke poured out of the engine as the bird suddenly shuddered and began to drop toward the ground again. It hadn't made it high enough to really crash, but it wasn't going to fly again anytime soon.

The incoming fire was intensifying, though. And they didn't have an infinite supply of ammunition to hold the Front's shooters off, either.

"Start falling back!" There wasn't a lot of cover up that valley, but they could still open the gap, especially with the helicopters disabled.

He'd made sure that the Shamans weren't going to go very far just after they'd ditched them, too. They *might* hotwire them, but Flanagan and Wade both had the keys. The bad guys apparently hadn't had enough time to notice that they'd spiked the tires, too.

With Price and Santelli keeping Vernon and Max moving, the team started to bound back.

As soon as their own volume of fired dropped, however, the enemy was moving. The Front's shooters had already been using what cover they had to spread out, and now they intensified their own fire, starting to bound forward in the teeth of the streams of bullets hammering at them in the dark.

These guys were good. They knew that the Blackhearts didn't have working night vision, and now they were using that to their advantage. Spread out, using the available cover and shadow, they were getting increasingly hard to spot.

Without surprise on their side, the Blackhearts were now on the defensive, and that was not going to end well against an enemy with night vision and suppressors.

Getting to his feet, Brannigan turned and sprinted uphill as fast as he could, even as bullets *snap*ped past his head, one of them striking the nearest spruce with a heavy *thunk*. He ran past Jenkins even as Price and Santelli dropped prone up ahead and started to lay down cover fire.

***

Jenkins waited for Brannigan and Bianco to get past him, then got up to move as the gunfire from above and to his right intensified. The incoming fire was getting awfully thick, too, and he couldn't see well enough to tell for sure where it was all coming from. He really, really wished he'd grabbed some enemy kit, especially those fancy GPNVGs. There just hadn't been time, though.

He got up to move, starting to sprint through the trees, when a rock rolled under his foot.

He felt his ankle twist, and felt the *pop* that told him something was very, very wrong, even before the shooting pain just about took his breath away and his leg folded under him.

Oh shit, oh shit, oh shit, oh shit...

He didn't need to look at the ankle to know he wasn't going to get far on it. His boot was holding things together still, but he was sure that it was already swelling even as he dragged himself behind a tree.

He glanced up at the mountains behind him, seeing a few of the Blackhearts falling back, their overwhites momentarily visible against the darker shapes of the trees. Morning was still a long way off, but the moon was shining through increasingly thin clouds overhead.

I'm probably not going to see the sun rise.

Dragging himself out from behind the spruce, he crawled and limped toward a boulder sticking up on the nearby hillside. More bullets smacked into the ground and the scrubby trees around him as he moved, but he ignored them. His ankle throbbed, and he knew he couldn't put any weight on it, but he still used it to push himself toward cover, gritting his teeth against the pain with every stabbing shock that ran through the limb.

Getting to the boulder, miraculously without getting hit, he laid his M4 over the top and got ready to reap some souls.

CHAPTER 32

Flanagan reached out and grabbed Curtis by the upper arm, pulling him up before he could faceplant in the snow and the rocks. The bodybuilder was working hard to keep up, but his legs were shorter, and even without the weight of a ruck, and after all the fighting they'd already been through that night, he was still carrying more ammo than most of the rest of them. He got his feet under him, nodded a breathless thanks, and kept going.

They were out of the trees, and unfortunately, that meant they were largely above the trees. A shooter down on the other side of the road might have a shot. Glancing back, Flanagan couldn't see much in the dimness, though he could still see and hear gunfire from down below.

He frowned, pausing as Curtis moved on ahead. Somebody was still back there, the unsuppressed reports of an M4 echoing across the valley from somewhere in the trees. Looking back up, he tried counting heads, but he couldn't get a precise count in the dark, without night vision.

Brannigan was somewhere up ahead. He couldn't tell exactly where the Colonel was.

Looking back down, he decided. The bad guys had all been running suppressed, which meant it was a Blackheart down there, hammering away at them with an unsuppressed M4. He knew the sound of 5.56 fire. He turned and started running back down the mountain, toward the enemy, and toward the teammate who hadn't gotten the message to break contact.

* * *

Jenkins was trying to be sure of his shots, to conserve ammunition if for no other reason. He only had about four mags left, and if these guys were wearing body armor, he was going to need every round.

He'd actually picked a good spot. He had good cover and a commanding view of the entire valley mouth below. Unless they wanted to turn into mountain goats, the bad guys had to come at him right into the teeth of his fire.

If any of the other Blackhearts had been there, he would have said that he'd totally picked it on purpose. That SEAL tactical magic at work. He knew it was bullshit. He knew they'd know it was bullshit. He'd found the first good bit of cover he could, looking through the haze of pain radiating from his ankle.

Not as young as you were on the Teams. Little sprain like that wouldn't have fazed you, back in the day.

Back in the day...

He snapped his rifle toward movement, catching sight of a dark shape against the white—pale gray, really, in the moonlight—of the snow, and fired. He might have hit the guy. Might have just grazed him. But the bad guy ducked back behind a tree and didn't return fire. Not yet.

Jenkins lifted his head from his rifle, scanning the scattered spruces just below his perch. They'd slowed down a lot after he'd smoked the first two dudes who'd tried to rush after the withdrawing Blackhearts. They knew where he was. He just was hard to get to.

He was kind of amazed how good his night eyes were, about half an hour after getting away from the lights of the compound. He'd never tried to fight this way, old school. Even *back in the day*, on the Teams, they'd always had NVGs. The nice ones, too. His first issued pair had been PVS-15s, the binocular jobs that helicopter pilots used. He still remembered talking to a Marine who'd trained with the old PVS-7Bs, the bulky relics with

258

two ocular lenses fed by a single objective lens. He'd been shocked. He'd thought those things had been out of use since the '90s.

More movement. A bullet spat rock chips into his face, and he returned fire, hammering three more rounds into the shadow where he'd seen something shift. He might or might not have hit anything, but the incoming fire stopped.

I'm going to die here. That wasn't something he'd ever thought he would contemplate with such calm. He'd been a SEAL. He realized he'd always thought, deep down, that somehow that fact had made him not only better than he'd actually been, but that in a way it had made him immortal. He'd known SEALs who'd been killed. He'd never been there when it had happened. He'd never seen it happen. So, there'd always been a detachment, an unreality to it.

Even after all his time as a Blackheart, seeing others go down, he didn't think that he'd ever considered that he might be the next one to buy the farm. Yet here he was, the rest of the team getting farther and farther away, knowing he'd never catch up, knowing that he *had* to hold this position because there was no cover up there, so if they were going to get away, somebody was going to have to take one for the team and hold the Front at the base of the valley.

You always did want to be a hero. Too bad the real thing doesn't involve praise and glory and booze and hot chicks. Just an epitaph, maybe read by men who might live because you held and died.

Maybe now they won't think you're such an asshole.

Two shooters suddenly came out of the trees off to his right. He turned and fired, almost blindly, and the first one staggered, as the second one dumped a burst at him, the suppressor spitting with sharp *crack*s in the cold mountain air. His movement had thrown the man's aim off, and the first two rounds went high, as he swung his weapon and shot back, the M4's report thunderous compared to the hissing *snap*s of the suppressed gunfire that was reaching for his life.

Even as he got a lucky shot off, the second shooter's head snapping back under the impact of the bullet just before he collapsed limply into the snow, Jenkins felt the fiery *thump* in his side that told him he'd been hit.

He ignored it, leaning out far enough to shoot the first man again. He was pretty sure the shot was low, going under the man's plate, because the guy doubled over with a scream, collapsing in the snow like he'd been kicked in the nuts.

Bad way to go. A pelvic shot would be extremely painful, while you bled out slowly, the contents of your veins draining into your waistline.

Only then did he slump back against the rock, the pain from his wound starting to radiate through him. He felt like throwing up. Putting a hand down to his side, he felt the warm dampness, just below his ribs.

Then he propped his rifle back up on the boulder, leaning against the rock as he looked for more targets.

***

Flanagan had half-sprinted, half-slid down the slope toward the nearest clump of trees above where he could still hear gunfire, and occasionally see a flash of muzzle blast in the dark. He had to move slowly now, since he was down in the spruces and could find himself at close quarters with one of the bad guys at any moment.

If he was judging things right, he was only about twenty or thirty yards away from their wayward teammate, but he was sure that there were already Front shooters between him and his target. A bullet had gone past his head with a distinctive *crack* only a moment ago, as there had been a fast-paced exchange of gunfire just downhill and to his left.

The gunfire had died down, and now he strained his ears to try to hear any movement nearby. Flanagan was a good man in the woods, but he'd be the first to admit that his hearing wasn't what it once had been. Too many gunshots, too many explosions, too many flights in helicopters or bare-bones military turboprops with no hearing protection. The harder he strained to hear, the more he just heard the permanent ringing in his ears.

There. A footstep crunched in the snow, just on the other side of the clump of spruces where he was crouched. Too close. And if he was judging the geometries right, he couldn't shoot this guy without possibly shooting his teammate who was holed up across the way.

The dark shape of a man in combat gear and helmet stepped out from behind the trees, barely three yards in front of him. And the man was looking the wrong direction, toward where Flanagan had heard the gunfire.

Slipping the carbon fiber stiletto he'd carried from the States out of his belt, Flanagan moved. He couldn't stop the snow from crunching under his boots, but at just that moment, more gunfire thundered from down the hill, covering what little sound he made as he closed the distance in three fast strides.

Grabbing the man's helmet, he wrenched his head to one side and plunged the dagger into the junction between shoulder and neck. His placement was just about perfect, missing the plate carrier's shoulder strap, and he had put enough force behind the spike to plunge it through utilities and underlayers, punching deep into the meat, wrenching it from side to side as he tried to find the subclavian artery with the blade.

The man under him shuddered and howled, but Flanagan was past trying to be quiet about this. He'd grabbed what he could, which had been the helmet and four-tube NVGs, and now he pulled out the spike and stabbed the man again and again, even as gloved hands reached back and battered at him, trying to get him off. He kicked the man's knee out from under him as he kept going like a monkey with a screwdriver, until finally, the Front shooter collapsed, hot blood surging out of the gaping wounds Flanagan had inflicted on his neck and shoulder.

Flanagan let him fall, snatching his weapon back up. He briefly considered taking the man's helmet and NVGs, but his eyes were already adapted to the dark, and he didn't have the time, anyway.

Keeping to the upper edge of the trees, he kept working his way around.

Linkup was going to be dicey, with no comms and no IR, and the enemy presumably all speaking English. But a moment later, that difficulty was somewhat resolved, as he stepped around a tree at the same time three more shooters tried to rush forward.

Flanagan didn't see that they were making for the big boulder just above him at first. He just saw three dark shapes moving, saw enough to identify them as hostile—the suppressed gunfire spraying overhead with hissing *snap*s was a pretty good indicator—snapped his rifle to his shoulder, and opened fire.

The man at the boulder opened up at the same time, and with a strobing series of flashes and echoing thunderclaps, the two of them blasted two of the three off their feet. The third dove for cover, but Flanagan tracked him behind a low spruce and put another three shots low into the dark foliage, being rewarded with a scream a moment later.

Then he sprinted for the boulder, yelling, "Friendly!"

Jenkins was leaning heavily against the boulder, still behind his rifle, dumping more rounds down toward the trees below. He probably couldn't see much more than Flanagan could, but he was just putting down cover fire at that point. Flanagan got behind the boulder, skidding to a stop on a knee.

"What the hell are you doing here, Joe?" Jenkins didn't sound good. There was a sick gurgle in his voice, and after a moment, Flanagan could make out the dark fluid staining the snow underneath him.

"You fell behind." He reared up over the boulder and took a shot at another dark silhouette moving from tree to tree, up higher on the mountainside above them. The figure disappeared, but he didn't think he'd hit it.

"Sprained my ankle. Then I got shot." Jenkins was starting to slide down the side of the boulder. He caught himself, dragging his body back up onto the rock to get behind his rifle. "I'm not going anywhere. Not in these mountains." He turned away from his weapon for a moment, to look over at Flanagan. "If you can spare a couple mags, I might be able to buy you guys some more time. But you've got to get out of here."

Flanagan didn't look at him. There were too many shooters out there. Two S-92s could have brought close to forty men. They'd killed quite a few, but probably not even half. And if the Front was really determined to get to them, they wouldn't let those losses slow them down.

He was a little astounded, though. George Jenkins had been a problem child for a long time. He'd kind of been the last man any of them would have expected to make the heroic, sacrificial last stand.

Yet here he was. It was possible that his injuries had taken away his options, but he could still have tried to surrender, to save his own life. It might or might not have worked, but by continuing to fight, he'd sealed his fate.

He'd hesitated a little too long for Jenkins. The man's next words came out in almost a groan. "Dammit, Joe, get the hell out of here! Go, or we're both dead!" He fired again, his M4 spitting flame down the slope.

Flanagan tore two magazines out of his vest and slapped them onto the rock next to Jenkins. "Give 'em hell, George." He gave the other man's shoulder a squeeze, then, a growing lump in his throat, he turned and ran up the valley, keeping his head down and trying to put as much terrain between him and the oncoming enemy fighters as he could, as fast as he could.

***

"Thanks, Joe." Jenkins didn't know if his teammate had heard him or not. His voice sounded like a thick mumble in his own ears, though they were ringing from the gunfire. He could feel his strength ebbing as blood kept leaking out through the hole in his side. It was getting hard to breathe. He probably was developing a tension pneumothorax. He vaguely remembered that that happened if the chest cavity was compromised. He didn't have long.

Waiting, straining to breathe, he watched for any movement. As weak and tired as he was getting, everything still seemed amazingly clear. The moonlight may as well have been high noon as far as he was concerned. He could see far more than he'd imagined he could in the night.

Movement caught his eye, and he slammed a pair at it. He saw something jerk and then whoever had been down there went still. With an effort, he shifted his position to see the slopes around him a bit better.

Breathing seemed to get a little easier. Or maybe that was just death coming, as he no longer really cared that much.

He shot at another advancing figure, but he might have missed. His bolt locked back on an empty mag, and he dropped it with shaking fingers, fumbling the reload once before he got one of Flanagan's mags into the mag well, slapping the bolt release clumsily even as two more shooters came out of the trees. He shot one through the leg, missed entirely with his second shot, then dumped five more rounds as fast as he could pull the trigger at the second, seeing the man spin away and fall even as he felt another fiery impact in his neck. He tried to ignore it, even as hot blood flowed down his side.

He never heard the shot that killed him. There was a brief, millisecond flash of pain in his head, then everything went dark.

***

Boyd looked down at the dead man, lying on his face in the snow. He'd put up one hell of a fight. Fully a third of the react force from Manas lay on the mountainside or out on the road, dead or badly wounded.

Brimstone was among them, somewhat to Boyd's relief. The Front's hatchet man had gone down immediately in that first burst of machinegun fire, taking a bullet to the side of the head, just below his high-cut helmet. He was down there in the snow, head-down in the ditch below the road, going cold and stiff, leaving what command there was left to Boyd.

He looked up the valley, where the intruders had disappeared. He couldn't see any of them, even on NVGs. He was pretty sure he could follow them, but he had to consider the state of the force he had left. Most of Brimstone's shooters had been getting steadily more cautious as they'd seen more of their compatriots go down, and when he looked up that valley, he suddenly got a very bad feeling.

They'd have to cross a lot of open ground if they went after those bastards directly. Open ground, covered in snow, while every one of them were in darker-colored camouflage. The bad guys had overwhites. They could even be up there right then, watching and waiting.

"Fall back." His voice was a croak.

"We're letting them go?" He didn't know the man who spoke, but his accent sounded vaguely Swiss.

Boyd waved at the snow-covered mountainside. "That's an ambush waiting to happen. We've got other ways. They're not out of the country yet." He pointed downhill. "We can move faster than they can."

CHAPTER 33

It was three days later when Boyd landed back in Manas, riding one of the backup S-92s that had needed to fly out to the base to pick him up. He'd made the call not to use the advanced Racer helicopters, despite Karesinda's screaming that he had to use any and every resource to get her subjects back—especially after Core and Vargas had followed protocol and killed the rest—because raising their profile even more was not a good idea.

Coming down the ramp, he ducked his head and turned sharply left to avoid the tail rotor, hustling toward a man he knew only as Gordon. They shook hands without a word, then hustled toward what had once been the US Air Force's Manas Airbase.

Gordon was a man of medium height, medium build, without a single distinguishing feature about him. Boyd, as trained as he was, would be hard pressed to give a detailed description if he had to report on the man's appearance. He was one of those consummate "gray men" who just disappeared into a crowd. Boyd didn't know much of anything about him, except he was a team leader for Epoch Solutions, a small, low-profile PMSC that the Front kept quietly on the books for just this kind of cleanup operation.

Gordon led the way into one of the semi-permanent tents, and Boyd took a look around. The Epoch team wasn't large, but it shouldn't have to be for what they had in mind. About ten men stood around the otherwise empty building, each in nondescript civilian clothes and heavy jackets, all long enough to conceal the B+T APC 9 submachineguns they'd brought. Boyd hadn't specified weapons, but the fact that they'd brought the subgun versions of the carbines his team had used was just an added bonus as far as he was concerned.

"Okay, here's the deal." There was only so much information he was allowed to pass to these guys. They were shooters for hire, and could *generally* be trusted to keep their mouths shut for enough money, but all the same, they weren't read in. They weren't a part of the Front.

Not that you're a huge True Believer, yourself. He ignored the little voice in the back of his mind and concentrated on the brief.

"We've got a high-value target that just popped up. This is *probably* time sensitive. We have a location, and our source has confirmed that the target is there." He hauled the tablet out of his pack, which also carried his APC 300 with the stock folded, and brought up the imagery with the target house marked. It was on the southern edge of Bishkek, out in the farmlands, right up against the foothills that had been terraced for farming. "The target is believed to have up to ten or fifteen shooters, but we not only have you, we have the source's own backup."

He hesitated a little at the next part, even as the Epoch shooters leaned in to look at the imagery. There was the potential that the next bit of information might give away a bit more than the Board wanted the Epoch guys to know, but there was no getting around it. *Winter's killers are probably waiting to clean these guys up at any time, anyway.* "The target himself is this man." He scrolled to a photo of Price. "He is to be taken alive at all costs."

"The rest?" Gordon didn't sound all that invested. In fact, he sounded downright bored.

"Kill or capture." The way Boyd said it prompted a nod all around. *Either works.*

"You said you have assets on site already?" The speaker almost looked local, but his accent was pure Southern California.

Boyd nodded. The Epoch shooters didn't need to know that they still had Price's local QRF suborned. The Kyrgyz PMC had been easy to turn. They were every bit as greedy as Epoch, they just lived in a country where a lot less money went a lot farther. He was frankly surprised that Price had been naïve enough to contact the group again. Maybe he didn't have many other options, and believed that Boren had been the sole turncoat. Maybe the man had convinced himself of that, to justify the lack of options in Kyrgyzstan. Price was a powerhouse, but he was still a man. He was still fallible.

"Our informant has a small local security company that the target hired for his protection. We believe that the target is trying to get out of the country, so we do need to move quickly."

The Epoch shooters had zoomed in on the house, a combination farmhouse and barn slightly isolated from the surrounding buildings, and were already planning their approach and how they would cordon off the building and make the hit. They kept their voices low, and there wasn't a lot of extraneous talk. These men had worked on this sort of job dozens of times before. It was old hat. And if the target thought that he was secure, while his security was suborned, it should be fairly easy.

It took only a few minutes before they were in the vans and moving out.

***

"Targets incoming."

Tackett heard the call over the radio, looking down at Nurlan Sadykov where he sat in a chair, his hands flex-cuffed behind him. Sadykov had been right hand man for Boren, Price's chief support contact in Kyrgyzstan. Price had assumed, once they got over the mountains, that Sadykov was every bit as compromised as Boren had been. That had been why it had taken several days to get back to Bishkek. They'd hired a farmer's truck in Boz Uchuk, using some of the cash that Brannigan had brought, thanks to Hauser, and ridden to Yuri's place in Kichi-Kemin. The day and a half they'd spent there had been expensive—Yuri wasn't running a charity—but they'd given the team time to contact secondary support networks.

Price had had his own backup, and as soon as he'd gotten some working comms, Brannigan had contacted Chavez to put him in contact with Abernathy's group. With confirmation that the Front was active and working on weapons of mass destruction, Abernathy had managed to get some assets moving their way.

Now it was just a matter of cleaning house.

Tackett tapped his trigger finger against the MPX submachinegun's receiver. The big man named Hauser had shown up with two others and a crate of weapons and gear, getting it all past Kyrgyz customs with quiet conversations, IDs that raised some eyebrows, and a pile of cash. Now the Blackhearts—and their strap hangers—had working comms, NVGs if they needed them, and more compact weapons for the show that was coming next.

Sadykov didn't look up. The Blackhearts had showed up on his doorstep, in a van that Hauser had acquired, and Price had called him from inside the van while the Blackhearts got ready to take him. He'd walked out right into their hands and been hustled into the vehicle and off to this safehouse, quickly purchased through a front company by Abernathy's group.

Tackett still had no idea who this Abernathy was, and the operators who'd showed up sure were tight-lipped, but he had a sudden feeling that he'd gotten in deeper than he ever had before. That the Blackhearts were familiar with these mysterious special operators was plain, and Santelli was even on a first-name basis with Hauser.

He wasn't going to look a gift horse in the mouth, though, not after what they'd just been through. It was nice to have this kind of support.

It might even make him reconsider signing onto the occasional contract.

Sadykov had sung like a canary. He'd been compromised, all right, and he'd called the man he knew as Boyd as soon as he'd heard from Price. Which meant that the Front's hitters were on their way.

Now it was confirmed.

Tackett wasn't going to be any part of the main effort this time. He was here inside the house, guarding Sadykov along with Max and Vernon.

Neither man had flipped out on the way there, as everyone—most especially the two of them—had been a little worried might happen. They'd been thoroughly wrung out by the time they'd gotten down out of the mountains at Boz Uchuk, neither having the strength to stagger another step. And Price and Tackett had been helping them both for the last several miles.

Tackett was worn out, himself, even after two days of relative inactivity, waiting for Price and Brannigan to make their arrangements. He hadn't exactly been in mountain trekking shape before this, and half-carrying Vernon for several miles, at or above ten thousand feet, had just about crushed him. He was just as glad that he was staying in the rear for this, even while a part of him wished he was out there with Flanagan and the others.

Vernon was up, sitting in a chair against the wall, though he still looked like hell. Max was still asleep in the other room. Vernon still didn't have a weapon, but he could still call targets.

And Sadykov didn't know how beat up he was, either. He still *looked* intimidating enough.

"They're coming." Tackett looked over at Vernon, who didn't have a radio, either. He got a tired nod in return.

"Hopefully this is all over in the next few minutes. One way or another."

***

Flanagan heard the alert at the same time. He felt the squeeze at his elbow from Hauser. The big man was down next to him, also ghillied up, watching the road through the scope on his CSASS, a modified version of the HK G28. Flanagan was behind a Surgeon CSR, also ghillied up and lying flat behind a bush on the edge of one of the terraces above their safehouse.

He took his eyes off the scope and scanned their surroundings. The Kyrgyz police—who had been quickly brought around after a short conversation with Hauser, in which Flanagan didn't doubt the word "terrorism" had been thrown about liberally, doubtless backed up by another pallet of cash—were staged on the other side of the hill, out of sight from the road. The busted-down looking van sitting next to the house was full of most of the team, just waiting to pop out, and the two bent old men working the farm were Wade and Brannigan, dressed as poor Kyrgyz, each man with an MPX under his coat.

Flanagan settled in a little better behind the Compact Sniper Rifle and waited for the enemy.

***

Price came out into the main room with Lee, one of Hauser's operators. He had Sadykov's phone in his hand. It was ringing. He held it out, his thumb hovering over the "Accept" button. "Make it good."

He held the phone to Sadykov's ear. "Yes. Yes, Mr. Boyd. The team is in place. No, they suspect nothing. As soon as you arrive, we will take him and turn him over to you." He paused. "Yes, Mr. Boyd. You want us to hold the outer perimeter. Of course. You are the commander. Yes, Mr. Boyd."

Price had kept the sound turned up enough that everyone in the room, all of whom had stayed dead quiet, had been able to hear, and tell for sure that Sadykov wasn't selling them out. He shut the phone off as the call ended and got on the radio.

"Two minutes."

***

The van wasn't out of place. It was an old, rust-pitted, blue UAZ 452, trundling along the dirt road like it belonged there. Only the timing made it stand out, and as Flanagan turned his scope on the windshield, the magnification cranked up, he could see that the driver was definitely not Kyrgyz. He might be Russian, but Flanagan was pretty sure he'd seen that face on the base in the mountains.

"Target in sight." Hauser was on it, too.

Neither of them would open fire until it was time. Hauser and his operators wanted some live prisoners. They'd probably be quickly whisked away to a black site somewhere deep in the Nevada desert or somewhere. Abernathy wanted information.

From what Hauser had said, Flanagan suspected that a B2 from Missouri was already winging over that valley in the Tian Shan, its bomb bay laden with obliteration. That base, intel value or not, was about to get wiped off the map.

The van slowed, almost as if it was going to turn into the small cluster of bungalows still surrounded by construction debris just to the left, then suddenly accelerated, pushing toward the safe house.

So, they were going to do this fast and dynamic.

Fine. We'll play your way.

Flanagan shifted his hips, following the van as it raced up to the safehouse. Pulling alongside, the side door opened at just the same moment that the rear doors of the panel van next to the house flew aside.

The exchange of gunfire was short and sharp. The Blackhearts, joined by the third of Hauser's operators, a grim-faced dude named Therien, had been ready and waiting. Bodies dropped as the van shook and shattered glass cascaded to the ground.

The driver threw himself across the cab and bailed out the passenger side, putting the bulk of the van between himself and the gunfire.

Flanagan watched him through the scope. The man had pulled a full-length, suppressed APC 300 out of his pack, flipping open the stock as he went flat and turned onto his side, bringing the rifle to his shoulder to shoot under the van.

Letting his breath out, Flanagan tightened his finger on the trigger. Hauser wanted a prisoner, but it wasn't looking likely, this time.

It was a two-hundred-thirteen-yard shot. Hardly even a stretch with an M4. With the Surgeon, it was child's play.

The suppressed rifle *crack*ed, surging back against the bipods and his shoulder. The bullet smacked through the man on the ground, punching right through his clavicle and down into his torso. He jerked, then shuddered and slumped to the ground, blood soaking the light tan jacket as he died.

Flanagan worked the bolt, ejecting the spent case and chambering the next, but there were no more targets.

It was over.

EPILOGUE

Hauser handed a tablet across the cabin. "It's done."

Brannigan accepted it, looking down at the imagery. The valley was recognizable, though most of the snow had melted around the base. Or, perhaps more accurately, where the base had been.

He didn't know exactly what ordnance the B2 had dropped, but both main buildings had been leveled. The helipad was cratered, and what looked like the burned-out remains of one of the fancy, high-tech helicopters—that were supposed to be experimental—lay on its side nearby. Two of the three hangars had also been smashed.

"Any luck on retrieving my boys?" The Blackhearts hadn't been able to go back up there after Javakhishvili's or Jenkins' bodies. They'd needed to get out of Kyrgyzstan, before the local authorities started asking too many pointed questions. Price had brought in one of his Global 7500s, and now they were currently winging over Uzbekistan, heading for the Caspian Sea and Europe beyond it.

Hauser shook his head. "I'm afraid not. Looks like they grabbed them along with their own. They were probably in there, if they hadn't already been incinerated." He waved at the wreckage on the screen.

Brannigan looked around the cabin. The rest of the Blackhearts were still awake, and they'd all heard it. There was no visible reaction, at least not obviously, but he saw a few stares move off into nothingness.

More teammates gone. More friends and brothers left to unmarked graves in the middle of nowhere.

It was probably coming for all of them, eventually. Brannigan's eyes strayed to Santelli. The former sergeant major had known that, and had tried to back away, but he ultimately couldn't. He doubted Santelli would sit out another mission.

None of them had probably ever really expected to die in bed, anyway.

He handed the tablet back. "Thanks for checking, anyway."

Hauser nodded as he took the device and turned it off. "Least we could do." He grimaced. "If we hadn't been tied up elsewhere, we'd have been right here with you the whole damned time." Hauser seemed like a generally level-headed dude, but he clearly had just about the hate-on for the Humanity Front that the Blackhearts did.

"We had plenty of reasons to take this job." Brannigan wasn't going to turn down Abernathy's group's help, but he wasn't going to bow out if the Front came up on the target deck, even if Abernathy's guys were on it. "We've had a bone to pick with the Humanity Front since the beginning."

Price came forward from where he'd been on comms in the back of the plane, and sat down in one of the vacant seats on the other side of the aisle from Brannigan and Hauser. "Well, gentlemen, I have to thank you. All of you." He looked at Hauser. "I probably can't offer to pay you, given what I can determine about your affiliation, but as for you and your guys, John…" He turned to Brannigan. "I'll make sure that you are all compensated handsomely for this. You saved my life and the lives of two of my best operators. That alone means I owe you more than I can pay with mere money. On top of that, you helped quash a program that I'm sure would have led to global havoc in short order."

Brannigan nodded his thanks. The money would certainly help. He wasn't sure about the last part though. "That's assuming that this was the only research station where they were working on this stuff."

Hauser looked grim, but didn't say anything. Brannigan and Price both looked over at him. "Do you know of more facilities like that?"

"Not specifically." That was probably about all he was cleared to say. "We've been tracing some more of the Front's operations over the last couple of years. A lot of them are buried deep, not only under layers upon layers of front organizations and shell companies, but they're also all over the world, set up in austere, obscure places like an old Soviet base high in the Tian Shan." He shrugged. "It's going to be a long time digging them all out."

"Well, you know where to find us." Brannigan looked over at Price. "What tipped you off to this place, anyway?"

Price looked thoughtful. "It was an anonymous source, actually. Someone who knew far too much about not only my operations, but the Front's. They gave me enough that I couldn't ignore it."

"You think they set you up?" Hauser asked.

"Possibly, but I don't think so." He rubbed his chin. He'd shaved since they'd boarded the plane. "I think that Boren was already on their payroll. His group was brought in after we got on the ground. I'm sure whoever they have in my organization called them, then they called Boren. Like I said, I still have an extensive security audit to do."

"That doesn't mean they weren't trying to draw you in." Brannigan still wasn't sure.

"That would mean potentially exposing one of their actual operations just to get me. They're cocky, but they're not stupid. They would have to know that it might not go their way." Price shrugged. "I've done some damage to their ops lately, but hardly enough that they'd risk exposing their EMP and mind control

277

research just to take me out of the picture." He shook his head. "No, I think this was something else."

"Like what?" Brannigan was mulling it over, and developing some of his own suspicions, but he wanted to hear Price's idea.

"Like there are factions within the Front, some of which don't agree with this particular course of action. I think one of them decided to take matters into their own hands, and sicced me on them." He inclined his head toward Brannigan. "And, eventually, Brannigan's Blackhearts."

Brannigan glanced at Hauser. "What do you think?"

"It's possible. It's going to take some more digging to say for sure, though. These people are buried deep, and getting information's been difficult. Especially given how many political allies they have, who will raise all sorts of hell if we start getting too close to their darlings." Hauser sounded like he would very much like to unleash that B2 on some of those "political allies."

"Well, that's why you have us on call." Brannigan leaned back in his seat. "Now, if you'll both excuse me, it's been a long week."

***

"Thanks again for coming after us, Dan." Vernon was leaning back in his seat, finally allowing himself to relax a little. He hadn't slept much. He still seemed vaguely afraid to close his eyes. As if he was afraid that this was all one more hallucination, and he was going to wake up in that cell. Or worse, in the tank.

"I couldn't just leave you guys out here." Tackett had been catching up with Max and Vernon since they'd taken off. It had seemed like there hadn't been time before. He still wasn't officially one of Brannigan's Blackhearts—at least, he didn't think so—but he'd filled a slot as well as he could, especially since Javakhishvili and Jenkins had been killed. "It's been a few years, but..." He trailed off, not sure how to put it.

Vernon just reached across the aisle and squeezed his hand. He got it. Tackett didn't need to say anything. "So, you gonna go back into retirement?"

Tackett glanced at his old friend sharply, noticing that Santelli, a row ahead of them, had looked back as if wondering at his answer. Then he relaxed and really thought about it.

"I think I'll go back to semi-retirement." He met Santelli's gaze. "What I saw back there... I won't go back out just for the money. The time away from my family's not worth it. But if these bastards come up again..." He nodded to the old sergeant major. "Then I'd say, give me a call."

Santelli nodded back, a look of some satisfaction on his face.

BRANNIGAN'S BLACKHEARTS

MARQUE AND REPRISAL

They strike out of nowhere...

...And leave no survivors.

Have they met their match, or their next victims?

Piracy has remained a major security problem in the modern world, ranging from the coasts of Africa to Southeast Asia. But none of the pirate bands of the modern day have ever been quite this bloodthirsty.

And no one knows who they are.

A string of ghost ships, bearing the mutilated bodies of their crews, have maritime security forces baffled. Only one company CEO decides to take matters into his own hands. He wants the best security money can buy.

Even if it means going on the offensive.

Brannigan's Blackhearts are going to sea, to face a shadowy enemy unlike any they have ever met before.

AUTHOR'S NOTE

Thank you for reading *Blood Debt*. Some of my more dedicated readers have been asking for some time whether Dan Tackett was ever going to return to the action, and I figured that the tenth book in the *Brannigan's Blackhearts* series was as good a time as any. I hadn't initially planned on it, after finishing *Kill Yuan*, but after connecting that book with the Blackhearts in *Doctors of Death*, it became more a matter of "when" than "if." I hope that I did him justice, once again.

To keep up-to-date, I hope that you'll sign up for my newsletter—you get a free American Praetorians novella, *Drawing the Line*, when you do.

If you've enjoyed this novel, I hope that you'll go leave a review on Amazon or Goodreads. Reviews matter a lot to independent authors, so I appreciate the effort.

If you'd like to connect, I have a Facebook page at https://www.facebook.com/PeteNealenAuthor. You can also contact me, or just read my musings and occasional samples on the blog, at https://www.americanpraetorians.com. I look forward to hearing from you.

Made in the USA
Middletown, DE
18 May 2024